PRAISE FOR CRAZY FOR YOU

ِؤ authentic local flavor, swoon-worthy hometown ِؤroes, and gorgeous scenery, Michelle Sass Aleckson has crafted a heartfelt return to Deep Haven, Minnesota. This latest installment in the Deep Haven series will surely delight Susan May Warren fans and those who love sweet romances.

— GABRIELLE MEYER, AUTHOR OF *SNOWED IN FOR CHRISTMAS*

Michelle Sass Aleckson has created an engaging story with characters who keep you turning the page and a setting readers have come to love. Crazy for You will leave romance fans with a warm glow of happily ever after.

— TONI SHILOH, AUTHOR OF *AN UNLIKELY PROPOSAL*

D0920525

CRAZY FOR YOU

A DEEP HAVEN NOVEL

SUSAN MAY WARREN
MICHELLE SASS ALECKSON

sunrise
PUBLISHING

A NOTE FROM SUSIE MAY

You want to write about a fireman in Deep Haven? Yes, please!

This was my response to Michelle Sass Aleckson's proposal for her first book in our Deep Haven collection. And, you want to make him a local, and related to nearly everyone in town? Oh, double yes!

And, oh by the way, what if it's a Hatfield and McCoy feud set in a small town?

Ding, ding, ding! This book rang all the winner bells for me from the first pitch.

And then I read the book... **She blew me away.** To say that I love this story doesn't do justice to the amount of exclamation points I'd like to add! I fell in love with Peter Dahlquist from the first page—and to pair him with a fiery Latina EMT who moves to Deep Haven is perfect. She's exactly what calm and steady fire chief Peter needs to ignite a fire in his heart.

Add to that the tension between the two warring families— the Dahlquists and the Zimmermans—who have definite ideas about how Peter should vote in an upcoming town meeting, and you have the makings for a hilarious yet poignant story about being caught in the middle between people you love.

As for Ronnie Morales, she's got a big heart and isn't afraid to stand up for what she believes in, starting with her kid brother. They're hoping to make Deep Haven their permanent home. But is small-town life right for this big-city girl?

You will love this country mouse versus city mouse story about finding your place in a small town.

And, did I mention it has a fireman?

All I'm going to say is...enjoy. And thank you for reading!

XOXO,

Susie May

To Jesse, who has always been my biggest fan and constant encourager from the moment I spoke out loud this crazy dream to write.

You have sacrificed, invested, and given so much to make my dream a reality. You are my first dream and my favorite dream come true.

Love you forever and a day.

CHAPTER 1

*T*he plan was easy. Bring Oreos, kiss his mother, and skedaddle.

No need to stick around and get caught in another fight.

The last thing Peter Dahlquist needed this Memorial Day weekend was another fire to put out. At least, the family relations type. A good old-fashioned barn blaze—he'd be all in.

He stood on the apex of Zimmerman Mountain and looked out on the land that had been in his family for more than eight generations. Eighty acres, about half of it developed now with log cabin and A-frame Zimmerman homes, all nestled in a valley of birch and pine forest. And sprawling out at the foot of the acreage was the glorious blue of Lake Superior, calm and barely frothy against a pebbled shore.

For the annual family picnic, all seventy-two of his closest relatives were gathered in the field behind him, in the yard of the family lodge, the first homestead—now remodeled—of Luther and Agnes Zimmerman. The fragrance of fresh cut fescue and other field grasses mixed with the smoke from the usual bonfire. Uncle Martin held camp talking politics in his grizzled voice with the dozens of other uncles and aunts, most of whom Peter didn't know.

Okay, he knew them all. But sometimes, he wished he didn't. Especially when it came to local politics.

"Uncle Pete, watch out!"

He turned just as a football shot toward his head. But instead of ducking, he reached out and nabbed it with one hand.

He still had it.

His second cousin, once removed, held up his hands and Peter chucked it back to fourteen-year-old Ben. He'd heard the kid was hoping to make the Deep Haven Huskies football team this fall.

"Wanna play with us?"

Toss around a ball and avoid getting roped into discussion? Definitely.

He opened his mouth to say yes when Elton stepped up and dropped a heavy hand on Peter's shoulder. "Sorry, Ben, I've gotta steal Pete to help unload wood for the fire. As soon as we get it going, we'll eat. Tell the others, son."

Great. See, he should've made a run for the hills as soon as he was done stacking wood for the fire. And running back to town for more ice. And after the game of hide-and-seek with his younger cousins.

Okay. Peter just couldn't find the words to say no.

Which was, of course, why he was in this mess.

"No problem," Peter said as he grabbed the wheelbarrow from Elton and followed his older cousin to the wood pile behind the family lodge, a simple one-room cabin they used for all the family events.

"So. Pete, you know which way you're voting, right? We could really use that property."

Yep. Ambushed. He knew it was coming.

If he kept his mouth shut, what were the chances of being struck by lightning? Peter glanced at the wide expanse of clear blue sky stretching over Deep Haven and the glistening sapphire of Lake Superior down the hill. Not a hint of a storm. At least not the kind he could appreciate.

"I'm still researching all the options." And a way to bring about a peaceful end to this longstanding family feud. It all started with him. He had to find a way to end it.

Elton grabbed a small log and faced him. "The Westerman Hotel should be brought back to its former glory. We can do that. We've got the Grand Moose Lodge here on the ridge and the Mad Moose Hotel down in town, but the Westerman with all that lakeshore could really help us draw in a different clientele. And it would be great for the community. We can use that big ballroom for weddings and events." He threw the log in the wheelbarrow. "Besides, we're family. What other options are there?"

Peter bent down and pitched a log onto the pile. "You know the other options. Ever since Pierre's burned down, people have been wanting a pizza place. That could be good for the town too."

"People? Oh?" Elton made a face and shook his head. "You mean the Dahlquists. Isn't it enough that they own half the county? They've got four other restaurants." He threw another log into the wheelbarrow with a violent *thunk*. "How many more does Deep Haven need?"

Everyone just needed to calm down. Peter took a breath. "El, if Dahlquists own half of the county, Zimmermans own the other half. You've got two other hotels besides the resort and Mad Moose."

"No, you're just saying that because you're a Dahlquist."

"Hey, I have Zimmerman blood. You know that—"

"Exactly. So show some loyalty, dude."

Peter took a breath. "I am being loyal. But—"

"But nothin'. Are you a Zimmerman, or aren't you?" Elton

chucked the last wood into the wheelbarrow and stepped up to grab the handles. "Don't betray the blood, man."

He didn't wait for Peter as he trundled the wheelbarrow away.

Are you a Zimmerman, or aren't you?

The answer should be obvious. Apparently not.

Now might be the exact time to leave.

Except, by the time he got back, Grandma Zee and the aunts finally brought out the hot dogs, buns, and store-bought potato salad. Family units clumped together and moved through the line. His cousin Katie, first cousin once removed, handed him her shih tzu while she piled up her plate. She'd inherited the Zimmerman dark hair and tall basketball legs. He followed her to the fire pit where she sat with her husband, who held a babbling toddler.

"Peter, you don't mind watching Daisy while I feed the baby, do you? Then Paul can make a plate."

Paul Hamlin, of the lesser known Hamlin clan. He'd played football a couple years after Peter.

"Sure."

"She probably needs a trip out to the woods, but be careful. She's a fraidy-cat and might bolt if she hears any strange noises. And I forgot her leash, so you need to carry her."

If it got him out of Elton's crosshairs, he would watch the spoiled dog all night. There was no way his outspoken cousin was done with the discussion. He'd probably track him down with one of those logs.

Peter tucked Daisy under his arm, his stomach rumbling. By the time the dog did her business and he got back to the gathering, the food table was as bare as the dusky sky. He watched the teenagers start up their touch football game again. Ben and one of the older kids snuck out into the woods beyond the field.

Oh, he knew exactly what they were up to. Some things never changed. He'd probably wander over later and make them all put out their cigarettes and warn them about the current level three fire warning.

But the Zimmerman clan weren't the troublemakers in town. Well, not usually.

His mom came up to him, her smile bright. She wore her favorite purple Deep Haven Huskies football sweatshirt with white capris. "Hey, Pete." She patted his arm and handed him a Rice Krispies bar. "I noticed you didn't eat."

He took the treat. "Thanks."

"I also saw you brought Oreos again."

"If you want me to show up, you'll have to be prepared—"

She held up her hand. "It's fine." She smirked. "I'm just glad you showed up. It's hard to be in enemy camp."

"Mom, you're hardly in enemy camp—"

"I'm a Dahlquist now. Yes, your father was my first love and I married into the Zimmerman family, but I think they would've been happy if I'd *stayed* married to his memory and never looked at another man. I'm not sure that they ever got over Gary adopting you and giving you *his* last name when I remarried."

"Mom, you're not the enemy. Grandma wouldn't insist that you come if you were."

"You're right. And if I miss this, then I miss Grandma Zee's famous rhubarb cake." She winked.

Truth was his mother was his one reason for coming. This was one of the only times he got her to himself while his dad took his two younger brothers camping. Abby, his sister, had opted to stay in the Twin Cities with friends.

"Cute dog." She patted its head.

They found seats near the fire. He had to give it to his great-grandparents—when they built this cabin, they took maximum advantage of the grassy slope and the view. The firepit was in the perfect spot. The outside speaker system of the lodge pumped out country tunes. Bright colors lit the sky as the sun sank lower. If only he could relax and enjoy it like every other year.

"Dad and the boys make it to the camping site yesterday?"

"Yup, their annual trip. But they'll be at the Dahlquist get-together tomorrow evening." She rubbed her arms. "It's going to be a cold one tonight. I hope Gary packed his good sleeping bag."

"I'm sure they're fine."

"Probably. But it's a wife's prerogative to worry. And a mother's."

He saw the concern in her look, but better to pretend he didn't. He stared into the flames, watching the glowing coals burn, seeing the warm faces of his relatives as they joked and roasted marshmallows for s'mores. He didn't look at Elton, but he felt a simmer of conversation, as if it buzzed in his blood, just as Elton suggested.

"Are you doing okay, Peter?"

"Ma, I'm fine. You know me."

"I just want you to be happy."

"I am." Really. He was. He had a great job, great family. So what if, at times, it felt like something was missing?

Grandpa Zim lumbered over and plopped down next to Mom. "There's nothing to worry about, Barb. Peter's a good boy. And he's going to make the right decision in that vote next week."

And here they went again. Back into the crossfire. His mother's lips curled into a tight smile. The others probably didn't see the pinch around her mouth as anything significant, but the smile she gave Grandpa was as fake as the artificial sweetener in his pop.

Elton spoke from across the circle, where he sat on a bench, his mouth full of food. "Yeah, Peter knows what he needs to do."

The chatter ceased. And he didn't count, but nearly everyone, including Grandma Zee, pinned their attention on Peter. The dog squirmed in his lap.

Uncle Al's voice boomed from across the pit where he sat in a lawn chair. "Of course, he knows what to do. We're counting on him. Right, Peter?"

At any time the Lord could open up those skies and bring that deluge. Or earthquake. Tsunami. He'd even take a tornado. He wasn't picky.

Instead his newly engaged cousin Ree—just an ordinary first cousin—and her fiancé, Seth Turnquist, came up from the driveway holding hands. He liked Seth. Big guy. Had saved lives last fall when a town dock collapsed. And Ree had harbored a crush on big Seth for as long as Peter knew her. Now, she glanced at Peter, a twinkle in her eye. She never had any problem mixing it up with the Zimmerman brood. "Come on, guys. Give Peter a break. This is supposed to be a family picnic, not the Deep Haven City Council Meeting."

"Thank you, Ree." At least someone understood the position he was in. Of course, she'd also asked for an exclusive interview for the *Deep Haven Herald* once he decided, so maybe she was just trying to stay on his good side.

Daisy picked that moment to rush out of Peter's lap and inspect the crumbs under the tables. He followed her. Might as well see if there was a lone hot dog bun or something left.

Vivien Calhoun, third cousin by marriage, joined her best friend Ree at the food table, scooping up the last Oreo in the package. "What's this vote about?"

Seth dropped a bulky arm around Ree, pulling her close. "The Westerman Hotel is up for grabs."

Vivien brightened. "Oh, I love that old building!"

Old was right. If Adrian Vassos had purchased the property like Peter had hoped, this wouldn't be an issue, but as soon as the place was available again suddenly everyone wanted it. And he'd regretted running for city council ever since. He couldn't go anywhere without one side or the other of the family pushing him to vote their way.

Worse, the place was a fire trap waiting to blaze over. As fire chief of Deep Haven, all he could see was a potential fire hazard sitting right on the harbor shore, vacant for the local kids to play in, get trapped, and die. Something needed to be done with the place soon. Seb Brewster, their mayor, had already called for a vote—which, of course, Peter had stalemated with a tie.

Seb expected him to break it at Tuesday's meeting.

Change of subject needed now. "Vivien, what are you doing in town? Are you back from New York for good?"

She came and sat next to him, petting Daisy while he bit into the burnt hot dog he'd scrounged up. Her wavy brown hair hung down her back, long legs in skinny jeans tucked under her. Her blue eyes gleamed in the firelight. "I am. I'm running a summer theater program."

"Where?"

"Here. In Deep Haven."

Uncle Charlie laughed from his lounger nearby. Not really an uncle—his father's cousin. But every man over fifty was monikered with "uncle." Uncle Charlie wore his typical Twins cap, a pair of jeans, and a flannel shirt he couldn't quite button over his girth. He held one of his grandkids on his knee. "Who's going to do summer theater?"

Vivien glared at him. "The kids. I started working with a children's theater back East and loved it. Kids have so much potential and they usually aren't as self-conscious as adults. Besides, what else are they going to do all summer?" Daisy shuffled over and Vivien pulled the dog onto her lap. "And how about you, Petey? Dating anyone?"

He stared down Vivie. "No. No time for that around here."

Seth smirked as he roasted a marshmallow for Ree, the skin turning a delicious golden brown. "Yeah. That and the fact that you're related to pretty much everyone in Deep Haven has put a serious damper on your love life, man."

Vivien shrugged a slim shoulder and flipped her dark hair. "Then why don't you move?"

Move? Moving wasn't the answer.

Yeah, this big crazy family drove him nuts, but he loved it here. He loved walking into the Loon Cafe and knowing every person who sat at the counter or in the red-padded booths. He loved his job as fire chief, helping people, fighting fires, running the annual Fire Prevention Week at school. Loved to see the awe in the kindergartners' faces when he brought the fire trucks to school. He loved the lake, the town, and every festival they hosted. And it was because of his love for Deep Haven that he'd run for city council. He'd wanted to give back and make Deep Haven an even better place.

No, he wasn't going anywhere. If God wanted him to have a love life, He'd have to plop someone in the middle of his lap.

Someone called his name, shaking him from his thoughts. "Yeah?"

"So you already met him?" Uncle Charlie was asking, clearly by the raised eyebrow, for the second time.

"Who?"

"The new paramedic we're getting. Cole Barrett said he was moving up here soon and taking Eli Hueston's place now that he's retired to Florida. Said the guy's name was Ross or Ron or something."

Peter stood and glanced at Seth, good friend to Kirby Hueston, the one most people in town thought Cole should've hired. Thankfully he was deep in conversation with Ree, paying no mind to the talking on this side of the fire. "I haven't met the guy. He's supposed to come next week. But if Cole knows him, I'm sure he'll be fine. Besides, it's not my choice. It's Cole's."

Uncle Charlie shook his head. "I don't know about that. Sounds like he's from the Cities. Minneapolis. You know those guys can't drive for beans. Especially in the winter. He should leave driving the rig to me and Dean. We know how to handle the ambulance on these roads."

Thankfully Uncle Chuck turned to his son, Elton, to complain some more about all the tourists that came up and quadrupled the population of Deep Haven during the peak summer and autumn weekends, completely discounting his family's hotels' dependence on them.

Peter made a noncommittal grunt and kissed his mother's cheek. Time to escape before the stupid vote came up again.

He dropped off Daisy with her family and walked away from the warmth of the fire with a wave goodbye.

His mom followed him down the long dirt road to the field where he'd parked his truck.

"Mom, I can walk to my truck by myself, you know."

"Oh, I know. I just...uh, I wondered what you were thinking."

"About what?"

She looked back at the gathering around the fire pit and dropped her voice. "Well...the vote."

His shoulders tensed. Blitzed by his own mother.

Her hand rested on his arm. Squeezed. "I know the Zimmermans want that place for their next moose-themed hotel, Peter, but it would make your dad so happy if you would vote for the restaurant."

Aw... "But Elton and Grandpa Zim have a good point too. A family-centered hotel on the lakeshore would bring more tourists for the restaurants and other businesses."

She stilled, staring at him. "Are you serious? Honey. You can't vote against the Dahlquists. It's—"

"Disloyal?" He stopped and turned to her. "I'm in trouble either way. No matter how I vote, some family is going to hate me."

She sighed. "Not me. I'll always love you. You know that."

He refrained from rolling his eyes. Barely. "Thanks. Guess I was hoping for a bigger argument."

She laughed, a quick chuckle that had more to do with pity than humor. "I'm sorry you're in this position." Her voice grew quiet. "I do understand."

Yeah, she did. She had once been married to a Zimmerman —Peter's biological father. After he died, she worked hard to stay connected with them for Peter's sake. Like coming to their Christmas party and this picnic every year.

But she'd remarried, had three more children, and now she had to live with the Dahlquists and the repercussions of Peter's choice.

Peter kissed her cheek and pulled the keys out of his pocket. "I know, Mom. I know."

She caught his face in her hands. "I know you'll make the right choice."

And what exactly was that?

A gust of lake wind whipped through his sweatshirt as he watched her walk back to the crowd. Then he turned, and in the wink of a sunset walked out to his truck.

How could a guy have the biggest family in town and still be so alone?

Five hundred miles might not be far enough away, but Ronnie Morales had done more with a lot less.

Not that she had a choice. She'd learned early on that no one was going to hand her anything on a silver platter. She rolled her shoulders back and took a deep breath, wiggling her fingers on the steering wheel. She would make this work. She had to. For Tiago.

The SUV headlights barely pierced the darkness in front of them. The scent of stale french fries clashed with the floral air freshener attached to the vent. Muted rap music spilled out of her little brother's headphones. It grated on her ears. The vibrations of the road put her backside to sleep.

She should stop, find a bathroom and a decent meal, because those Cheetos she ate hours ago were not cutting it.

She checked her rearview mirror. Nah. Better to push through and get to Deep Haven. Besides, where would she stop?

Nothing but a hill covered with forest on one side of Highway 61 and Lake Superior on the other, a black abyss with reflections of moonlight lurking on the water.

No other vehicles on the road. No lights.

She was heading to the backside of nowhere.

Still, if she had to go to the end of the state map to find a safe place and keep Tiago out of trouble, so be it. He was only ten. Probably didn't realize how big a deal this was. Uprooting from their North Minneapolis neighborhood, moving to the opposite end of the state, and starting over...

Hopefully in a place where gangs weren't recruiting at the local elementary school.

Of course, if Mom had spent an ounce of attention on the poor kid instead of her latest loser boyfriend, or better yet, if she had a smidge of backbone, maybe they wouldn't be in this mess.

But coming home off her tour with the Army to find her mother in jail and her brother in foster care facing arson charges meant something had to change. Ronnie would not sit by and let Tiago throw his life away like Mom had.

So goodbye, military career. Goodbye, Minneapolis. Hello, Deep Haven.

If they ever found the place.

Man, it was dark out here.

But no turning back now. Like Papa always said, *Press on and move forward, Veronica. Find something good to focus on.*

The job Cole offered her was certainly a good fit. Paramedic for the small town. Using her skills for this Crisis Response Team she could totally get behind.

She just needed to help Tiago find some new friends, some *good* friends, and something for him to do in his spare time besides setting fire to public property. And it wouldn't be so bad to find a cute little house to fix up and call their own eventually. Something without bars on the windows would be nice.

Ronnie glanced at the clock. It was already after eleven. They had to be getting close. Maybe she should've called Cole. Hopefully, he wouldn't mind her coming in a few days early. Once she was done with her discharge paperwork, put in her notice at her temp job, and packed, it didn't pay to stick around the Twin Cities any longer.

A faint glow in the sky ahead beckoned.

Ronnie nudged Tiago in the passenger seat. "T, wake up. We're here."

He mumbled and retreated further into his hoodie. His soft snores resumed.

The light grew stronger as she crested the hill. A sign for a cabin resort on one side of the road. A mini golf place and a Welcome to Deep Haven sign on the other. Yes. This was it.

From the top of the hill she spied the town below, one stoplight up ahead. The hill above the harbor was dotted with porch lights, and a small cluster of businesses along the lakeshore gleamed a rainbow of colors onto the surface of the lake.

It looked so peaceful. So...small.

Wow, it was small.

She checked the navigator, drove to Third Avenue and turned left just as the highway started to curve. One and a half blocks up, and their rental, Cole's garage apartment, shone in her headlights. The detached garage apartment sat next to a cute gray Victorian. Or maybe it was white. Hard to tell in the dark.

Ronnie exited the car and stretched. Brrr. She dove back

into the SUV for her jacket. This was cold for late May. Then again, she'd never been this far north. They were practically in Canada.

"You're early," a voice called. She looked over her shoulder. "Thought you wouldn't be arriving until next week."

Cole Barrett. He still looked good—tough, focused, all intensity as he came down the sidewalk of the front door.

Ronnie zipped up her fleece and turned with a smile to the former Army Ranger. "Why delay the inevitable, Sergeant?"

Barrett shook her hand. "Good to see ya, Morales."

"Likewise." She studied him. Something was different about him. Good different. "Small-town life seems to agree with you. You look good."

That was an understatement. Because under the lights, under close scrutiny, gone was that haunted look in his eyes, the tortured soul that had walked away from the 75th Ranger Regiment after his buddy almost died. Now that slight smile he wore seemed...genuine. No more anger flashing just under the surface of his words. The man radiated something calm. Steady.

If Deep Haven could do that to Cole Barrett, maybe it would live up to its name and work some of its magic on Tiago too.

A cute blonde walked out the door of the main house and tucked herself under one of Cole's arms like she belonged there. He looked down at her, grinning like a fool.

Ah. Not the small-town charm. A *woman* was responsible for this new version of Cole Barrett.

"Ronnie, this is Megan, my wife."

Megan approached with open arms. "Nice to meet you, Ronnie. Cole has told me so much about you. He said you saved his friend's life."

Apparently they hugged upon first meeting here. Uh. Okay.

Ronnie gave her an awkward pat on the back and tried to smile when she stepped away. Megan went back to Cole's side. Her blonde hair was thrown up in one of those cute little messy knots on the top of her head and even in a sweatshirt and leggings, she was absolutely adorable. They looked like some fairytale couple.

Ronnie felt more like the Beast after a long day of packing and driving. She tried to smooth back the hair escaping her ponytail.

Fairy tales had never been her thing. She had never believed in happily-ever-afters and handsome princes to save the day with a kiss.

Tiago stumbled over, rubbing the sleep out of his eyes.

"This must be your little brother. Santiago, right?" Megan asked.

"It's Tiago. Or T," he grumbled.

Ronnie nudged him. "Hey. Manners."

He rolled his eyes.

It didn't seem to deter Megan, who turned to Tiago. "I have a son about your age. Josh. He's asleep now, but you guys should come over tomorrow and you can meet him. He'd love to have a new friend."

"Yeah, maybe." Tiago toed the ground, kicking a pebble away. Then he looked up at Ronnie. "Do you know where we're sleeping? I'm tired."

Megan nodded. "Oh, here, let me show you the apartment while Cole helps Ronnie unload your luggage. Josh helped me put a few things up in the bedroom you'll be using."

Was everybody this...nice in Deep Haven?

Tiago must've had similar thoughts, the uncertainty written all over his face, as his eyes asked, *Do I go with this crazy lady?*

Ronnie nodded toward the garage apartment. "Go ahead with Megan. I'll be right there."

He must've been tired since he didn't put up any more of a fight.

Ronnie and Cole went to the back of the SUV. She opened

the hatch and grabbed her duffel. "So. This is Deep Haven, huh?"

He reached for Tiago's suitcase. "Yup."

"We're pretty far off the beaten path."

"True, but we've been in worse places. At least no one is shooting at us here."

She gave him a smirk. "Okay, so straight up. What am I in for, Sergeant? What's the civilian life like?"

"It takes some getting used to. For one thing, you can drop the 'Sergeant' and call me Cole. But, not gonna lie, it's great not having someone telling us what to do all the time."

Yeah, that would be a nice change. "And the paramedic position?"

"You'll answer to me but will work with the town fire chief quite a bit. He'll have jurisdiction within Deep Haven city limits, but you'll be the one calling the shots if we're dealing with anywhere else in the county. There's a lot of square mileage we cover, a lot of wilderness and hard-to-reach areas. We have two or three EMTs and a handful of first responders, but everything is on a volunteer basis, so they all have other jobs. You're the only full-timer. Hopefully our summer won't be too busy as you learn the ropes. You know how it is—when it's crazy it's really crazy and then there's a lot of downtime in between."

She picked up her duffel bag and followed Cole toward the door. "What's this fire chief like?"

"Peter? Great guy, but don't get on his bad side."

"Why? Is he hard to get along with?"

"No, he's about as easygoing as they come. But Peter Dahlquist is a Deep Haven legend. They love him around here."

She stopped in the middle of the sidewalk. "So, why the warning?"

He stopped at the bottom of the stairs and gave her a pointed look. "Ronnie, you're not exactly the plays-well-with-others type."

She dropped her duffel and faced him, hand on her hip. "So, you don't think I can do the job?"

"Calm down. If I thought that, I wouldn't have offered it to you. You just need to work with the system here. It's different. Small-town volunteers, not military ops, not big-city EMS staff. More salt-of-the-earth folks helping out their neighbors. So, you're going to have to go easy."

"Just because we're in the sticks doesn't mean I'm going to drop my IQ to fit in and keep people happy. I won't risk people's lives to salvage someone's pride."

A rumble of frustration escaped Cole's throat. "I'm not asking you to risk lives, Ron. Just...be aware that the people you're working with are the same people bagging your food at the grocery store. They'll be Tiago's teachers and the barista making your coffee at the Java Cup. You ruffle too many feathers here and you're going to have a tough time fitting in. Your brother too."

"That's what you're worried about?" She picked up her bag again. "Seriously, Cole. Since when did you become such a Mother Hen?"

"I'm being serious, Ronnie. I've seen you in action. You're great at getting results and making things happen, but you can't bulldoze people around here. The mayor, Seb Brewster, insisted on a ninety-day probationary period. You can be fired for any reason. He wants to make sure you'll be a good fit for the town. He's one of our EMTs, so he'll see you out on calls. And you might already have some opposition since you beat out one of the locals for this position. You, hands down, have more medical experience, but you'll have to break out your kid gloves around here."

"What are those? Tiny mittens? Come on. If you say I'm qualified, what's there to worry about?"

"Ronnie..."

"Fine. Kid gloves. Got it." As long as Tiago made friends and she could do her job, they would be fine. A little challenge never scared her. She climbed up the stairs inside the garage and walked into the apartment.

It was small, but nicer than any place she'd ever rented. A cozy living room done in tasteful neutrals, furnished with sofa, loveseat, coffee table, and entertainment center. It opened to the black-and-white kitchen/dining area. The place definitely needed some color, but the wood laminate flooring throughout gave it a warm feel.

She walked into the master bedroom off a short hallway and dropped her duffel on the queen-size bed. Tiago trudged in from what must be his bedroom directly across the hall.

He plopped on the bed and whispered, "Are we going to be okay? These people are weird."

"They're not weird. They're being nice. Something that might take a little getting used to, but, yeah, we're okay. Just wait and see. It will be great here."

Tiago didn't look convinced.

A piercing alarm broke the quiet. Ronnie rushed back to the living area. Cole grabbed his phone, an EMS signal spouting off an address.

"House fire. All available emergency personnel report to—"

Megan stepped out of the kitchen. "You better go, Cole. I'll help Ronnie settle in."

Ronnie rounded on Cole. "What? Settle in? No, I'm going too."

Except, well, maybe Tiago—

"I can stay and watch Tiago since Josh is just in the house," Megan said.

Oh...the old spark ignited inside her again, flushing all her fatigue away. She glanced over at Cole and he was giving her a skeptical look.

"I have to jump in sometime. Besides, this is the perfect opportunity to see your Crisis Response Team."

Cole hesitated a second more and then blew out a long breath. "Not exactly the Deep Haven orientation I had in mind, but let's go. Remember. Kid gloves."

"Yeah, yeah. Time's wasting, Boss."

It didn't matter what size mittens she wore—Ronnie was going to prove she was exactly the person they needed to save lives in this backwoods town.

Because if she didn't, she'd have to get back in the car and keep driving. And she'd just about run out of road.

CHAPTER 2

*T*he rumors were true.

Old man Gust Hagborg was a hoarder and he might die in the midst of his clutter, his addiction to holding on to the past.

Peter stood at the entry of the house, smoke billowing from the garage roof. Flames were licking out the windows of the one-story ranch home in the middle of the woods. A few distant neighbors in bathrobes watched from the edge of the yard.

Around him, his crew—Seth, Uncle Charlie, Dean Wilson, and a few others—uncoiled hose from the truck. A siren whining through the night suggested Sheriff Kyle Hueston might be on the way. Hopefully his brother Kirby, one of the few EMTs in the area, would be too.

No Jensen Atwood. His wife, Claire, was in labor.

And especially, no sign of Gust Hagborg.

So, Peter had a skeleton crew to save a mid-century home that belonged to his eighty-one-year-old former Sunday school teacher.

Who was hidden somewhere in the smoky minefield of his house.

Towers of papers, magazines, files, and cardboard boxes blocked all access in the front entry. The smoke alarm screamed over the crackling of the fire. By the roar of the flames on the other side of that wall, they didn't have much time. Gust created a fireman's worst nightmare, a maze of tinder just waiting for a spark. Once flames reached that far wall, the whole place would go up in a matter of seconds.

Peter threw his irons into the first pile and started knocking down a path with brute force and adrenaline. Once he had a small clearing he started his thermal imaging.

No sign of Gust.

With Seth right behind him, they wound their way around heaps destined to become piles of ash. By some miracle, Peter found his way through the smoke and the towers to the hallway. Stacks of containers lined the wall, narrowing the passage to the point his shoulders touched each side. He hunched them together as he squeezed through the hazy tunnel on his hands and knees. He prayed the way Gust had taught him to, like God understood everything, even the desperate pleas he couldn't voice. Even though the elderly man didn't fear death, this was an awful way to meet his Maker.

Peter opened the first door. No Gust. Next door, a bathroom. Empty. He tried the door at the end of the hall.

There.

The red orange blob on his screen indicated warmth. A body.

Peter picked his way across the room, tossing containers to Seth who threw them off to the side. They slowly fought their way through the crowded bedroom.

Gust, in his pajamas, was sprawled on the floor next to his bed, as if he had tripped and a pillar of boxes fell on top of him.

A crash sounded. Voices called through the radio.

"The fire breached! It caught in the living area."

Which meant their escape was blocked.

Peter reached Gust and felt a light pulse. He most likely had internal injuries, but there was no way they could get a back-board in here or even have time to strap him on it.

"Dahlquist, you better get out of there! This place is going down!" A voice thundered through the radio.

Peter looked behind him. The hallway they just passed through was already a tunnel of fire.

Perfect.

"Through the window!" Seth pointed through the haze at a grimy window.

Yep. But first they'd have to get to it. Stacks of books and a cluttered nightstand stood in the way. And as soon as they opened the window, the rush of oxygen would feed the fire.

Backdraft.

But that window was the only exit.

He stepped over Gust, and the two of them threw the books on the bed, the one open surface in the room. Peter motioned for Seth to pick up Gust. The local lumberjack had no problem pulling the brittle man over his shoulder.

Rescue first. Then attend to his injuries. He yelled into the walkie on his shoulder. "Dean and Charlie, come to the far window! But stand clear—I have to break the glass."

Peter cleared the nightstand with one swoop of his arm, then shouldered the bulky piece of furniture. With one hefty move, he launched it through the window, shattering the glass.

The surge of fresh air hit the fire. The inferno behind them roared as flames shot up the walls and across the ceiling, hungry for more.

Dean and Uncle Charlie stood outside ready to catch. Peter stood at the window and steadied Gust as Seth handed him over. They threaded him through to the men on the other side.

"Out now!" he shouted to Seth, and the big man went through the window like a buffalo through a fence.

Peter followed him. He hit the ground and ran as flames tore through the window—fingers grabbing at him.

Peter yanked off his mask, bent over to suck in air.

"That was close," Seth said, doing the same. But he smiled at him. "Fast thinking."

"Good work." Peter straightened, ignoring the shakiness in his legs. "Grab some water and then we need to put this fire down." Already, the night sky misted from the water hose now manned by John and Casper Christiansen.

At the edge of the yard, a woman with long dark hair pulled back in a ponytail kneeled by Gust. She wore a pair of gloves, had a medical kit out.

"Who is that?" Seth asked. "And where are Seb and the ambulance team?"

"Not sure, but I'll find out. Why don't you go help John?" He ran over to her. "Hey—"

She looked up. "We need a backboard. Don't you have one on your truck?"

"Yeah." He slowed.

"Then go get it! This man could have a serious spinal injury. What were you thinking just tossing him out the window?"

Well for one, he'd hardly tossed him. And then there was that little matter of him almost dying—

"We're about to lose him if we don't get him to a trauma center now!" She turned back to her patient.

Right. "Dean, grab the backboard and collar." Peter ripped off his gloves and ran to the truck for the oxygen kit. He found the tank and mask and headed back to Gust.

The woman was checking his airway. She didn't even look up as she grabbed the kit from him. "This man should've been collared and backboarded before he was ever moved. That's basic emergency protocol." She shined a light into Gust's mouth.

Dean and Uncle Charlie came up with the backboard. The short jog left both of them wheezing for breath.

"It's about time," she mumbled. She directed her gaze to Uncle Charlie. "You, kneel at his side and put your hands here." She pointed to Gust's shoulder and hip.

Peter didn't wait to be told, just knelt next to his uncle and placed his hands on Gust's hip and knee. While the bossy woman directed Dean to get ready with the backboard, she collared Gust.

"On my count we roll. Keep his back straight. One, two, three."

They rolled Gust on to his side while Dean slipped the board under him.

She looked up at Peter. "Where's the ambulance?"

Right. As if her question had conjured it, the old Deep Haven EMT unit pulled up. Cole Barrett hopped down from the front seat. Peter jogged over to him.

"Where are Seb, Kirby, and the rest of the EMS crew? I know first responder protocol, but I should be with my guys."

Cole pursed his lips. "Don't know. Heard a lot of people are gone for the holiday weekend. And the hospital ambulance crews are already out on another call in town. I dropped off Ronnie and drove to the fire hall, then found what I could to stock this old thing and rushed back."

Forget trying to track down everybody. They still had a life to save and a fire to put out.

Peter helped Cole get the cot out of the back. "Do you have this?"

"Go. I'll get this to Ronnie."

"Who?"

Cole nodded toward the woman treating Gust. "That's Veronica Morales, the new Crisis Team paramedic. She's one of the best. Gust is in good hands."

So that's the woman who'd beat out Kirby Hueston for the Crisis Response Team position? Good to hear that the brusque Ronnie was at least competent. Then Peter could concentrate on trying to put out the fire. And maybe make sure Seth didn't have to deal with her tonight. He was still sore about Kirby being passed over.

He slipped his gloves back on and checked in. Nathan Decker and a few more fire volunteers showed up. Peter switched out the hose crews and called to his nearest captain. "Seth, check for propane tanks and outbuildings. Anything else we need to be aware of."

"On it, Chief."

The fire was close to being under control simply because it had already consumed most of the house. Peter started another line and sent John to refill the truck at the lake access.

Seth came up. "There's a propane tank all right. Behind the house at the edge of the woods. Also a small shed back there."

"Let's get another hose on that side of the house, wet down those trees and grass, and keep the fire as far from the tank and shed as we can."

They threw on another hose and more volunteers showed up in bunker gear. Peter put them to work.

Over the noise of the fire, the sirens, pump trucks, and hoses, a woman's wailing reached Peter.

Gretchen Riggs, Gust's daughter, cried at the door of the ambulance while Ronnie and Uncle Charlie tried to load the cot.

"Daddy! Daddy! Is he okay?"

Dean tried to hold her back, but she pushed him off and reached again for her father. She blocked the ambulance doors.

Ronnie nudged her out of the way as she stepped up into the rig. "Ma'am, I'm trying to save his life. Please move. Now."

Sheesh. Yeah, they were all on edge and stressed. But couldn't she show a little compassion? Peter ran over. "Gretchen, you need to let them go so they can help your father."

"Oh, Peter. Thank goodness you're here. They won't let me

see him!" She clawed at his arm, tears coursing down her wrinkled cheeks. "That woman won't let me near my own father."

"They're helping him, but they need to get him to the hospital right away."

"Then I need to go with him!"

"I'm sorry. Only emergency staff can ride. But I'm sure we can find someone to take you to Duluth."

"Duluth?" She let out another wail. "Is it that bad? Oh, Daddy!"

He got it. Gust and Gretchen were the only family the other had left. He couldn't imagine if it were his father being loaded in the back of that ambulance. "They'll do everything they can to save him. We have to let them go. The sooner they get him to the hospital the better chance he has." He waved Kyle over. "Maybe the sheriff can help you find a ride." He tried to move the woman away from the rig. But for such a little thing, her planted feet wouldn't budge.

Ronnie was focused on Gust but called out, "Why aren't we moving?"

Uncle Charlie stood by Peter, waiting for Gretchen to move in order to close the doors. "We've gotta go. I need to drive."

Ronnie's head snapped up. "You're not driving. Cole will."

Gretchen clung harder to Peter's jacket, pulling his attention away from his uncle and Ronnie's argument. "If I can't ride then you have to go with Daddy in the ambulance."

"Mrs. Riggs, I've got a fire to put out."

"I don't care about the house! You have to save my father. I trust you, Peter. Please!"

In the reflection of the flames, the haggard woman begged. Her hair was a mess, her eyes bloodshot and weepy. "I know what he means to you, Peter. *Please*."

His heart wrenched. How could he say no to her?

Kyle reached them and gently pried Gretchen's hands away. "Come with me, Mrs. Riggs."

"No! Not until Peter promises me that he'll go!" She stood resolute in the ambulance doorway.

Peter looked out across the yard. The fire was dying. There wasn't much more to burn. The crew had watered down the small shed and all the grass and trees on the lot. He could already see the backyard over the rubble and diminishing flames.

"Let me tell my crew."

"Oh, thank you, Peter. Thank you. And I won't move until you come back." Gretchen let go of his arm and guarded the back of the vehicle.

Peter ran to Seth. "I'm riding with Gust. Gretchen won't let them go without me. Can you take over here?"

"We're good. It's almost out and we have more volunteers now." Seth looked back at the ambulance. "So is that woman the new Crisis Response medic? The one Cole hired?"

"Yeah. Cole says she's one of the best. She was an Army medic."

Seth shook his head and concentrated on the fire. "Whatever. It should've been Kirby."

And how was he supposed to respond to that? Kirby was a great EMT. But he also wasn't here. Peter clapped Seth on the shoulder. "Take care of our crew."

"You know I will." He walked away and moved toward what was left of the house with a shovel.

Peter checked out with the safety officer and climbed in the back of the ambulance. Uncle Charlie—scowling, probably due to being pushed out of the rig by Ronnie—shut the doors behind him. Cole started the sirens from the driver's seat, and they left. Out the window Peter watched Kyle, who tried to comfort Gretchen in the middle of the dirt road. She cried as she waved goodbye to her father.

Possibly for the last time.

He studied the woman, his new partner on the Crisis

Response Team. Her long dark hair pulled back in a no-nonsense ponytail, her brows knit together in concentration. "You could've let her say goodbye, you know."

Something in her eyes softened as she kept her laser focus on Gust. "I'm not a counselor. I'm a paramedic. My job is to save his life."

Okay then. He must've imagined the softness.

He didn't know where Cole found this woman, but she needed to go back to where she came from. She would never fit into Deep Haven or their newly formed team with an attitude like that.

And the last thing Deep Haven needed was more trouble.

The sirens screamed and lights flashed as they raced down the opposite lane of Highway 61 Ronnie had driven up just a couple hours earlier. This time, Ronnie's only view was the harsh fluorescent lighting in the back of the ambulance. The reflection bounced off the chrome surfaces and highlighted the victim's wrinkled pallor and bluish lips.

She couldn't lose her first patient in Deep Haven. She had too much riding on this. And if people would just get out of the way and let her work, maybe she could do that. First those responders being so incompetent and then the daughter showing up on the scene. Couldn't she see she was trying to save her father's life? That she wanted to do everything possible to keep him alive?

Ronnie didn't have the luxury of dealing with emotions when lives were on the line.

Now she just needed to tune out all the shouts and sirens around her, ignore the smell of smoke in her hair, and her cold legs where the damp grass had seeped through her jeans. Concentrate on her patient.

But the bulky fireman sat on the bench watching her, something of a snarl on his face, clearly disapproving of her treatment of the hysterical daughter.

Yeah, maybe Ronnie could've been nicer. But nicer didn't save lives.

And see, this is why she missed Army life. When a man was bleeding out on the field, there was only one objective—keep your teammate alive. It didn't matter how, and no one cared about feelings. Only efficiency. Competency. Grit.

Things were clearly going to be more complicated in Deep Haven, if the fireman's glower was any indication.

Ronnie reassessed her patient. Still unresponsive, gray lips, rasping breath, contusions already forming on his bald head, face, and one exposed arm with second—possibly third—degree burns. She opened up one compartment after another.

"What are you looking for?" Fireman asked.

"This truck is a mess. I can't find anything." She slammed a door and opened another. "Gotta clear that airway. I need to intubate. His breathing is too labored."

"Here." Fireman opened one of the cupboards above his head and pulled out the kit. "By the way, his name is Gust. Gust Hagborg."

She nodded and prepped the laryngoscope. Fireman moved to her right, where her partner would usually assist. He picked up the tube and had it ready. When she found the vocal chords, he passed it to her.

Maybe he *would* be helpful.

She kept a steady hand while inserting the ET tube down Mr. Hagborg's trachea. "Now that I've got him intubated, pull out that stylet and bag him. Keep a steady rhythm. Three to five breaths—"

"I know what I'm doing."

She watched to be sure. He squeezed the BVM forcing air

into the lungs. The ET tube fogged up nicely. Mr. Hagborg's chest rose and fell. Hopefully his oxygen levels would rise too.

Ronnie got the monitors set and an IV going.

The patient started to stir, moan.

"Mr. Hagborg, don't try to talk. We're taking you to a hospital. I need you to stay calm."

He reached for the tube in his mouth. He was coming to and growing agitated.

Fireman leaned closer to the patient. "Hey, Gust. Just relax. You're okay. We've got a tube down your throat to help you breathe."

The rumbling bass voice seemed to calm the older man for a bit, but then the patient started to grab for the ET tube again. His eyes opened, panicked. Heart rate shot up.

Ronnie dug through the meds for the Versed, measured the correct amount, and administered it to his IV. The last thing she needed was the guy to rip out his ET tube or IV line.

He calmed, dropped his hand back to the cot, the sedative kicking in.

Good.

His pulse decreased to a normal beat. But one touch indicated his hands were cold and clammy. Those oxygen numbers were still too low.

The monitor started beeping. Blood pressure dropping.

"Come on, Mr. Hagborg. We didn't come all this way to lose you now." Ronnie spoke quietly in his ear as she made sure his tube placement was correct. She pushed more meds and fought to stabilize the older gentleman. "That's right, Gust. Keep breathing."

Slowly his numbers improved, but not by much. There was nothing else to do but watch over him.

And still Fireman steadily squeezed the bag in perfect rhythm.

At some point he had shed his coat and helmet. His long

dark hair curled past his shoulders. Same dark-colored beard. He looked like he belonged in the north woods, but instead of lumberjack flannel, a navy Deep Haven Fire Department shirt stretched across his broad shoulders and thick biceps, and red suspenders held up his bunker gear pants. Yeah, his brawn took up a lot of room. But go figure. The fireman knew a little emergency medicine.

His eyes locked onto her. "Thanks for saving him."

She stilled for a moment. Not sure what to do with the gratitude, she shrugged. "Don't thank me yet. He's still critical."

Not that the old monitors and outdated gear around them were a huge help. "That defibrillator is ancient. Do you even have a LUCAS or something for mechanical compressions for CPR? I maybe should've checked the expiration date on the meds."

A muscle in Fireman's jaw ticked. "This is a backup vehicle. Usually an ambulance would come from the hospital, but they were already on other calls. We're trying to raise funds for our own Crisis Response Team rig now that you're here. But it's a small town."

"Tell me about it." She blew out a short breath. "Well, let's hope we get those funds sooner than later. This is borderline ridiculous. If they want us to save lives, we need the tools to do that."

She checked Mr. Hagborg again. Steady heart rate. Oxygen improved but still not what it should be.

"I suppose you're used to state-of-the-art equipment." His hazel-green eyes cut back to her. His words sounded more like a judgment than an observation.

What was his deal? "I know how to make do. I've worked in war zones and in the middle of the wilderness. I'm up for whatever it takes to save this man's life, but it would be a lot easier with gear from this decade and people who are trained to use it. Have those two guys back there ever boarded somebody?"

"Usually we have more seasoned EMTs on site. But with the holiday weekend and one guy having a baby, Charlie and Dean were the only first responders available."

"Seriously? That's the best they could do? No wonder Cole said you needed help." She readjusted her gloves. "Do you need me to take over the bag?"

"I've got it."

Despite his tight lips and scowl, he'd been helpful, so she'd let him continue.

Cole called to the back, "We're almost there. They have the ER standing by."

Good, because she had done all she could for Mr. Hagborg and he was still on the verge of tanking—and Ronnie couldn't bear to lose him or any patient in her care.

With Cole and Fireman, they exited the ambulance and wheeled the cot into the ER in far less time than it took to load him. Amazing how working with competent people made this so much smoother. They released the patient to the hospital's staff, and Ronnie leaned against the wall of the waiting area to draw her first full breath since the alarm sounded. See? Despite the ancient equipment, the long drive, and all the other obstacles in the way, she could totally do this backwoods paramedic thing.

She should hit the head while they waited for one of the staff to bring their backboard. But that would require moving. And now that she'd stopped—

A split second of panic jolted her. She pushed off the wall. Tiago!

She'd forgotten her brother. Here it was, three in the morning, and she was over a hundred miles away from him.

"You, okay?" Cole asked. He handed her a water bottle as she paced the hall and patted down her pockets to find her phone.

"My brother. I need to check on him. Can I have Megan's number? I didn't even ask—I mean, I didn't know—"

"Ronnie. Don't worry. He's fine. She texted me earlier that she has someone staying with Josh so she could watch Tiago. But I'll call her. She'll be expecting me to check in anyway. I'll meet you back at the ambulance, but take a deep breath. He's okay."

Fireman said nothing as Cole walked out—at least not with his mouth. But his eyes said it for him.

How could you forget your own brother?

Ronnie's cheeks burned. Some guardian she made.

Like Cole said, Tiago was fine. Thank goodness Megan was close by and willing to help.

Okay, so maybe this new job wasn't a breeze. But she had to make it work. She *would* make it work. Because really, what other choice did she have?

She'd start by bringing their EMS into this century.

She didn't anticipate having to ride in an ambulance two and half hours one way just to reach Level III trauma care. Apparently, the Deep Haven ER was only equipped for minor emergencies. That meant major calls would be a long time for Tiago to be alone.

She just had to find someone, maybe even Megan, to keep an eye on him when she was gone. It had to be better than Abuela's house where he was exposed to her delinquent cousins and their druggie friends or wandering the city alone with the kids in their neighborhood looking for trouble. She wanted a better life for him than what she'd grown up with.

One of the nurses brought the board and another bag to them. "Sorry for the wait. I grabbed a new collar for you. Oh, and some more things to restock your ambulance."

Ronnie took the collar and bag from her. "Finally, something up-to-date for our rig."

But the nurse only had eyes for Fireman, her gaze running over him. She called out, "Deer are out tonight. Be careful driving back, Peter." She sent a flirty wave to the guy, who just nodded and marched away with the backboard in hand.

Ugh. Why did women do that, throw themselves at men just because they were good-looking? She headed outside, Fireman beside her.

Under her breath she mocked the nurse with a falsetto voice. "Be careful driving back." She chuckled to herself. "You mean when we go back to the Podunk town in the middle of Nowheresville where people don't know a hair dryer from a defibrillator?"

She glanced at the fireman. Surely he'd appreciate a little humor after all the stress.

He stopped and glared at her.

Or maybe not.

"We may be a small town, but we have each other's back. We don't have all the latest and greatest gadgets, but we're all about family and community. If you don't like that kind of thing, you're welcome to go back to where you came from. We were fine before you came."

He stowed the backboard in the ambulance, got into the passenger side of the vehicle, and slammed the door.

What was that all about?

Go back to where you came from.

No. She couldn't go back there. She needed a safe place far *away* from there. And, hello. She'd just saved that guy's life. No way those other responders could've done that. If she'd been back in Iraq, the guys would've given her a pat on the back, not a door in the face.

What was with this place?

Ronnie crawled into the back of the truck and plopped on the bench. She fought the fatigue and emotion pushing against her eyelids and sore muscles. She leaned her head back and closed her eyes. After the long day packing and driving, Ronnie had no more fight left. The imminent adrenaline crash washed over her. A few tears escaped.

Wait. She smacked her forehead with the palm of her hand.

Peter. That's what the nurse had called him.

Wasn't that the name of the fire chief that Cole had warned her about?

The one everybody loved?

Wonderful.

She may have saved Gust Hagborg's life, but she'd apparently insulted her brand-spanking new partner.

Her time in Deep Haven was off to a stellar start.

Ronnie curled onto her side and fell asleep somewhere on the road to Deep Haven—a place that didn't want her.

What else was new?

CHAPTER 3

One down, one more Memorial weekend family function to go. The Dahlquist Rib Cook-off. Peter clutched his package of Oreos and walked up to the Cook County High School football field, his game face on. The smell of smoky sweet pork in the air stoked his ravenous appetite. A shrill whistle and a rumble of male voices indicated the game had already started.

Exercise and food. After the stressful midnight call, arriving home close to dawn, and sleeping most of the day, that's all he wanted. No, needed.

His stomach growled.

Thankfully, he was in the right place. Every one of his dad's siblings and cousins competed tonight for the title of Rib Master on his old high school football field, thanks to Uncle Gordy, generous donor to Deep Haven athletics and member of the school board.

They would feast as they filled out score sheets with each delicious rib entry. And Mom always made sure he went home with a week's worth of leftovers.

He could count on it, sure as he could count on a fierce game of football between the older and younger generations, Grandma Doris's apple pie for dessert, and each restaurant-owning family trying to corner him and persuade him to vote the Dahlquist way. But the food would be worth it.

Hopefully.

With a wave for his mom, Peter bypassed the women congregated near the concession stand where they set up for the meal. He searched for his cousin Nick on the field.

Wait a minute. Why was Dad facing Uncle Gordy on the forty-five-yard line? The brothers should be on the same team, the forty-and-older team, not opposing ones.

"Peter's here! Time out." Nick broke the line and ran over. As his closest cousin and friend, Nick always felt more like a brother. They were in the same grade growing up, played foot-ball together, and even shared a dorm room at the University of Minnesota in Duluth for a couple years. And with a similar height and dark brown hair, they were often mistaken for siblings, even though they weren't blood-related and Nick had a leaner frame. Made him a great wide receiver.

"Bro, where have you been? We need you to block for our running game. We're down two touchdowns." Nick grabbed the Oreos out of his hand, threw them to the sidelines. "I don't know why you bother with those when Grandma made bars. Now, come on. Your dad's waiting."

Bars? What happened to apple pie? Peter looked at the variety of ages in the huddle, from his younger brother Johnny to Great Uncle Joe to ten-year-old Grayson—second cousin once removed. "What happened to the Old Fogies versus Young Bucks game?"

"Get with the times, Peter. Uncle Gordy and I picked teams. Wanted to mix things up a bit." Dad slapped him on the back then got down to business and called the play.

But Peter couldn't pay much attention to it. What was going on? The Dahlquists didn't "mix things up." And yet, the huddle broke, and Peter took the line next to eighty-year-old Great Uncle Joe on one side and Nick on the other, at defensive end.

A sliver of hope took root. If they were willing to switch up the game, maybe they would lay off on the vote talk too and let him decide in peace.

Maybe.

Abandoning his worries, Peter threw his all into the game and forgot about the vote—and everything else weighing on him—for one glorious hour. The only thing that mattered was stopping the opposing team, then turning it around and moving his team down the field to victory.

Which he did.

After congratulations and high fives for running the ball to the winning touchdown, Dad called for Peter to join him as he checked on his smoker. "Nice game, son. You really helped us turn the tide."

He should feel a rush of pride. Instead tension in Peter's shoulders flared. Another attempt to bring up the vote? It was only a matter of time.

Dad slipped his Kiss the Cook apron over his athletic shirt. Like all the Dahlquist men, he was tall and lanky. They may be skinny, but they sure knew how to cook and how to pack it away. He opened the smoker and checked the meat temperature.

The mesquite aroma escaped and filled the air. Dad moved the ribs from the smoker to the grill and brushed them with his secret sauce. "I've missed the win the last three years, but mark my words, I will be wearing that crown by the end of the day."

His father always seemed to ooze confidence, always knew what to say or do. If only he could've passed that gift on to his adopted son.

Still, the dreaded subject didn't come up.

For now.

They joined the rest of the adults sitting in camping chairs circled around the coolers at the edge of the field. Peter popped open a Mountain Dew, taking a long swig as he studied the new Huskies scoreboard towering over them. This town sure loved their sports. And their festivals. There were so many good things about Deep Haven, even if *certain people* couldn't see it.

"Heard about the fire last night at Hagborg's, Peter. What happened?" Aunt Alice asked. She sat on a folding chair and knitted away on her latest Christmas sweater. Everyone in the family had one.

"Space heater in the garage. A piece of insulation fell on it and poof." He didn't mention the clutter.

"Well, that place was a fire waiting to happen with all the hoards of junk Gustav kept. The poor man. He hasn't been the same since his grandson Monte died," Grandma said from her place by the dessert table.

"No, but can you blame the guy, Mom? All alone in that house. What a sad existence." Aunt Connie shook her head as she stirred her homemade barbecue sauce on a camping burner.

Peter took another swig and tried not to think about his own lonely cottage. "The house is a total loss, but we were lucky enough to get to Gust in time."

"It wasn't luck." Uncle Gordy joined the group, tugging down his Vikings hat to cover up his bald spot. "It was pure grit. Heard you were the one to pull him out of there, Pete. Had to escape through the window right before the roof caught fire and collapsed."

"Peter, is that true? Are you okay?" Mom looked worried again, like she always did when a fire rescue came up.

"I'm fine. Better off than Gust anyway. But the doctors are hoping he'll make a full recovery."

"Talked with Dean Wilson. He said they should've hired Kirby Hueston since that new paramedic that helped on the scene is worse than a wounded grizzly bear. Dean's ready to quit. You meet her?" Gordy asked.

Every muscle went taut at the mention of his new Crisis Team partner.

And here he thought the vote would be the worst thing someone could bring up. He'd managed thus far to put the ornery woman from last night and this morning out of mind.

Until now.

"Yep. Met her." Peter kept his gaze on the can in his hand, trying to keep his voice even and look as nonchalant as possible even as he crushed the empty beverage container into a solid block of aluminum.

"So, what's she like? It's not every day someone new moves to Deep Haven," Nick said from where he fished through one of the drink coolers.

"Her? She?" Mom straightened in her chair. Her eyes lit. "It's a woman?"

Great. Now Mom would never let the subject drop. All the other side conversations came to a halt.

Throw them a bone and run. That would work, right? "Uh, yes. A woman. Veronica, but she goes by Ronnie. She seems to know her stuff. Probably saved old man Hagborg's life. She's got a younger brother with her, and that's all I know." He turned to his dad. "We should go check those ribs."

"Nah, we still have time." Dad settled back in his chair and took a sip of his beer. The smirk said he knew exactly what he was doing too. "Tell us more about this Ronnie."

Peter stood. "I'm going to go check on the kids."

"I'll come with you." Nick matched his pace as Peter bolted away from the group. The snickers behind them grew to full-out belly laughs by the time they were halfway across the field.

Yeah, he wasn't kidding anyone. The woman affected him. Like a virus.

He owed her an apology. A huge one. He still couldn't believe the words that had come out of his own mouth. *Go back to where you came from.* He'd never talked like that to anyone in his life. He was supposed to keep the peace, not start a fight. But she kept griping about the town, and the way she pushed aside Gretchen and barked at the crew, it ate at him. And, yeah, maybe he felt a little for Kirby.

"So, tell me the truth, what's this Ronnie like? She cute?" Nick asked with a grin.

Peter snorted. "Kinda hard to tell as she ordered everyone around, insulted our entire EMS, and growled at anyone who came close. The woman is infuriating."

Nick froze. "Wow. That's gotta be the most unflattering thing I've ever heard you say about...anyone. What happened, Mr. Diplomacy? You always find a positive spin on people."

"I said she saved Gust's life. That's positive."

"She really got under your skin, huh?" Nick's grin grew.

"Shut up." Peter turned and started walking again toward the kids.

"She's pretty, isn't she?" Nick's voice filled with mirth.

Pretty? He supposed. But snippy brunettes with sharp amber eyes weren't really his type. How did anyone see past the fangs in her words?

At the hospital, he'd been on the verge of marching up to Cole to demand that he find another paramedic. Okay, he probably wouldn't have demanded, but he would have strongly encouraged it. Only then she'd surprised him.

She had been freaking out about her brother, worried about him. Asking Cole to use his phone to check on him.

That tiny glimpse of a beating heart beneath the razor-sharp armor was the only thing stopping him.

That and the gentle way she'd treated Gust, whispering for him to keep fighting for his life.

So he was a sucker for second chances. Maybe she'd had a bad day and the stress of moving was getting to her.

Still, his mother would be ashamed of how he'd spoken to her.

How he was supposed to work with her, he hadn't a clue. But she was the last thing he wanted to think about right now. He turned to his cousin. "You know who's back in town and pretty enough to turn *your* head?"

"Who?"

Peter walked away. "Never mind. You won't care—"

"Come on, Pete. Don't hold out on me now." Nick pulled him to a stop. "Who is it?"

"Vivien Calhoun."

Nick swallowed. *Yep, that's right, buddy.* Vivie, Nick's high school crush.

It paid to know everyone in town.

"Oh, really?" Nick said. He looked away. "What...what's she doing in Deep Haven? Just visiting, right?" He made a show of picking at a callous on his hands, but the gulp of his Adam's apple spoke volumes.

"Sounds like she's sticking around. At least for the summer. She's leading a theater camp for kids."

"Yeah? Good for her."

Before Peter could tease Nick anymore, Grandpa Dahlquist called everyone in for prayer, and the meal began. No bonfire or amphitheater here. Instead the children scattered to sit on blankets dotting the field, while the adults moved their camping chairs to sit in a large circle under the evening sky.

Peter's mouth watered as he piled his plate high with smoked baby back ribs, gourmet potato salad, molasses baked beans, and some kind of fancy coleslaw. He headed toward the drink coolers when his uncle called him back.

"Whatcha need, Uncle Gordy?"

"Got a seat for ya here, Pete." He patted an empty chair between him and Grandma Doris, right in the thick of the crowd. "We wanted to hear your thoughts about the vote."

Peter's appetite died.

Sure. They could switch up the football game. Grandma

made apple bars instead of pie this year. But some things never changed.

And, clearly, there was no escape.

Everyone watched him as he sat and bit into a rib. "Wow, Dad, these are good. I think you're right. That crown might be going home with you tonight."

"Thanks, Son. But back to the vote. With new building restrictions, we can't rebuild Pierre's Pizza on the old site the way we want to." He leaned in. "We need you."

Wow. Way to go straight for the jugular.

Uncle Gordy spoke up. "Your Uncle Gunter and I have already talked to architects to design a restaurant with a large outdoor seating area and an authentic brick pizza oven. That hotel property on the lake is perfect. And we would have enough room to build apartments above the restaurant. You know Deep Haven could use more rental units. It will help offset costs during the slow season. Your vote will make it happen."

They all looked at him with so much hope and expectation. Mom winked. Dad gave an encouraging nod. Aunt Karen came around with a second helping of potato salad and plopped it on his plate.

And then, silence.

Peter cleared his throat. "You know I want what's best for Deep Haven—"

"That's all we're asking, Peter. Asking you to think of what's best for the town." Grandma patted his cheek. "And for your family. We're depending on you."

She passed him a wrapped loaf of zucchini bread. "I made this just for you. It's your favorite. And more importantly, it's made with love."

Yeah. And a heaping dose of familial obligation.

"Thanks, Grandma."

"Don't worry about those Zimmermans. They don't need

another tacky moose hotel. Just think of your family when you vote."

The rest of the group gave their hearty agreement and launched into a Zimmerman-bashing session. The few bites Peter managed to swallow landed like lead in his gut. He got up, threw his plate in the garbage bin, and made his getaway. Memories of food flying and fist fights destroyed his appetite.

He didn't even care about the leftovers.

He pulled his truck into his driveway and killed the engine. He studied the house in front of him. Sure, the cottage was on the small side. But the navy blue siding with white trim gave it a classy, clean look. The yard was neat and well maintained. It was a good home.

And as empty as Gust Hagborg's charred lot.

No porch light shining in welcome or bright windows glowing with warmth. Just a cold, dark, empty house.

He sighed. Maybe it was time to get a dog.

A dog who would be happy to see him and whose loyalty didn't depend on how he voted in town politics.

Ronnie refused to call the prickly sensation that settled into her head doubt.

It couldn't be. Because doubt meant she might have made a wrong choice. And moving Tiago out here was the *right* thing to do. They couldn't stay in Minneapolis. Therefore, this itchiness in her brain was simply the need to be active. Maybe the transition to civilian life manifesting itself. That's all.

But whatever it was, it refused to budge.

The uncertainty lingered even as she approached the apartment at the end of her five-mile morning run. Much of it had been up and down the hills with the new day's sun shining on the small town and bouncing off the ripples of the Great Lake.

She pushed to sprint the last block and checked her time before walking in. She went straight to the fridge, grabbed a water bottle, and downed it in one long draw.

Tiago didn't look up from his video game in the living room. "Where'd you go?"

Ronnie swallowed the last gulp of water and stood on one leg to stretch her quad. "I left a note on the table. Didn't you read it?"

"I know you went for a run, but where? There's no place to go in this stupid town."

"It's not stupid. It's quiet, I'll give you that. I had to find a city-noise app to help me sleep last night. But look outside. You walk two blocks and you have all of Lake Superior at your feet."

"Whatever. What are we doing today? I'm bored."

"Thought we could try that mini golf place."

"I don't want to do some lame mini golf course." He sat cross-legged in front of the TV, still in his pajamas. His dark brown wavy hair flopped in his eyes.

"Oh come on. Have you even been mini golfing before? We'll grab a donut before we go. Saw a place called World's Best Donuts. It'll be fun."

Tiago threw down the controller and finally made eye contact. "Why did you bring me here anyway?"

She wouldn't react to his anger. Instead she switched legs, pulling on her foot until she could feel the stretch down the front of her thigh while she counted to five. "Come on, T. We talked about this. We needed a clean break from the Cities. You and me. We're on an adventure, right?"

"An adventure?" He huffed. "No! You're punishing me for something I didn't even do, no matter what the freaking judge said. You took me away from all my friends and moved us to the middle of nowhere. That's not an adventure—that's kidnapping!"

Okay, that was it. Forget trying to stay calm. "T, we had to leave. And now you have to give this a chance. We're not going back to Minneapolis."

"I don't like this place!"

"We've been here, what? One full day? And besides—"

A knock interrupted. Great. Probably neighbors complaining about the yelling.

Ronnie opened the door to find Megan and a boy about Tiago's age standing on the step. His dark hair contrasted with wide blue eyes.

Sure, the first chance Tiago had at meeting someone his own age and it was during a fight. Great first impression.

She stepped aside and held the door. "Hi. Uh, come in. Sorry if we were loud, we were just…"

"Oh no, you're fine." Megan placed a hand on the boy's shoulder. "This is my son, Josh. And we wondered if you two would like to join us for a little backyard barbecue this after-noon to celebrate Memorial Day. It's just a few friends coming over, and I thought Josh and Tiago could get to know each other."

Megan offered a sweet bubblegum pink smile, standing there in the entry in a pristine white sundress and cute strappy sandals, while Ronnie dripped sweat down her back, her gray workout shirt stained, black leggings streaked with dust, limp hair falling out of her ponytail. And if the smell lingering in her kitchen was any indication, she might've forgotten deodorant.

She had their day planned, but what the hey. Tiago needed friends. "Yeah, that sounds great. When and where?"

"Come on over to the Black Spruce Inn, right next to our house. We'll be in the back yard, eat around five, but you can come any time after three."

Josh spotted Tiago's game. "You have Madden NFL 20?"

The two boys started talking video games.

See? This would work out. Even if she'd forgotten him briefly during that call. He didn't even know she was gone all night long. And Megan had been as gracious as could be when Ronnie and Cole woke her up. She probably had a sore neck from sleeping on the couch, but she never said a word.

Every indication was they would fit in just fine. And the sooner Tiago made some friends, the better. "We'll be there."

Later, in the cleanest leggings and sports tank she could find, and plenty of deodorant, Ronnie showed up in Megan's back-yard with a case of pop and a bag of Cheetos. Tiago and Josh already tossed a football around. In the shade of the tall spruce trees, another couple sat at the picnic table with Cole and Megan.

"Glad you could make it, Morales," Cole called from his perch.

She walked over to them. "Thanks, Sergeant—I mean, Cole. I'll get it one of these days."

He laughed, and the hard clench in her chest released even more.

Megan took her meager offerings—thanking Ronnie as if they were some Pinterest-worthy homemade appetizer—and introduced her to the very put-together couple across the table.

"This is Ella Bradley and Adrian Vassos. Ella makes eco-friendly cleaning supplies and Adrian, among other things, is helping fund the Crisis Response Team by providing Deep Haven with a helicopter."

Ella, another golden-haired beauty with big aqua-blue eyes, made the simple gray T-shirt dress and flip-flops she wore look elegant. Adrian wore laugh lines framing deep-set green eyes, his expensive-looking polo immaculate. They looked like another fairy-tale couple. Sheesh. Was Deep Haven a breeding ground for blonde beauties and gorgeous men? Maybe she should've made more of an effort to dress up.

Then again, some things were more important. "Did you say helicopter? Here in Deep Haven?" Ronnie sat across from Adrian and leaned in on her elbows. "Because, let me tell you, that would've been really handy Saturday night. It's ridiculous that we are over two hours from any kind of trauma center and there's no helo. Especially with all the wilderness around here. Cole says the busy season is about to start. We need to be ready."

Adrian held out a hand to shake, wearing a too-handsome smile. He should probably be in politics. "You must be Ronnie, our new paramedic Cole was telling us about. I like that go-get-'em spirit. As far as the helicopter goes, we're just waiting for one more person to sign off. The fire chief has the final say in which type we get."

"Fire Chief? Peter what's-his-name?"

Megan handed her a Mason jar of lemonade with strawberry slices and green leaves floating on top. "Peter Dahlquist. He'll be here soon. You met him, right, Ronnie?"

Oh, perfect. "Yeah, we met the other night." When instead of a "Nice work saving Gust Hagborg's life," he'd basically told her she didn't belong.

But it wasn't the first time she'd encountered a cold reception.

Except for his touchiness about all things Deep Haven, he had been competent and helpful. She could work with that. She was here for her brother and to do her job, not to make life-long friends or anything. Ronnie took a sip of lemonade.

"Great! Maybe you can get Pete to sign off on this thing and get that chopper here ASAP."

Not likely. But, "I'll try."

Adrian gave her a high five. "Sounds like a plan."

"How do you like Deep Haven so far?" Ella asked as she looped her arm through Adrian's.

Before she could answer, Tiago laughed. He legitimately cracked up at whatever Josh had said. She watched the boys in wonder. When was the last time her brother even chuckled?

Huh. A little Deep Haven magic working already.

She turned back to Ella. "Deep Haven is great."

"You're settling in okay?"

"Sure. Takes a little getting used to being so far from everything. And the EMS team needs a lot of work, but I'm up for the challenge. We'll get them whipped into shape in no time." She took another sip from her jar.

"Get who whipped into shape?"

Ronnie didn't have to turn to recognize the voice behind her. She'd heard it in her head all night long.

We don't have all the latest and greatest gadgets, but we're all about family and community. If you don't like that kind of thing, you're welcome to go back to where you came from.

Why Peter's voice was stuck on repeat in her mind, she had no idea. But no better time to get going on that plan to bring the helo to Deep Haven. This EMS team needed all the help it could get.

When she did turn around and got a good look at the newcomer holding what looked like homemade chocolate chip cookies, she swallowed hard, the lemonade in her mouth not quite wanting to go down.

She'd thought he was good looking enough in the ambulance in his firefighter attire, but sheesh, he had turned into a full-out North Woods lumberjack—red flannel, cargo shorts, and hiking boots.

Now, he towered over her, one brow raised, those hazel eyes peering into hers with a question.

Shoot, he even smelled nice. Something woodsy and clean. Totally went with his lumberjack vibe.

If a girl liked that sort of thing. Thankfully she knew better. No guy was going to take over *her* life.

"Peter. Hi." Ronnie cleared her throat. "We were just talking about your EMS team. But, more importantly, Adrian here tells me we're waiting on your signature to bring that med-evac helicopter to Deep Haven. What's the hold up?"

Out of the corner of her eye she caught Adrian and Cole

making a beeline for the grill. Megan took Peter's cookies and Ella followed her to the table arranged with drinks and snacks.

What was this—people running for the hills at the first spark of tension? Please. Besides, they wanted this helicopter, right?

Whatever. She could handle Peter what's-his-name.

"Sit down. Let's talk about this." She patted the seat next to her and lined up her arguments for convincing Peter to sign off on the helicopter as soon as possible.

He ignored the hint. "Uh, actually I need to apologize."

Huh? "Apologize?"

He curled a hand around the back of his neck, a sheepish look crossing his face. "Yeah, I was way out of hand talking to you like that yesterday morning at the hospital. Especially after you saved Gust. I was stressed and tired, but it's no excuse."

Ronnie lost all words. She couldn't recall the last time anyone apologized to her. For anything.

Not like she hadn't heard a lot worse from people. Her own family even. Give her direct orders, sarcasm, blunt talk. But what was she supposed to do with an apology?

She brushed away a fly and found her voice again. "It's...uh, fine. We were all tired."

"Well, it's no excuse. Sorry again." He started to walk toward the grill.

No. She needed him to sign off on that helo. And forget this apologizing business. It was too...uncomfortable. She scrambled after him. "What about the helicopter? Deep Haven could really use it. Gust could've used it."

"What about it?"

"You're the one they're waiting on, right? They just need your signature."

"Can I get you a drink?" Peter craned his head, like he was looking for something.

"No, I've got one." She gestured toward her jar. "So, what's the hold up?" Since he wouldn't sit down, she stood facing him.

"Uh, I'm sorting through all the information. It's a big decision."

"What's your timeline?"

"Hmmm?"

"Timeline? Due date. At some point you have to pull the trigger. So what is your timeline for making this decision?" Finally getting back into her groove, she moved in closer.

"I don't know…"

"And what are you going to do about this EMS team? Your people need more training. And you need more people."

He finally looked at her, folding his arms across his chest. "It's not that easy to get volunteers, coordinate everyone's schedule for training, and find the money for supplies and teaching. But we're working on it." He glanced over at the boys. "Is that your brother playing with Josh? I should meet him."

He started to walk away but she grabbed his arm.

Okay, yes, he had really strong arms. But of course he did—he was a firefighter. "I'll introduce you in a sec. But first, I'd like to see your equipment, list of volunteers, and training schedule. I need to know what I'm working with here. We've got to bring the group up to speed on procedures. People's lives depend on it. We can't have another repeat of that last call."

"Yeah, we should set something up." He smiled and tried to walk away again.

Ronnie stepped in front of him, blocking his path. "When?"

He let out a sigh. "When what?"

"When are we going to go over the equipment and list? I'm free tomorrow."

A beat passed as he stared at her. Then, "Fine. Tomorrow's… great." He tried to step around her.

Ronnie stepped too. "Where's a good place for breakfast then? The sooner we get this going, the better."

His mouth opened. Closed. "The Loon Cafe is good, I guess." He looked back at the boys. "So, what's your brother's name?"

"Tiago. What time are we meeting? I'd like you to bring—"

"Watch out!"

Just that fast, Peter put out his arm and yanked her against his chest.

With his other hand, he caught the football that must've been headed straight for her head. He lifted the ball in one hand, like a superhero stopping a runaway train, and looked down at her. "You okay?"

Um. Her hands rested on his rock-solid flannel chest. *Maybe?*

One thing was for sure—thank goodness she'd remembered deodorant.

Before she lost herself in his woodsy scent and hypnotizing eyes, she pulled away and swiped the hair away from her face. "Yeah. I'm fine."

"Good." He tossed the ball to Josh. "Hey, bud. Better be careful with that thing. Why don't you introduce me to your new friend?"

This time, she let him walk away. She needed another drink. Now.

Ronnie stood, watching him high-five Josh and meet Tiago, tossing the ball to the boys, laughing, smiling.

The hero of Deep Haven.

But she wasn't here to make friends. She had a job to do. Mark her words, despite their breakfast meeting, before that man left this yard, she would have a firm date for signing off on that helicopter and a detailed plan to make the Deep Haven EMS staff a cohesive, well-trained team.

CHAPTER 4

*A*ll a hardworking, stressed-out guy wanted was a quiet day off. Here, away from all family connections, Peter should have that.

But no. Megan had invited Ronnie Morales. And man alive, she was relentless.

At least for now, she headed in the opposite direction to join Megan and Ella. He would make this helicopter decision in his own time, thank you very much. He didn't need her pressuring him too.

Peter released a long breath. Time to enjoy the holiday and forget all about the vote and helicopter business.

He walked to the back of the yard where the sun trickled through the branches of the shaggy spruce tree border. Josh's face lit up, but Ronnie's brother stepped back, jutting out his chin in a way too familiar way.

"Hey, Josh." Peter gave him a high five. He nodded in greeting to the other dark-haired boy. "It's Tiago, right? You're Ronnie's brother?"

"Yeah. What about it?"

Not much muscle or meat to the kid. Josh actually stood an

inch or two taller. But like Ronnie, Tiago gave the impression of being bigger than he was, tougher.

"Welcome to Deep Haven." Peter tossed him the football. "You play football?"

His eyes narrowed in challenge. "Wanna find out?"

"Show me what you got." Peter backed up, giving the boy space to throw.

Tiago launched a perfect spiral.

Peter nabbed it with one hand, bringing it in easily. "Not too shabby." He tossed it to Josh, who caught it two handed, grinning.

Josh spiraled it out to Tiago, just like Cole had taught him. The kid was really catching on.

Peter's shoulders loosened as the three of them zigzagged across the backyard with the football. Now, this was what a day off should be like. The smell of sizzling burgers on the grill. Sweet lemonade to quench the thirst. Tossing around a pigskin.

"Go long, Peter!" Josh yelled.

The football sailed in a perfect arc. Peter reached out and—

Ronnie swooped in from the side and intercepted the catch.

What?

She danced away with the ball, laughing.

And sure, impressive, but seriously? What was it about this woman butting into things?

She turned to face him, smirk and jutting chin matching her little brother's. She tossed the ball back and forth in her slender hands, that glint in her amber eyes.

Oh no. The bulldog was back. Better cut her off before she got started. "Nice catch. You want to join the game, Ronnie? We could make it two-on-two." He offered her his most charming grin.

"What's it gonna take for you to sign off on the helicopter?"

He stifled a groan. Clearly this woman did not know what the word *holiday* meant. "We have plenty of time to talk about that later. Let's take on these boys and see if they can score against us."

"After you give me a decision on that helo, I'm in."

Re. Lent. Less.

Okay, new tactic. "On second thought, I'm going to see if Cole needs any help with those burgers. I bet we're close to eating. Can I bring you a plate?"

"No, I'm—"

"Ronnie, stop hogging the ball!" Tiago called from across the yard. "Toss it here."

She turned away and Peter escaped to the grill. He glanced at Ronnie. Good. The boys lured her into their game, so she was occupied for the moment—hopefully a really long moment. That meant he could hang with the guys and relax a little.

Cole flipped one of his handmade burgers. "So, what do you think, Dahlquist?"

"I think those burgers look amazing. Can't wait to eat."

Megan came over and handed him lemonade in a Mason jar with a lemon slice floating on top. Peter thanked her.

Adrian laughed. "Nice try, Peter. Cole means what do you think about our new paramedic?"

Them too? "Uh, she's very…persistent." He took a swig of his lemonade.

"That's a nice way of putting it." Cole flipped the next one. "She'll be a real asset to the team if she doesn't scare everyone away. That's why she needs you."

"What do you mean—"

"Listen. I know she can be a little rough around the edges, but she's good at her job. And I know a lot of people in town thought I should hire Kirby, but she has more medical experience as a paramedic versus his EMT certification, and she has more time in the field. But we've got to get her through this probationary period. Ninety days. Just…help her fit in. You know—put out any fires she starts."

Perfect. Like he didn't have enough of that in his line of work or his family life. "Why me?"

Cole looked up from the grill. "What can I say? You're good at it."

"Gee, thanks a lot. But I don't remember that being on my job description when you approached me about the Crisis Team."

"Come on, Peter. I've never met anyone as calm as Ronnie when the world is blowing up around her. She gets things done. She just needs some help relating to people. So much of the town is stacked against her because she's not Kirby Hueston. She just needs someone to pave a way for her."

Yeah, but how much trouble was she going to get him into in the process? And ninety days to get her to fit in? Might as well be ninety years.

She threw the ball to Tiago, laughing with the boys. Okay, maybe it wouldn't be too horrible. She had to be a pretty decent person to take care of a little brother like she did.

Cole pulled the last burgers off the grill and called everyone to the table. Ronnie ran up with Tiago and Josh, breathing hard.

"Just in time! I'm starved." She picked up a plate just as Cole said, "Let's pray."

She stiffened even as Peter bowed his head.

"Lord," Cole said, "thank You for the food and the freedom we celebrate today. We are humbled with gratitude for those who made the greatest sacrifice. And thank you for Ronnie and Tiago who were able to join us. Amen."

Though Peter's eyes were closed, he could feel Ronnie shift at the mention of her name. He peeked, caught the surprise in her expression, like it was a strange thing for someone to pray for her.

Interesting. Might be a reason for all that edginess.

They sat down at the long picnic table. Peter took one bite of his burger and moaned. "Aw, man, this is good."

Ronnie cut into her bunless meat with a fork. "Does anyone know how Gust is doing?"

"Gretchen said he's much better and will probably be released later this week." Peter turned to Cole. "So, what's your secret with these burgers? Do you use some kind of special seasoning for the meat?"

"You know, we should get your EMS and rescue teams together and debrief after that call," Ronnie said. "There were so many people not following protocol. We could use it as a teaching time. Examples of what not to do."

Did this woman ever stop thinking about the job?

Peter turned to her. "Everyone on that call is a volunteer. They're doing their best." He looked back at Cole. "So, is the seasoning homemade?"

Ronnie leaned in. "Well, if that's their best, then we definitely need to debrief and get some training done."

He sighed. "Look, we try. We do what we can."

"But you can be better. You need everyone on the same page. Do you want a team that saves lives, or do you want to continue to bumble around?"

"Of course we want to save lives and help, but—"

"Great. Then, see? We're on the same page." She took another bite. "He's right, Cole. These are amazing."

Wow. She was a piece of work. He glanced at Cole.

Who was smirking.

And yeah, as an emergency response team, they could use a lot more training and practice with so many of the older, more experienced players retiring and not enough new volunteers filling in. But couldn't a guy just relax a little on his day off and not be reminded of all the responsibilities awaiting him tomorrow? He bit into his burger once more, but it had cooled off and lost a little of its flavor.

Ronnie and Cole started talking old times—something about grill recipes in Afghanistan, and he should have guessed she'd done time in the military. He finished his burger and helped Megan and Ella clear the plates from the table.

The sun was just falling toward the horizon, bathing the lake in a beautiful rim of gold.

"So, Peter. Helicopter. What's your decision?"

He looked at her. She stood, wiping her hands with a napkin, her dark hair pulled back, those brown eyes locked on him.

Fine. "Look, I know you want an answer, but it's not that easy."

"So explain it to me."

He crumpled a paper cup and threw it in the garbage bag he held. "There's just a lot of options to go through."

"Like what?"

She really wanted to do this? "Okay...do I get one built for speed and best for the medical evacuation calls that EMS wants, or the one that's sturdier, better for wilderness rescues? Or there's one that the fire department wants with firefighting capabilities for the few times that will be helpful. Then I have to think about pilots. Some choppers are easier to fly. We'll have more pilots available with the proper training. But the more multi-function choppers will need two pilots with specialized training. Then we could potentially have a helicopter without anyone to fly it. And there's the storage issue. Which helos are easiest to maintain and find parts for and which will be held up when we have to get a part from Germany or Italy because that's where they're made. See? Not a clear-cut decision."

Around him, the chatter had died. Perfect. This was almost as fun as a council meeting.

She didn't seem to notice. "Sure, it's a big decision, but it has to be made." She scooped up the dirty napkins on the table. "Just make it." She threw away the napkins and stood toe to toe with him.

"Just...*make it?* I'm responsible for making a million-dollar decision. The people of this community are counting on me. I don't take that lightly."

"Good, then you're probably the right person to make the choice. But you can't wait forever. This is too important."

Oh that was just enough. "I know it's important! And maybe if you would get out of my face and let me think, I could choose!" He narrowed his eyes at her. "We will get the chopper. We'll get the training. And I'll have a decision by next Monday."

His jaw hurt, it was clamped so tight. His heart pounded as he stared down into those sparking amber eyes.

She smiled.

Honest to goodness smiled.

"Okay." She gave him a playful punch on the shoulder. "That wasn't so bad, was it?" She turned and walked over to where Josh and Tiago sat with an orange tabby cat.

What. Just. *Happened?*

Ella and Adrian stood like statues. Eyes wide, mouths agape. Cole and Megan were probably right behind him with similar expressions.

And he was shaking inside.

But what was he supposed to do? She dug her claws in and would not relent.

And then just like that she trotted off with a grin like he hadn't just completely lost his cool, raised his voice, and shocked his close friends with a side of him he didn't even recognize.

Peter plopped down on the picnic bench while everyone else moved to the decorative fire table and dug into ice cream sundaes Ella handed out. He closed his eyes and counted to ten.

"Hey." Megan handed him a bowl, one of his cookies stuck into a mountain of vanilla ice cream and swirls of warm caramel drizzled all over. "Your cookies are delicious. Did you make them yourself?"

"Yeah. Mom's recipe." His monotone voice was barely more than a whisper. "Peanut butter chocolate chip."

She made a sympathetic hum. "Uh, you okay?"

Good question. Was he?

Not in the least. He hadn't even recognized himself there for a while. But Ronnie—she didn't seem upset by their fight at all.

In fact, if he wasn't mistaken, she'd almost looked like she respected him before she walked away.

He nodded slowly. "I'm okay. I think."

Megan shook her head with a quiet chuckle. "And here I thought my pretty new neighbor might be a good match for you. Finally, someone in Deep Haven you're not related to. But obviously..." Her voice trailed off as she made a face.

He met it. "Yeah, sorry. No."

From the firepit, Ronnie's laugh carried over. Her hands gestured wildly as she jumped into some story. Her eyes shone. Her tan skin glowed.

The boys and the others were captivated by whatever she was saying.

Maybe she was pretty in a tomboy, exotic way.

But he didn't like exotic and especially not annoying and stubborn and...

Although, maybe she was right about the EMS team. Uncle Charlie and Dean never could've handled that last call alone. They needed more volunteers and to step up their game if they were going to keep citizens and visitors to Deep Haven safe.

But with her around, he'd be lucky if his entire team didn't quit.

If *he* didn't quit.

"She has one thing going for her though," he said as Megan got up.

"What's that?"

He took a bite of his ice cream and looked back to Megan. "At least she's not my cousin."

She just might like it here.

The night felt almost perfect. Ice cream sundaes and laughter around propane flames of the Black Spruce fire table. Tiago was making a friend. And to finish it off like the cherry on top, she'd talked Peter into signing off on the helicopter within the week.

Admittedly, he'd surprised her with all the things he had to consider in choosing a helicopter. He really cared about covering all his bases. But he'd just needed a little push.

She'd helped him, like a good partner should.

Yes, she might survive this small town. She didn't even know who her neighbors were in the city. They never had backyard barbecues like this. But it was…nice.

Looked like she'd made the right decision to come. Now she just had to find a way to stay. She took one last lick of her spoon and set the dish to the side.

"Ronnie, you should've seen Adrian when he first came to Deep Haven. Or the first time we went camping. It was a disaster." Ella smiled from across the fire.

"What? You're not all from Deep Haven?"

Ella shook her head. "Oh, no. Adrian, Cole, and I are all transplants. Megan and Peter are the natives. But we're hoping to put down some roots. In fact, my stepsister is moving here soon."

"My first night here was spent in jail, so you're already doing better than me," Adrian said. "Although, I think I managed okay." They all laughed as Adrian sweetly kissed Ella's cheek. "So, Ronnie, why Deep Haven? I heard you're a fantastic paramedic. Why not stay in the Cities?"

She looked at Tiago. His gaze sank to the ground and his thin shoulders slumped. He didn't need a reminder of what had spurred this move. And wholesome small-town folk like this group wouldn't last a day in Abuela's neighborhood. She had to show them she and T belonged. "It's Cole's fault."

Cole held up his hands. "Guilty."

Tiago raised his head a little. Sneaked a glance at her.

Good. She needed him to keep coming out of that shell. "Yeah, Cole told me about the paramedic position and I just got out of the Army not too long ago, so the timing and the job were perfect. Couldn't miss out on the opportunity."

Ella rested her head on Adrian's shoulder. "Why did you leave the Army?"

Oh. That. Holding the smile got a lot more difficult. She could still hear Abuela's shaky voice telling her that Tiago had been taken to a temporary foster home. Mom was back in jail. Not exactly the kind of thing that would give her a ticket of welcome.

"The Army was a great choice for me after high school, but I didn't want to miss my brother's life, watching from afar. So, when my time came to re-up, I told Uncle Sam that I had a better offer and came home. I worked with one of the ambulance services down in the Cities the last few months, but North Minneapolis isn't the greatest place for a kid to grow up, so when I got the call from Cole about the paramedic job here, I pounced. And here we are."

Adrian looked down at his girlfriend. "Deep Haven is a great place for a fresh start."

Everyone around the fire nodded, but Ronnie's back stiffened. Fresh start, huh? She'd never really been a fan of those, mostly because those were the same words Lara Morales said the last time she left Ronnie and newborn Tiago with Abuela.

I just need a fresh start, baby. Then I'll be back for you.

Sure, and all the money Ronnie had saved up for a car just happened to disappear at the same time. And the creep with Mom was apparently the only one who could give her the fresh start she wanted no matter how much Ronnie begged her to stay.

Well, they were better off without her. She hoped her "fresh start" had been worth it because Ronnie and Tiago had paid too dear a price for it.

She shook the memory off as Megan called her name. "This must seem really boring after working in combat zones and living in the Cities."

"Yeah, but I've always wanted to help people. That's one of the reasons I joined the Army in the first place. Here, I feel like I can make even more of a difference." She turned to Peter. No time like now to try to make amends and forge a good working relationship. "I know I come off a little strong, but I mean well. I really want to help you—I mean, help the people here."

Megan stood and started collecting dishes. "Of course you do. Look at what you did for Gust. We're glad you and Tiago are here." She took Ronnie's dish and moved on to the boys. "Josh, I've got work tomorrow, so you should head to the house and get ready for bed."

"Yes, ma'am."

Ella and Adrian said their goodbyes and left. Peter moved closer to Tiago and showed him a trick with the football.

He seemed like a good guy. Most guys she knew wouldn't take the time to get to know a kid like Tiago. Josh adored the man. Cole respected him. Megan and Ella had nothing but nice things to say about him.

She sighed. He probably had a girlfriend somewhere. A guy that hot who was good with kids and willing to run into a burning house and save people didn't stay single long. Yes, he might as well have *Hero* tattooed on his forehead.

Even if he did have a hard time making decisions.

But now that he'd given a date for making the chopper decision, they were one step closer to putting together a serious Crisis Response Team.

And that's why she was here. To recruit volunteers. Train them. Streamline policies and procedures. She had the will. She would make a way.

And Tiago would have this cute little town to grow up in.

Things were looking up.

"Hey, T, why don't you head up to the apartment too."

"It's summer now. I can sleep in."

Before she could say anything, Peter piped in. "Dude, I'd listen to your sister. Otherwise you'll get grounded and I'll never get to come play Madden with you."

Tiago rolled his eyes. "Fine." He trotted back over to the garage.

Once he was out of earshot, Ronnie turned back to Peter. "Hey, thanks for hanging out with him. He could use some positive male influence in his life."

"No dad in the picture?"

He had to go there.

Still, he might as well know a little of what he was getting into if he really did want to hang out with her brother. And something about his steady stare, the way he'd saved her from a football concussion earlier...Peter seemed safe.

And he'd probably figure out that she wasn't like any of the other women he worked with—if he hadn't already. "My dad died when I was young. Not even sure who Tiago's father is, but probably no one worth knowing anyway. It's pretty much just me and him."

He gave a soft nod. "That's gotta be rough. I lost my dad when I was a baby. But Tiago seems like a great kid. He's lucky to have you." He got up, clearly ready to end their conversation.

She didn't know why, but she sat there, not quite ready to leave. "So, I'll see you tomorrow at the Loon Cafe? Seven a.m.?" Sheesh, and she sounded even a little...what? Needy?

Please.

He glanced at her. "Yep." Then he said goodbye to Cole and Megan and hopped in his truck.

Apparently, the campfire was over. Ronnie thanked the hosts and headed to her own apartment. She slipped into her pajamas and thumbed through a running magazine as she sat on her bed, back propped up on the pillows, her thoughts back to the fire-table discussion.

That group jelled. Like they'd all grown up as best friends or something, even though they *hadn't* all grown up here. What would that be like? Not that she needed friends. She'd done fine up to this point. But it would make things easier to fit in at least a little. And her job did kind of depend on staying in the town's good graces and getting along with Peter.

The nice guy with spectacular arms who wasn't afraid of their not-so-pristine background.

Shoot. She might even like him.

Tiago came in with fresh minty breath wearing his favorite fuzzy pajama pants. He plopped down next to her but didn't say anything.

"Ready for bed?"

He nodded, but he didn't move. She knew that look on his face though. "What's up, T?"

"I...I'm sorry."

She put down her magazine. "Sorry? For what?"

He blew out a short breath. "For everything. That you had to give up the Army and take care of me."

Ronnie leaned over and looked deep into Tiago's brown eyes. "You have to know. I would do anything for you. We're family. That's what real family does. Forget about Mom and all our crazy cousins and stuff. You and me. We're in this together, 'kay?"

His face softened for a few beats but then twisted in frustration. "It's not fair."

"What's not?"

"Ronnie, I didn't set that fire. It's not fair that I got in trouble and you had to leave everything." He buried a fist in one of the throw pillows. "But you gotta believe me. I didn't do it."

"I do believe you, Tiago. But you might as well learn now, not much in life is fair. You gotta watch out because there's a lot of messed-up stuff. This world...well, it's a hard place. Cruel even. You know that. No one else will look after us. All we can do is be on our guard, put it behind us, and move on. Try to make something of ourselves."

He looked skeptical. "You really think we can do that here?"

What was it that Adrian said? *Deep Haven is a great place for a fresh start.*

If she were going to have a fresh start—and not the variety of Lara Morales—but if she were going to have the *right* one, this would be the place to do it. And unlike her mother, she would stay with Tiago and keep him safe. Not let some guy come into their lives and take over.

Tonight was the happiest she'd seen her brother since she'd come back to the States, so she would do whatever it took to give him a good home here.

"Yeah, I do," she said to his question. "We can build a new life here."

She would make sure of it.

CHAPTER 5

*K*nowing her, Ronnie would be on the rampage this morning, ready to whip their EMS into shape. And, okay, maybe they did need a lot of help. But the last thing Peter wanted to do was lose his cool.

He really was a competent chief. And Deep Haven was a fantastic place to start over.

And he didn't have to prove that to anyone, thank you.

Yeah, he needed coffee. Vats of it.

Peter opened the glass front door of the Loon Cafe, its bell above clanging in welcome. The smell of pancakes and Italian dark roast met him in the entry. Pastor Dan and Kyle nodded from the barstools. Edith Draper and her silver-haired cronies stopped their conversation in the booth long enough to wave hello.

He let out a sigh of relief when no one struck up a conversation. He slipped into the last booth along the back wall and flipped over his coffee mug.

Within seconds, Thelma filled it. "Morning, Peter. What'll it be today? One of your aunt's caramel rolls? She just pulled a pan out of the oven."

The bell above the door sounded again. He tucked himself farther into the booth, keeping Thelma between him and everyone's prying eyes. "Uh, I'm actually meeting someone later. So just coffee for now."

And with the day he had ahead of him, he'd need it strong—something to steel himself for meeting with Ronnie and that dreaded vote.

Interest twinkled in Thelma's eyes. "Oh, really? Who are you meeting?"

"That would be me," a loud and familiar voice answered.

Peter's first sip of coffee spewed from his mouth, showering the table and Thelma's apron. "Ronnie?" He coughed. "You're early."

She materialized from behind Thelma, her eyes bright, her expression chipper, as if she'd been awake for hours already. "So are you. Good. We can get started. After this gets cleaned up, that is."

Should've known. Five seconds in Veronica Morales's presence and he'd already lost his composure. He took the damp rag from its usual spot behind the counter and wiped down the booth and table while Thelma brought them fresh full mugs and silverware.

Kyle didn't bother to hide his chuckle. And Peter felt pretty sure Edith almost fell out of her seat trying to see around Thelma. A few scowls were sent Ronnie's way. People must've figured out she was the one Cole hired instead of Kirby. Even Thelma was rather cool toward her, and Thelma loved everybody.

Ronnie finally sat down and asked for a menu, apparently not noticing the displeasure in the room. After Thelma left, she looked around, taking in the mural of Lake Superior painted on the wall right above them. "So this is the Loon Cafe?"

Peter tried another sip from his mug, ignoring the fact that all the cafe customers still looked their way. At least this time the coffee went down. "Yup. Been in the family for five generations."

"Your family owns it?" Ronnie's eyes widened in surprise.

"Yeah, the Dahlquists own four of the restaurants in town. My dad runs the Timberwolf Bar and Grill. It only serves lunch and dinner, so I come to breakfast here a few times a week. My Aunt Connie and Uncle Gunter run this place."

"I thought your father died."

"He did. My mom remarried."

"Oh. Okay, so what's good here?" She lifted the menu.

"Everything. Most people come for the caramel rolls or the biscuits and gravy, but the pancakes are good too. Aunt Connie makes her own maple syrup. Oh, and the cook makes a great omelet."

She smirked. "Ah. So you're indecisive about what you eat too."

He bristled. "Not always. Besides, you asked for recommendations. There are a lot of good options."

"Mmmhmm." Her sights dropped to the menu.

She wore bright pink, completely impractical earrings, her dark hair pulled back all businesslike, and the kind of outfit his sister wore to work out in.

He just didn't understand this woman.

She looked up and caught him staring. "Is there something wrong? Do I have something in my teeth?"

"No. I just..."

"What?"

Thelma approached again, saving him from having to admit he'd been studying her weird earrings with the exercise ensemble. "What'll it be, folks?"

Ronnie ordered an egg-white omelet with turkey bacon. Thelma said nothing as she wrote down the order.

"You, Peter?" she asked with her usual warmth and smile.

He said the first thing that came to mind. "I'll have...the

Cascade omelet." He closed the menu. "And we'll take a caramel roll to share." See? He could be decisive.

"You sure you want the Cascade? It has mushrooms in it. You hate mushrooms."

Oh, yeah.

"Uh, just ask Vlad to keep the mushrooms out."

Thelma glanced at Ronnie and sent him a concerned look before walking away.

Why did he choose this place again?

Busy digging through a bag, Ronnie didn't notice. She pulled out a folder and notebook and slapped them on the table. "Let's get down to business. Did you bring your volunteer list?"

Don Berglund walked by and frowned at the back of Ronnie's head. Thank goodness he was behind her. Cole wasn't kidding when he said she'd need some help fitting in.

"Peter. List?"

His attention snapped back to her. "Sorry. I didn't write them down. I just know."

"Okay, so who's in charge of the EMS?"

"Ellie used to be in charge, but she retired. Then Dan, the pastor there at the counter by Kyle, took over, but he's dropped down to part time. Eli Hueston ran the place the last few years, but he just moved to Florida."

"So basically no one. Okay." She wrote something in her notebook. "How many EMTs do we have?"

"Well, Jensen, but his wife just had a baby. And usually Seb, the mayor, and Kirby Hueston when he's around. They both just happened to be gone Saturday night."

Ronnie nodded. "So, I'm left with Dumb and Dumber, the first responders on that call with Gust."

Seriously? "Hey—"

"Admit it. They were both dangerously out of shape. And clueless. Sorry to say it, but your team is pitiful."

Peter's shoulders stiffened. "They showed up. They're volunteers. They do this for *nothing*!"

Great. He was getting worked up again. And why? He'd had the same thoughts, questioned Uncle Charlie's and Dean Wilson's abilities and motives too, so why did it bother him so much to hear her say the very same thing?

Maybe because she was just so...blunt. His grandmother might even call it rude.

No, all of Deep Haven would call it rude.

Not that she even seemed to notice that he was upset. She continued to write notes. "The biggest problem is lack of organization and manpower. We need more volunteers and to establish a training schedule. But we can do—"

"Peter! There you are." Vivien called to him from the front door and walked over. "I've been looking everywhere for you. Scoot."

She shooed him over and plopped next to him in the booth just as Thelma set the steaming omelets on the table. Vivien helped herself to the caramel roll. What was it with these women encroaching on what was supposed to be the most important meal of the day?

"Viv, what are you doing here? And since when did you become a morning person? You didn't make first hour all of senior year. It's not even seven."

"I'm looking for you. And don't worry, I'm still not a morning person. I've been up all night. Now, about my idea—"

"Excuse me, who are you?" Ronnie asked, head tilted to the side. "You're interrupting a meeting."

Vivien extended a hand. "Vivien Calhoun. And I'm sorry to interrupt, but I need Peter's help. It's crucial. You don't mind, do you? Oh, I love your earrings!"

Ronnie's lips thinned as she stared Viv down.

And he was trapped against the wall.

"I'm Ronnie. What's so crucial?"

"Oh, these rolls are heaven. You have to try this." Vivien tore off a piece and handed it over to Ronnie.

Who stared at it as if it might be a cigarette offered to a child. But she took it. Ate it.

"It's good," Ronnie said quietly.

"Right?" Vivie picked up a fork and dived into Peter's eggs.

It was a gift. Vivien could tame anyone. And finally, Ronnie had one more person in town on her side.

But then Vivien turned and set her sights on him. "So that big town meeting tonight...you said it's about the Westerman, right?"

Peter set his mug down on the table, splashing his napkin. "Ugh, you too, Vivie?"

"What?"

"I suppose you want me to vote for the Zimmermans. Did Elton send you?"

"No! Like I would listen to him even if he did. Besides, I have a better idea. A *brilliant* idea." She squeezed Peter's arm. "What if we made it into a youth center? A youth center with a theater and a gym!" She squealed. "Wouldn't that be great?"

A youth center?

Ronnie set down her fork. "A youth center sounds like a good idea."

"Yes, see? I knew I liked you! These kids need something to do in the summer and a warm place to hang out in the winter. A youth center would be perfect."

"There are already two proposals on the table—Pierre's Pizza and the resort."

"Yeah, but you know the town needs something like this." She turned to Ronnie. "Do you have any children?"

"My little brother lives with me. He's ten."

"And wouldn't you want something constructive and positive for him to do?"

Ronnie nodded.

Vivien continued, her passion growing. "Just think, we can offer tutoring, year-round theater productions, more community sports and activities, maybe even an art studio. Basically, a safe place to hang out and have fun."

The idea had potential. But—

"What do you think, Peter?" Vivien asked.

What did he think? Too many thoughts. What would the Zimmermans say? What would the Dahlquists do? What would be best for the town? What would Seb think? "A youth center could be a good idea, but you'd have to have a proposal ready tonight. And I can't present the idea. It would have to come from you. Could you come up with a plan before the meeting?"

"Don't worry about that. I already have Ree typing something up. She's the writer."

"All right, then present it tonight, and we'll see what happens."

"Do you think there's a chance?"

"There's always a chance."

"That's all I needed to hear." Vivien swiped the last bit of caramel off the plate with her finger and licked it. "So, Ronnie, you should bring your brother to the musical tryouts on Friday. I'm leading a children's production of *West Side Story*. It'll be great."

"Children's theater? I don't know. Tiago is more of a sports or video game kind of kid."

"He should at least come try out. He might love it. Even Peter did theater back in the day."

Peter groaned. "Viv, don't…"

Ronnie leaned forward. "Really?"

Then she smiled. And something about her smile changed her entire face, just like last night at the fire. And oddly, it did something in him too. Made him stop. Look at her.

Yeah, she *was* pretty…when she wasn't biting his head off.

"He was the best—"

Oh no. Vivie! Peter reached over to clamp a hand over his cousin's mouth, but she squirmed away.

"—Danny Zuko."

Ronnie's jaw dropped. "Danny Zuko? From *Grease?*"

"Please stop talking." He buried his face in his hands.

Of course she didn't listen. "Oh, yeah. He made slicked-back hair, black leather jackets, and penny loafers cool again."

Peter lifted his head. "Let's remember it was seventh grade, I was the only boy who could sing bass, and I broke my arm, which meant I couldn't play baseball that year."

Vivien sighed. "Ah, the good ol' days. I got to be Rizzo. The illustrious start to my stage career." She popped up and ruffled his hair. "Well, I'm off to see how far Ree is with that proposal thingy and then to find a job. I'm hoping Casper will have a kayak instructor position at the Wild Harbor Trading Post that'll be flexible enough to work around the practice schedule. So see you tonight, Petey. Nice to meet you, Ronnie. Oh, and I'd better see you both at tryouts on Friday!" Like the whirlwind she was, she zipped through the cafe and out the door, everyone smiling and waving at her before she left.

Peter grumbled as he took a bite of his now cold omelet. Well, that went well.

He held up his empty coffee cup to Thelma. "More, please?"

Of course he had a girlfriend—she should have guessed it.

Ronnie watched Vivien walk out the door, her long dark hair in perfect beach waves. For Vivien being up all night, somehow her cute maxi dress draped down her thin frame flawlessly and without a wrinkle.

Obviously, she was born for the stage. Beautiful, elegant. Ronnie couldn't fault her good taste in being with a guy like Peter.

And, no. That pinch of envy had nothing to do with their relationship. She had no interest in romance.

None.

Even if the guy did have great hair.

Ronnie gave herself a mental shake and finished her last bite of omelet. Focus. She had an EMS group to organize. She set her fork down. "Why don't we go up to the fire hall and look over the equipment?" She slid out of the booth to wash her hands.

When she returned, Peter stood by the table. "Let's go."

"Wait. I didn't pay." Ronnie opened her bag and dug for her wallet.

"It's taken care of."

She looked up and narrowed her eyes at him. "You better not have."

Peter shrugged. "It's no big deal."

"It's a big deal to me. I pay my own way."

His mouth tightened around the edges. "Then you can pick up the tab next time. Let's go." They moved to the door. Some of the customers glared at her. Even the sheriff's stare wasn't the friendliest. Others just looked irritated.

She tipped her chin up but lowered her voice. "Fine, but this is the only time. And if you're saying 'next time' hoping I'll forget, you have another thing coming."

He shook his head as he held the door for her. "We just met, but I know you well enough not to underestimate you. In any way."

She didn't know why, but his tone didn't suggest this was a good thing.

Ronnie got into her SUV and followed his truck to the fire hall. The big white metal-sided building was situated on the bay as if it were a sentinel looking out over the town. A cute town, but a confusing one.

She walked over to where Peter was unlocking a side door.

"Can I ask you a question? I thought small towns were supposed to be friendly, but it seemed like people in the cafe were upset with me. Am I missing something?"

He glanced over his shoulder at her, a pained expression on his face. "You noticed that, huh?"

"So it's not just me." She folded her arms across her chest. "What did I do? I've only been in Deep Haven three days."

"Yeah, but after that call at Hagborg's, Gretchen wasn't too happy with you. She's a talker, so I'm sure people have already heard about that. And Charlie Zimmerman was mad that you wouldn't let him drive the ambulance. But mostly, I think people are upset because Cole hired you rather than Kirby Hueston. He's the sheriff's brother."

"So people were already against me before I even came? I'm here to help! Can't they see that? I did save Gust's life."

He walked into the fire hall after her. "I think people will come around. But it wouldn't hurt if you were a little more…"

Ronnie spun to face him. "What?"

"Friendly."

So she was back to that kid glove thing. "Yeah, but Cole said the first ninety days is a trial period. I could be as friendly as Mr. Rogers, but if this town doesn't like me, what am I supposed to do? I can be fired for *any* reason."

"Then don't give them a reason." His stare was direct, but not cold or mean in any way. He leaned against the bright yellow fire truck. "Cole also said you're a great medic, so keep doing that. Just remember, a little kindness goes a long way around here."

She tried not to squirm as he watched her. For some reason, it mattered what Peter Dahlquist thought of her. If she could win Peter over, the town would probably follow.

A hint of his woodsy scent wafted around her.

Her job. That was the *only* reason why Peter's opinion of her mattered.

"Kindness. Right. I can do that." She nodded. "So, show me around. Please." Ronnie gave him a saccharine smile.

After a chuckle, Peter turned all business, showing her the ambulance and rescue medical equipment. Much of it was terribly outdated. "This is the Deep Haven Fire Hall. We're sharing the space, but Cole and Seb are looking for a better location for the Crisis Response Team HQ. This is what we have for now."

She had learned how to work with what she had, but with all the technology developed in the last fifteen years, their kits could be so much better. She swiped her hand across the old training dummy. "This won't do."

Peter shoved his hands into his pockets. "We're not a big county. I mean, it's big in land area, but not heavily populated. Not a lot of funds."

"How do we get more funds? They can't expect us to save lives with this equipment. How am I supposed to teach all the volunteers we need to train on one decrepit dummy?"

"We do fundraising events when we can, but beyond that, we could apply for grants or try to secure private funding like Adrian donating the helicopter. We just haven't had anybody able to tackle that."

"All right. That's what I'll be working on then. I'll start researching available grants and apply for those."

"Really?"

"Yeah. That's why I'm here. What are partners for, right?" She gave him a grin—and immediately wanted to cringe. For goodness' sake, was she *flirting* with him? *C'mon, Ronnie.*

For one thing, he and Vivien were obviously close. Their easy banter. The way she made herself right at home next to him in the booth at breakfast. Ronnie wouldn't go after someone else's boyfriend.

And besides, relationships—boyfriends—made women

weak. Gave a man a welcome mat to invade and take over. She would never be helpless like her mother. No, thank you.

She erased the stupid smile. "So, are you ready for that meeting tonight?"

A look of uncertainty flashed across his face. "Yes and no. I'm ready to get that vote over with, but I still don't know which way I'm going to go."

She shrugged. "Don't overthink it. Just pick the better option."

"That's the problem. Both proposals are decent options. There's no obvious choice."

"So it's the helicopter decision all over again and you're afraid."

His mouth opened, then he gave a snort and shook his head. "No, I'm *not* afraid. But this time I have family on both sides of the issue. And as you've already discovered, in a small town choices have lasting repercussions. Someone is going to get hurt, and I hate having to be the source of it."

"What about Vivien's idea?"

Peter kept walking toward the back of the fire hall. "Vivie's idea would actually be really cool. But I'm not sure if Vivien and Ree can pull it off in time. Don't get me wrong. I love Viv. She always has amazing ideas. But she's not so great at the follow-through. She's the queen of unfinished projects."

He walked into the kitchen, which was actually more of a kitchenette with a small fridge and a two-burner stove. Not the kind of place that could foster the camaraderie they'd need for their Crisis Team.

She glanced at Peter, who had moved over to the window, staring out at the parking lot. The guy looked so conflicted that for some reason she longed to ease some of his discomfort. "Well, who needs a youth center anyway? It's like living in a fairy tale here. You have backyard barbecues and how many summer festivals?"

He turned. "It's a small town. Not Utopia. Kids get bored, get into trouble. Drinking, partying, drugs…it's all here."

What? "No. This is so far from…everything. Drugs and gangs—"

"You don't need inner-city gangs to get into trouble. You can find bad choices in Deep Haven just as well as Minneapolis, Chicago, or LA. But maybe providing an alternative for the kids here *would* help…"

Ronnie's stomach tightened. Here she thought she'd yanked Tiago out of all that temptation and trouble. And now Peter was telling her it might not be far enough away?

She could kick herself. She knew better. Hadn't she just said something similar to Tiago last night? This world was a messed-up place. How foolish to think she could hide him away from it all.

Maybe she should check on him—

"You okay?"

She looked up, not realizing she'd gone silent. Peter was considering her, frowning.

Ronnie offered him a fake smile. "Yeah. I'd better go and check on Tiago, and then I'll start on a training schedule and researching grants."

He nodded, slowly, then followed her out to the driveway. She opened the SUV door and he held it open. "You know, if you really want to get to know the town, you should come to the town meeting tonight, see how things work, who the players are. It'll help you in this job."

It probably would. "I'll be there." And not just for her job. She needed Deep Haven to be safe, which meant she'd better get to know what she was up against and figure out how to fight it.

He stood in the parking lot, his hands in his pockets again, watching her as she pulled out.

Interesting.

Ronnie drove to the skate park, which was just a few blocks

uphill from the apartment. She spotted Tiago and Josh riding their boards over the cement forms, helmets on, high-fiving each other. Good. She breathed a little easier. Nothing on fire, no empty liquor bottles, no gang-bangers offering them opioids or even cigarettes.

Nope, this wasn't the inner city, despite what Peter said.

They spotted her and ran over to the SUV. "Hey, sis," Tiago said. "I'm hungry."

"Hop in."

Tiago and Josh dove into the back seat and she drove the boys home.

Josh ran up the walk, and Tiago shouted at him, something about his Madden game.

Okay, he probably needed something else to do this summer. They walked into the apartment and she set down her bag on the table. "So, T, there's a play, a theater for kids, and I think you should try out."

Tiago looked at her, frowning. "Why would I do that?"

"Because it'll be fun. And you can get to know a lot of kids from your new school. Make some more friends this summer."

"No way. I don't want to be in a *play*. That's for girls." He kicked off his shoes by the door.

"Well, too bad. You have to."

"You can't make me." He headed over to the sofa and picked up his controller.

She followed and stood in front of the television, folded her arms across her chest. "Uh, yes, actually I can. What do you think 'guardian' means? You're going to those tryouts."

"Forget it!" He threw down the controller and started to get up, but Ronnie blocked his way.

"Listen, I dropped everything and moved here for you. Now I'm stuck here because of you. And we *will* make the best of it, but that means you're going to tryouts on Friday."

In the silence her heart hammered, her own words echoing

back to her. Okay, she sounded frighteningly like her...her mother.

She took a breath, intending to soften her words when—

"You're just like Mom. You don't want me." His voice was so small. A sheen to his eyes showed him holding back tears.

What—?

But a memory pierced. She was about the same age as Tiago, standing in a different doorway, her mother ignoring her pleas to get up and eat. *Go away, Ronnie. Stop bothering me.*

Oh, Tiago. I'm sorry.

Ronnie reached for her brother's hand, but he pulled away. "Tiago, I do want you. In fact, it's *because* I want you that I'm flipping out a little here. I just...I just want you to stay out of trouble. I don't want to lose you. And you heard what the judge said—he'll put you back in foster care or send you straight to juvie if there's another incident."

"I told you I didn't do—"

"I *know*. And I still believe you. But look what happened by just being with the wrong crowd. So that's why it's so important for you to have good friends and things to do. That's why you're going to tryouts."

"But theater is lame."

She sighed and sat on the sofa, pulling him down next to her. "Yeah, that's kinda what I thought too. But you need this. We missed the registration for summer baseball. This play will give you something to do that isn't gaming or boarding..."

He looked away, clearly undaunted.

Wait. "Peter was in a play. A musical even."

He looked at her. "You made that up. No way would a guy like him do that."

"I promise you he did. And there is nothing lame about Peter Dahlquist."

Nothing lame at all, in fact, from that long dark hair and

broad shoulders down to the six pack she'd felt beneath his flannel shirt the few seconds she was in his arms yesterday.

Yeah, she hadn't forgotten that.

"He'll even be at the tryouts."

Tiago paused. His brows knit as he considered her words.

"Please go to these tryouts. Just give it a chance."

"What if I don't like it? I mean, Josh is fine, but there's still nothing to do around here. And it's weird."

"I'll tell you what. You do these tryouts and at the end of summer, if you still don't like it here, we'll find a new place to move." With her job on a trial basis for the next three months, they might have to move anyway. Not that she wanted to go anywhere, but if she had to, she would. Tiago came first. He was the whole reason for moving up here in the first place.

She would simply convince her brother to like it here. She had eighty-seven days to do so.

He looked up at her. "Are you *sure* Peter did a musical?"

"He was the lead guy in *Grease*. Ask him."

"*Grease*? That one with the car race that Abuela likes?"

"That's the one." She held her breath.

He fidgeted with the edge of his shirt. "I'll see if Josh will do it too. If he'll try out, then I'll go."

She refrained from breaking out into a victory dance or even cracking a smile. And she'd make sure Megan talked Josh into going. "Thank you."

"If I do these tryouts, can I go out with Josh tonight too? He said there would be a group of guys at the skate park after dinner."

"Yes, but you have to promise me you'll stay out of trouble. I'll be at a town meeting."

He gave her a fist bump in agreement.

And that's how she got things done.

CHAPTER 6

The closer Peter's truck got to the Cook County Courthouse, the more his foot slid off the gas. He parked in the far end of the lot, took in all the fresh air he could before walking up the steps to the main entrance of the yellow brick, cube-shaped building, dragging his feet like a prisoner about to face the firing squad.

Or the Deep Haven City Council meeting.

"Peter, wait up."

Great. Seb Brewster. He liked Seb, but that title in front of his name changed things today. Just like the huge columns lining the front of the courthouse. They added a touch of grandeur to a small county government building. He still remembered the awe he'd felt as a little boy when he walked between them the first time to finalize his adoption all those years ago. Something on any other day he'd be proud of, happy to see.

But today the friend was now a mayor, a person of authority, and the looming pillars of marble only added to the dread pooling in his stomach.

"Hey, I know you're in a tough spot on this vote tonight,

Pete, but you've got to make a decision. We can't put this off anymore."

Sure. No big deal. But could someone tell him which side of the family to cut himself off from? Because if Vivien and Ree didn't present their youth center idea—and knowing Viv, the odds were *not* in his favor—he was doomed.

Peter took his seat next to the other four council members and Seb. The heat of so many bodies packed into the city hall room stifled him despite the cool evening air outside.

No doubt as the night progressed, it would get even more heated. Everyone went through the security checkpoint, so there were no weapons to worry about—at least the kind that caused physical harm. With so much riding on the issue, feelings and egos were bound to be bruised by the end of all this.

Probably Peter's most of all.

Reminders of what was at stake were stationed everywhere in the room.

Dad—who could never sit for too long—stood in the crowd against the back wall, Mom on one side of him, Uncle Gordy on the other. Tens of thousands of dollars already spent on architectural plans and pressure to rebuild Pierre's—a Deep Haven icon.

Meanwhile, Uncle Charlie had a front-row seat, with Elton Zimmerman on his left and Grandpa Zim on the right. The drive for them to compete with all the other lakeshore hotels and reclaim a property that was once theirs was understandable.

Each family had plenty of supporters with them too—employees and other business owners that benefited from one side or the other. So many people's lives affected by his choice.

Lord, what do I do? How am I supposed to choose?

Ree sat next to Seth, recorder and pen in hand, ready to report for the *Deep Haven Herald*.

Peter pulled at the collar of his T-shirt and searched the crowd for his one ticket out of this mess. Vivie.

Nope. She wasn't here. He was on his own.

His gaze landed instead on Ronnie. Her dark hair and golden-brown skin stood out among the pale Scandinavians in the room, and her eyes were full of honey-colored light—a beacon in the crowd.

Huh. He hadn't expected an ally, nor the weird feeling her thumbs-up and wink gave him.

Seb called the meeting to order.

They rushed through accepting the last meeting's minutes and all the usual agenda items. Councilman Lewis introduced the Westerman business proposal and opened up the floor for discussion.

No surprise, Uncle Charlie was the first to the mic on behalf of the Zimmermans. "I think we all know that the Westerman deserves a chance to shine again. We will make the place a wonderful getaway for families, a place where they can enjoy all that Deep Haven has to offer. It will benefit every other business in town to keep that property as a hotel."

Uncle Gordy shoved his way to the front and grabbed the mic from Uncle Charlie. "Now wait just a minute. Everywhere I go, people ask me when we're rebuilding Pierre's Pizza. And our plan includes apartments. Our long-term rental housing options are sorely lacking. We'd be killing two birds—"

And from there, chaos erupted.

Peter lost sight of the microphone, not that anyone using it could be heard over all the shouting. The other four council members, two on each side of Peter, yelled over his head and debated amongst themselves. Seb tried to hold Margaret Walker back from the very real threat of punching Bob Frasier in the face.

Peter's body absorbed the boiling tension, the pressure building through the room. To witness the animosity between his closest family and friends was like watching his own worst nightmare come to life—the one where he ran through a burning building toward cries for help but he couldn't get to them. The one where the heat blistered his skin and he could smell singed hair before he woke drenched in sweat.

A guy could only handle so much.

He stood. With one sharp whistle, all action ceased. "Come on, folks. We are better than this. Everyone, take a seat."

Chairs shuffled as people went back to their places. Movement from Ronnie caught his eye. She pointed to the entryway. Vivien.

Thank you, God.

Peter sank back to his chair and spoke into the microphone on the council table. "We've heard plenty from both of these parties. Now, if there are any *new* proposals, this is the time to bring them up."

A rumble sounded through the crowd as Vivien made her way forward. As always, she captured everyone's attention without even trying. And he'd never been so thankful for that.

Vivien smiled at the council members and Seb. "I would like to present another option for the Westerman property. An option that will greatly benefit Deep Haven and fulfill a felt need." She paused, and the whole crowd behind her leaned forward to hear her idea.

"I came back here to start a youth theater program. The school is overpopulated and has an undersized auditorium. As I was thinking about alternative locations to hold our summer production, I realized that we don't have many options for indoor space for our children and teens. The school gyms aren't even adequate to provide enough space for our sports programs anymore. Teams and school clubs are always competing for practice time. So, I propose we turn the Westerman Hotel into a youth center. A center with a gym and theater, a tutoring program, and indoor playground. We could—"

"A youth center?" Uncle Charlie sputtered. "And who's going to pay for that?"

Vivien opened her mouth to answer when Seb interrupted.

"Let's hear Vivien's idea and we will have a time for questions later."

Way to go, Seb.

Vivien outlined a rough plan for the Deep Haven Youth Center. Peter had to admit, she'd put a lot of thought into it.

Uncle Charlie's nostrils flared, but he held his tongue. Dad and Uncle Gordy wore their disdain on their brows, the same tight lips and clenched jaws, but also stayed quiet.

"Thank you, Vivien," Seb said as she finished. "As much as I really wanted to come to a vote and conclusion about the property, I think this bears considering. We need more information before we can make a fair decision. I propose we put this on hold and come back—"

The Deep Haven EMS signal echoed throughout the room from multiple pagers and phones.

Peter had never been more thankful for a call. Yes, give him a fire to fight over personal conflict any day.

Fire rescue and medical support were needed at Rusty's gravel pit up on the ridge.

The crowd dispersed and Peter rushed to the fire hall with Seb, now teammates again, the debate forgotten for the moment.

Rusty's was an abandoned junk car lot located outside city limits, a site that had long ago been reclaimed for late-night parties and local shenanigans.

No one needed directions.

Peter manned the pump truck with the other volunteers, Ronnie and Cole in the ambulance, as they headed out of town. The gravel road was dark, but he knew the way too easily and he swung the rig into Rusty's lot, the high beams on. Beer cans and empty bottles littered the ground, and the radios from cars and trucks blared music as the headlights created eerie shadows on the mounds and valleys of gravel and dirt.

A sunset pit party.

Of course. With most of the adults occupied at the meeting, the local youth decided to light it up and get drunk. Teens and older kids rounded up by the deputies stood a safe distance away from the out-of-control bonfire and a burning storage shed at the edge of the clearing. Their faces were somber in the flashing red and blue lights.

Peter organized his crew and got to work. Thankfully, someone shut off the last radio from the cars as the hose crews fought to put out the storage building and bring the fire back under control.

These kids were extremely lucky the sparks hadn't carried across the road to the small grassy field or woods surrounding the lot. Lucky the building didn't have anything explosive or flammable.

As it was, enough people were hurt. Ronnie was wrapping one kid's arm with gauze. A few more looked like they'd gotten into a tussle. Seb and Jensen were working on another kid lying on the ground with Kirby assisting. Some of the parents stood near the deputies, shooting angry looks of disapproval at their teenagers.

Megan was here too? Sure enough, Josh stood next to her, head hung low. And Tiago was with him. How did they get mixed up in all this?

Just as he walked over to find out, a blur rushed from the trees and jumped over the bonfire that started the whole thing, now a much smaller blaze, but not yet extinguished. With a whoop, a teenager ran away from Kyle, who tried to grab him.

Ben Zimmerman.

Ben lunged away from the sheriff. Backed up right into the fire. Yelled as he spun in a circle, flames catching his jeans.

Peter dropped the radio in his hand and rushed forward,

wrapping Ben in a tight hold and tackling him to the gravel. He rolled with him to smother the flames. The boy flailed and screamed.

Peter held him tight, grunting. "Stop fighting me, Ben. I'm trying to help you." His cheek scraped against the crushed rock on the ground as Ben's head slammed into his jaw and a bony elbow caught him in the ribs.

Ben kept yelping, even after the flames were out. When he finally settled down enough, Peter let go of him.

And to thank Peter for saving his life, the punk lay in the dirt and laughed. "Whoooeeee, did you see that, Uncle Pete?"

Seriously? To go from screaming and fighting for his life to hysterical laughter, the kid had to be high.

"What did you get into, Ben?"

"Just a little something for a good time." He giggled, then started making hand puppets and rocket noises.

Yeah, definitely high. And, sure, laugh it up now. But once Uncle Charlie showed up, there was little chance Ben's grandfather would find the whole thing so amusing.

Actually, where was Uncle Charlie? He had been at the courthouse and, as a first responder, he should be here by now. But no familiar Twins cap in the crowd.

Huh. He must've been serious about his threat to quit the team until Ronnie issued him an apology. But now someone needed to take Ben in hand before he injured himself anymore. Peter dragged Ben over to Cole. "Call Elton and then get this one to Ronnie to patch up."

"Good. This will give her something to do. The parents here won't let her treat their kids. They don't trust her yet or they're still upset she's not Kirby. She's just treating the minors whose parents haven't arrived."

Why couldn't people just get over it? Kirby was a great guy, but he'd only got into emergency medicine in the last couple years. And yeah, the woman could get under a guy's skin, but she had a lot more experience and really knew her stuff when it came to medical care.

Ben stumbled and gave another whoop. "What's a matter, Uncle Pete? Don't you know how to have fun?"

Peter didn't even bother to respond. As soon as Ben's father showed up, his "good time" would come to a swift end. And Elton wouldn't be the only concerned relative. He spotted Gina and Tommy Dahlquist among the troublemakers. Aunt Connie would have a field day with that. Thankfully Peter's own brothers weren't on-site, even though he recognized quite a few of their friends. In fact, he recognized each and every face around the fire.

The crowd grew as more parents arrived. He wouldn't be navigating the fire trucks through this anytime soon. His team gathered the hoses and other equipment and loaded up. While Peter stashed one of the axes, a disgruntled voice carried over. "It's not a pizza parlor or resort we need. That youth center would've been nice right about now. If we had an arcade or some evening sports, these teens wouldn't be setting fire to stuff."

Maybe this youth center idea was an answer to Peter's prayers—an option every family could benefit from. This was more serious than sneaking off and smoking a few cigarettes in the woods at the family picnic. These pit parties were becoming more common and more dangerous.

Ronnie's familiar voice spoke up in response to whoever was around the corner of the truck. "Peter and Vivien are working on it. Believe me, nobody cares more about these kids or this town than Peter."

Well, what do ya know? Maybe Ronnie as a partner wouldn't be so bad. Someone backing him up for once.

And she was right. He did care. If he didn't do something, chances were more kids and teens would get hurt.

But voting for the youth center would mean kick back from *both* the Dahlquists and Zimmermans.

And if he thought this bonfire had been nearly out of control...

A few sparks and wisps of smoke flew up into the night sky. The firefighter crew had the blaze under control, but if Elton Zimmerman wasn't careful, Ronnie would reignite it and set *him* on fire.

She'd never met anyone more stubborn. But for the sake of his son, she would give Ben's father one more chance.

"Ben needs to be seen by a medical professional. He has second—possibly third—degree burns on his leg. You've got to let me treat them."

Ben moaned on the stretcher.

"See? He's in pain. I can help him."

"You won't lay another finger on my son." Elton gripped Ben under his arm and lifted him off the cot and down to the ground. "He'll be fine. We have medicine at home."

"But he's *high*. You don't even know what drugs are in his system right now. If you won't let me treat him then at least take him to the ER where they can give proper dosing."

Elton got right into her face. "Ben isn't some druggie, and my son is my business. You better butt out."

Yeah, well a lot of bluster from the likes of Elton Zimmerman did not intimidate her. She moved in even closer. "He needs to be seen."

"Like it or not, you don't have a say."

And there he had her.

His son suffered and thanks to his father, there was nothing she could do about it. She squeezed the pen in her hand, holding herself back from releasing a solid right hook to Elton's jaw. But she would at least cover her bases and make sure it didn't come back to bite her if Ben's wounds got infected later and Elton wanted to blame her.

She wouldn't put a lawsuit past a guy like him. She held the release form out. "You can't take him without signing a refusal of treatment."

He ripped the clipboard from her hand and scribbled his signature on the line. "Now stay out of my business and watch out. We don't need any more trouble from you." Elton stomped out into the night, dragging Ben away.

Trouble? What was he talking about? She wasn't the one who'd lit up the night with weed and bonfires that had burned down a storage shed.

Insufferable jerk.

With all the patients taken care of—at least the patients whose parents hadn't shown up and refused to let her treat them—Ronnie yanked her latex-free gloves off and marched over to Megan, where Tiago and Josh stood. As if it couldn't get any worse, now she had to deal with her own charge. She couldn't believe it when she'd seen Tiago and Josh in the crowd. "So, anyone want to explain to me why you're here, Tiago? What happened to the skate park?"

"We didn't know what was going on here."

Josh nodded, his eyes red-rimmed. Hard to say if it was because of smoke or remorse-filled tears.

"This is the exact *opposite* of not getting into trouble. How did you even get here?"

He pointed to his bike lying in the dirt, next to Josh's. "Some other guys we were hanging with at the park said there were some cool jumps we could do with our bikes up here. I didn't know how far away it was. And once we got here, we saw the bigger kids and what they were doing. They wouldn't let us leave."

Megan looked to Josh. "Is that true?"

"Yes, ma'am." Poor kid's voice shook.

"Why don't you boys go put your bikes into the truck and wait for me there. We will be talking about this at home." When they left, Megan rounded on Ronnie. "This is not something Josh would do."

The words jolted her, like a slap. "What are you saying?"

"I'm concerned. He's never gone off where he's not supposed to be before. This isn't like him."

That's right, blame the new kid. Ronnie drew in a breath, very aware that Megan was Cole's wife. Despite this incident, she didn't want to pack up quite yet. "Look, I'm upset too. I'll talk with Tiago and make sure this doesn't happen again. But it doesn't sound like they were looking for trouble. Tiago wouldn't know anything about this place being a party spot. We just moved here."

Her words seemed to register with Megan, who took a deep breath and nodded. Then, "I'm not blaming him. I like Tiago, but I am very protective of my son. I want to make sure we're both on the same page." Her voice lost some of its hard edge.

"We are. And believe me, I'm not going to let Tiago get away with this kind of behavior." Not that Ronnie had any idea how to punish him. Any parenting he had in the past swung from extremes, from outright beatings—thankfully Mom had left that guy pretty quickly—to complete neglect. She needed to find some middle ground, consequences to help him make better choices. But right now, she just wanted to throttle the kid.

Megan's eyes softened, as if she sensed Ronnie's frustration. She sighed. "The boys need to understand how serious this is, but don't forget to listen too when you address this with him at home. He needs to know you still care even when you don't approve of his behavior." She looked around the site, still crowded with people but many starting to scatter and leave. "Why don't I take the boys to my place until you're done with the call? I know you'll have paperwork and cleanup." She offered a small smile.

A peace offering.

Ronnie could probably offer one back. "Thanks. And, Megan, don't worry. I'll talk to Tiago. This won't happen again." But Megan was right. She needed to listen, which meant she should cool off before saying anything else to her little brother.

Ronnie walked back to the ambulance, many of the other emergency workers and townspeople already gone.

Peter was standing at the fire truck nearby, working off his bunker jacket. She heard a grunt, as if in pain.

"Peter? Are you hurt?"

He spun around, his eyes wide. "You're still here?"

"Come on, Tough Guy. Let me see it."

"I'm fine."

"Sit."

He rolled his eyes, but complied, lowering himself to the bumper of the fire truck. "Are you always so bossy?"

"Yes. What are you going to do about it?" Ronnie took hold of his arm. From elbow to wrist, the skin was raw and red like a rug burn. Not much she could do for that. But the deep cut and scratches high across his cheek, probably from the gravel, she could address. She brushed back his long hair, his beard softer than anticipated beneath her fingertips as she inspected the lacerations.

She could feel her body heating from the core, all the way to her face. Perfect. She was probably blushing.

She should really have gloves on. And probably get herself checked out, the way she was reacting. Geez. It wasn't like she'd never treated a handsome, muscular man before. She was an Army medic, for goodness' sake. "Come with me to the ambulance so I can clean out these cuts."

"I'll take care of it at—"

"Not you too. I've dealt with enough stubborn men tonight."

She dragged him over to her rig and pointed. "Up." She donned a set of gloves and started working.

His body radiated warmth as well as a manly musk with a hint of smoke, and it weirdly reminded her of a cozy campfire in the woods—the kind where characters in a rom-com would roast s'mores and hot dogs and snuggle together to watch the stars.

Pull yourself together, Morales.

She opened up another drawer. What was she getting again? Oh yeah, saline. Tweezers. Gauze. She gathered up the materials and turned back to Peter.

She needed something to fill the silence, to combat the way his presence overwhelmed the tight space. "So that was some meeting, huh?"

He grimaced as she washed the wound with the saline solution. "You could say that."

"What is the big deal about this property that has everyone so uptight?"

"The Westerman? Well, two of the biggest families in Deep Haven want it." He sighed. "And I just happen to be related to them both."

"What do you mean?" She wiped the excess solution and dirt out of his beard.

"Remember how I said my dad and his siblings, the Dahlquists, own restaurants? Well, they want to rebuild Pierre's Pizza—which we lost in a fire years ago—and add some apartments. But Gary Dahlquist is not my biological father. He adopted me when he married my mom. My biological father was Dylan Zimmerman, who died when I was a baby. *That* side of the family owns resorts and hotels, but they don't have anything directly on the lakeshore in town, so they want to rebuild a hotel on the site. Both are equally good options as far as revenue and bringing income and what they could do for the town."

"And you're the deciding vote?"

"Yeah. But now Vivien has this youth center idea to throw into the mix. This call makes me realize she's right. These kids need something to do. So I think I know what to vote for, but I don't want to hurt anyone in the process. I'll be disappointing a lot of people." He winced as she removed the last bit of dirt from the deepest cut.

"You can't keep everyone happy. Some won't like your decision and that's okay. You're doing the right thing."

He looked up. Wow. This close she could see every burst of gold and jade in his eyes. Her fingers stilled.

"You really think so? Think I'm doing the right thing?"

"Well, yeah. Don't you?"

"Part of me does. Then I think of how upset people will be. People I care about. People I see all the time."

"Not that a youth center will solve all the problems, but you have to remember what you're fighting for. If you made a difference for some of these kids, gave them something better to do than getting high and drunk and hurting themselves or others, isn't it worth it?"

He took in a big breath and released it. "Yeah, it is." His voice was quiet, but sure.

Before she could do anything stupid, she finished with the last cut. "There you go. Try to keep these wounds dry, put some antibiotic ointment on them at home, and be careful with your arm."

"Thanks, Ronnie. I'm glad you were here tonight." He smiled, jumped down, and headed back to the crew as they were loading up the last few pieces of equipment.

He was glad she was here.

Huh.

She gathered the wrappers and garbage to throw away when a far-off scream cut through the rumble of the fire truck engines.

"Help! She's not breathing!"

The desperate cry came from one of the teens, a tall girl in a yellow sweatshirt and ripped jeans at the edge of the lot who stood over another teenager collapsed on the ground.

Ronnie grabbed her jump bag and sprinted over. "What happened?" She put on new gloves and knelt in the gravel.

"I don't know. Jordyn was kinda sluggish. I thought she was just drunk, but then she just fell and—oh my gosh. She's going to die, isn't she?" The girl cried, smudging her dark black eyeliner even more. Her hands shook as she wiped her cheeks, staining her sleeves with makeup.

Ronnie listened and felt for breath in the petite girl sprawled on the ground. Nothing. Pulse thready. She grabbed her light, pried open an eyelid. Pupils restricted to a pinpoint.

Ronnie looked around but could hardly see anything as they were practically hidden behind one of the rusted-out vehicles at the edge of the gravel pit. She needed help. Now. But Jensen and Seb were already gone with another patient in the other ambulance. Not sure where that Kirby guy was. "What's your name?" she asked the friend standing over them.

"Kayla." She sniffed. "Kayla Larsen."

She could send her to get help, but first she needed to know what she was up against. "Kayla, I need you to tell me exactly what your friend here took tonight." Ronnie quickly measured the unconscious girl's jaw and slipped in an oral airway.

Kayla shivered and shook her head. "Nothing."

"That's not true. And if you want to save your friend's life, I need to know exactly what is in her body right now." She hooked up the oral to the bag-valve mask and started bagging.

Kayla began sobbing. Another teenager, a guy in a purple football jersey, came up to them. "Whoa! Is that Jordyn? What's wrong with her?"

Ronnie sent him to find Peter or Cole. Anyone. Still no

breathing for the girl on the ground and her pulse was getting even lighter.

"Kayla, this girl needs help. I need to know."

"I promised Jordyn I wouldn't tell anyone. We were just drinking," she managed to sob out. Her gaze dropped to her friend.

"Did she take any heroin? Cocaine?"

Kayla shook her head. "No! We would never do drugs like that."

She was lying. The symptoms all pointed to drug overdose, but Ronnie had to be sure. "Did she take anything with the alcohol? Anything? Pain killers—"

Kayla's head jerked up. Her eyes went wide.

Aha.

Ronnie dropped her voice as other teens and parents started hearing the commotion and moved toward them. "What did she take, Kayla?"

"It was just some Oxycontin from when I injured my ankle. I didn't know it would hurt her!"

Yup. Oxy and alcohol. And with Kayla being taller and more muscular than the slight Jordyn, the dosing would be more than the girl could handle. The opioids were shutting down brain function.

Peter rushed through the growing crowd. "How can I help?"

"I need you to grab the locked narc box in the ambulance and keep everyone back," she said as she kept bagging.

As focused as Ronnie was on the thin blonde girl lying in the dirt, she couldn't help but overhear some of the parents and teens standing around them.

"Who is that? Is that the new paramedic that stole Kirby's job?"

"Does she even know what she's doing?"

"Oh my goodness. It's Jordyn Chase."

"My mom wouldn't let her touch me. She doesn't trust—"

Peter broke through again. "Everybody step back! The best thing you can do for Jordyn right now is pray and give Ronnie space to work."

He looked at her and nodded. It was almost like he believed in her. Like he was telling her to forget all the haters in the crowd and to do her job. He gently but quickly moved Kayla toward one of the other firefighters who joined him. Peter handed Ronnie the locked box and took over bagging.

Right. She had a life to save—because she couldn't find Jordyn's pulse anymore.

Ronnie did find the NARCAN though. It would quickly reverse the opioid overdose. She squeezed half a dose of the aerosol up one of Jordyn's nostrils, then half a dose up the other. With Peter's help, they rolled her onto her side. Silence choked out all sound as the crowd waited.

After a few minutes, Jordyn still wasn't breathing on her own. Ronnie gave her another dose of the NARCAN.

Jordyn's eyes opened and she gasped for air. The crowd sighed with relief. A few even clapped.

Ronnie rested back on her heels and took a deep breath herself. The girl would be okay.

The rest of the night flew by as Dean and Peter helped load Jordyn into the backup rig and they drove to the hospital.

In the emergency room, a petite blonde woman met them. The distraught Mrs. Chase clung to Ronnie after hearing what happened. "Thank you. Thank you for saving my baby girl."

Peter stood next to her after the mother left. "Way to go, partner. You just saved the principal's daughter."

Ronnie hid the smile that wanted to burst out and shrugged instead. "It's what I was trained to do."

And if everyone could just get on board and see that she was here to help, maybe she could keep her job.

CHAPTER 7

*P*eter should get back to the fire hall as soon as possible and chip away at the pile of paperwork on his desk. And if not that, there were a number of other things he could be doing. Like mowing Gust's lawn as promised. Helping Mom get her garden tilled. Doing the annual check on smoke detectors and extinguishers in Grandpa Zim's cabins.

Or...figuring out a way to see Ronnie again that wasn't awkward or creepy.

In fact, she'd settled in his brain for the past few days since she'd doctored his cuts. For such a feisty woman, she had a gentle touch with her patients. A gentle touch that stirred something he didn't quite want to acknowledge.

Maybe that was why he'd answered his scheming cousin's cry for help and now here he was stuck in his old high school auditorium in danger of being at Vivien's beck and call. Knowing Vivie, he was sure she'd find some way of tearing his male pride to shreds again—probably in front of an even bigger audience.

Fifty kids ran back and forth on the stage in front of them, sounding like a large herd of elephants. And without any air conditioning in the building, it kinda smelled like it too. Ripe.

All the older kids and teens moped in the front row of seats, as they stared at phone screens. A couple of them were snoring.

"See what I mean?" Vivien's whisper had a distinct whine to it.

Peter tried not to chuckle. "Yeah, you might have gotten in over your head. Maybe you should stick to kayak instructing. It would be safer."

She slapped his arm. "Don't laugh. This is why I called you. All these parents are freaking out about their kids being caught at that party so they're bringing them here. And I'm glad for such a great turnout, but I need help."

"That's your big emergency? What am I supposed to do?"

"You're a big strong guy. Seeing you on stage could pave the way to greatness, Peter. Think of the good influence you can have on these kids."

He lifted an eyebrow. "Laying it on a little thick, aren't you?" But she knew his kryptonite: *children*. Well, that and his inability to say no.

"Just stick around and help. Maybe do a little crowd control." She added a couple of flits of her eyelashes.

As if that had any effect on him.

A screaming game of tag rushed by them. The pull to join in, add a few lion roars, and watch the kids react tugged at him, a much more effective temptation.

But so were the many other things he needed to do.

"Pleeease?"

He looked down at Vivie's pleading eyes. Big mistake.

"Fine. I'll give you ten minutes, but then I have to get back to work."

It was sort of a "no." Baby steps.

"Wonderful. Now, to start, can you find out what's wrong with her?" She pointed to the little girl with a huge purple bow in her hair. While all the other kids ran around, she clung to the stage curtains.

He made his way to the stage and squatted down next to little Madison Baker, a third cousin once removed, and probably the smallest kid here. "What's wrong, Maddy?"

"Parker just told me there's—" Her lips wobbled. "There's dancing."

"That's what you're worried about?"

She nodded and looked down at the plastic brace wrapped around her calf helping correct her leg that turned inward. Water pooled in her eyes.

Oh no. Anything but tears.

"Hey, it's okay. Watch, there's nothing to it." Peter broke into his best dance moves sure to guarantee a giggle, including the Sprinkler, Running Man, and Macarena.

Maddy wasn't buying it though. If anything, her lips wobbled more.

"Come on, Maddy. Give it a try. It's fun." He took her hands and showed her the Macarena choreography. He added an extra flourish on his tush-shaking and jumped to the right.

Right into Ronnie.

"Hey!" she said, grabbing his arm to regain her balance.

Sure. *That* made Maddy laugh, and she skipped away with a friend.

And here he was once more looking like an idiot.

"Are you okay?"

Ronnie chuckled. "Oh, I'm fine. Don't let me interrupt. Nice moves there, Travolta." She walked away, still laughing.

Nice.

Her hair was back in its usual ponytail. Her Army T-shirt and workout leggings were paired once again with running shoes. A feminine scent—something sweet and rich—lingered after her as she walked with Tiago to the table where Beth Strauss was registering kids.

He checked his watch. Ten minutes were up. But maybe he should stick around a little longer and help Vivien. She definitely needed it.

Masking his newfound enthusiasm for the idea, he hopped off the stage and sighed as he approached Viv. "Fine. I'll stay and help. But I am *not* singing."

Vivien's worried expression morphed into a victory smirk. "Glad you came to your senses. As for singing, we'll see."

No way. But...

He glanced over at Ronnie still talking with Beth on the stage. "You know, you should ask Ronnie to help too."

That was totally nonchalant. Right?

Vivien looked at Ronnie. "You're right. We need all the help we can get." She marched down the aisle and clapped her hands. "All right, everybody, come up onstage and let's get started."

The children flooded the platform. Ronnie waved at him and turned to leave, but Vivien ran after her. Peter couldn't hear what she said, but Vivien always got her way.

And this time he was counting on it.

Sure enough, Ronnie walked over to him looking amused. "So, I've already seen your wicked dance moves, but word is if I stick around, I get to hear you sing too."

No! Peter whipped his gaze toward Vivien. She sent him a wink and a shrug.

Oh, he would strangle her. Not in front of the children, of course. But as soon as they left the building, she was toast.

"C'mere, Peter!" Vivie called from the stage.

He shook his head as he made his way center stage. Meanwhile, Vivien told her captive audience about his starring role in *Grease*, a slightly embellished version, yes, but all he had to do was stand there and not burn from embarrassment any more than he already was. And not that he would ever admit this to her, but she might be right. A few of the older guys straightened up, didn't look quite so bored. Tiago and Josh lost the skeptical looks on their faces.

Still, he breathed easier when she sent him off the stage.

Peter plopped down next to Ronnie sitting in the middle of the auditorium.

She nodded toward Vivien. "That's nice of you to help her out. Most guys wouldn't go that far, even for a girlfriend."

Peter looked at her. "Girlfriend? Vivien is my *cousin*. Well, a third cousin by marriage on the Zimmerman side, but still—" He shuddered. "Not a girlfriend. Family."

"Oh." Ronnie blushed.

Blushed, huh? He didn't expect that on her. "You really thought there was something between me and Vivie?"

The blush deepened. "I mean, she hangs on you and bats her eyes. And you're hot—oh!" She slapped a hand over her mouth. "I mean, I wouldn't blame her... Okay, I need to crawl into a hole and die now." She covered her eyes with her hands.

Peter couldn't hold back a grin. Hot, huh?

He gently pulled her hands down. "Please don't die. We were just starting to get along. And Cole really doesn't want to find another paramedic."

She looked up at him and made a face. "Maybe I've been in the Army too long. I thought she was flirting with you."

"Stick around long enough and you'll see that Vivien flirts with everybody. And, I'm single."

And why he'd said that, he had no idea.

She stared at him and oh how he wished he could read her.

A voice from stage snatched their attention.

They listened slack-jawed to Tiago belt out "Mary Had a Little Lamb" like nobody's business.

"Wow," Peter said. "He's good. Has he always been a good singer?"

"I don't know." Ronnie looked from the stage to Peter. "I don't know much about singing, but it sounded good. Didn't it?"

"Yeah and look at him up there. He's got some talent."

"He does." She smiled as they watched him. The next boy came onstage.

"Speaking of cousins," Peter said, "that's another cousin of mine. Grayson. But I already know he's tone deaf."

"You're related to that kid? Maybe I don't want to hear you sing."

"I'm related to most of these kids. See the blonde girl by the curtain, the one with the red shirt? That's my cousin Mandy's daughter. Mandy is a Dahlquist too, but she broke away from the restaurant biz and is a hair stylist in town. She started at a young age. Got in trouble for cutting my hair when I was eight. Uh, that kid—you know, the one from the fire—Ben Zimmerman, he's my cousin Elton's son. My cousin Ree used to babysit him until he accidentally set the cat on fire. She refused after that. And that little guy over there is a cousin too. Funny story. His dad used to sell raffle tickets to decide who would be his date for our Dahlquist Annual Rib Cook-off. It's family and significant others only, and it's amazing food. He made a killing off those tickets until he got engaged and his fiancée shut that down."

"What about the kid singing now?"

His gaze went to the blond-haired kid belting out "Happy Birthday."

"Let me guess. Second cousin, once removed." She glanced at him, grinning.

She smelled good. Fruity, or maybe floral.

Not at all like a fire station.

"Uh, no. That's Joe and Mona Michaels's son. No relation whatsoever." And it occurred to him that, for the first time in ages, he was sitting by a pretty girl also of *no relation*. And when she smiled at him like that, he forgot whatever it was he was going to say.

He cracked his knuckles. "So, do you know what part Tiago wants?"

"No clue. Never even seen *West Side Story*."

"I've never seen it either. But I think from what Vivie said, there's two gangs fighting, the Sharks and the Jets. A girl named Maria gets caught in the middle of it. Every kid will get a part."

Because no kid wanted to be left out. He should know.

She turned to him. "It kinda sounds like Deep Haven. Two families, with you getting caught in the middle, like Maria."

Just what every guy wanted—to be compared to a heroine of a musical. "It wasn't always like that meeting the other night. I mean, for the most part, both of those families stay out of each other's way."

And boy did he wish for the good ol' days, when he was just Peter. Not really a Zimmerman anymore, but not completely a Dahlquist either. A time when no one paid him much attention.

"Well, you probably don't get it, but having a part in this play will be good for Tiago. He needs a group to fit into."

"Oh, I get it. It really stinks to feel like an outsider, like you don't really belong. I mean, the Christmas when I was six years old, every one of my cousins got presents at our Christmas parties except me. Santa forgot me...twice."

"What? That's awful. My family is not what you would call functional, but my *abuela* spoils us all at Christmastime. She can't afford it, but she will make sure everyone has presents. How could Santa forget you?"

He tried to shrug away the weird sting of the old memory. "It was the first holiday after Mom and Gary married and I was adopted. There was a little confusion about the family parties. At the Zimmermans on Christmas Eve, all the grandkids have presents under the tree that my Grandma buys for us. But they didn't think Mom and I were coming. They were still a little hurt that Mom remarried. Anyway, there wasn't anything under the tree for me. And with such a crazy number of gifts and people, no one noticed until Grandma gave me my present a few days later."

"And the Dahlquists?"

"They had hired a Santa. But the mother of each child was the one that actually picked out and bought the gifts for their own kid. It was my mom's first time there and she didn't know. So, Santa came and he had a present in his bag for everyone there—except me."

"You must have been devastated!"

"I was convinced I did something to be on Santa's naughty list. But don't worry, my older cousin Tracy set me straight. Said it was because I wasn't really part of the family. I was only adopted. And since I didn't have a present at the Zimmermans' party, I concluded that I didn't belong there either."

Ronnie frowned. "I don't think I like Tracy."

Peter bumped her elbow. "Careful. Don't want to say that too loud. That's her son over there."

She laughed. "So, I guess you can have a huge family and still not have a place to belong, huh?"

Maybe like Tiago, they all wanted a place to fit in. And for some strange reason, he wanted Deep Haven to be that place for her.

Before he could say anything, Vivien came up to them. "I'm going to need your help. Both of you."

Ronnie sat up straight, almost panicked. "Don't expect me to get onstage. I have no acting skills at all."

Made sense. She was blunt. Direct. Nothing pretentious about Veronica Morales at all.

But the calculated look on Vivien's face worried him. She was scheming again. "Can you build?"

"I know my way around power tools," Ronnie said.

"Great, then you and Peter can build the set. I'll get you some sketches and ideas."

More time with Ronnie?

Finally, one of Vivien's schemes that he didn't mind at all.

Ronnie slurped her creamy coffee drink as she walked between the yellow fire trucks. The move to Deep Haven was worth it for the amazing Java Cup iced mochas alone. But it didn't hurt that Tiago was actually excited for play practice today too. Vivien was going to have the cast list ready. He was hoping to get a part as one of the Sharks.

It was nice to see him excited about something again. It had been way too long. And now that she was getting to know the town, she was ready to attack her job with gusto. All in all, not too shabby for a Monday morning.

Ronnie headed to the office in the back of the fire hall. Time to see which chopper Peter chose. Now *there* was something to get excited about. The helicopter would be such a big step to bringing this Crisis Response Team into the current century.

And any excitement about working with Peter was just because she was making progress in getting along with her work partner. Finding out he was single didn't change anything.

Well, not much.

She turned past the last pump truck. The office door was open. Peter sat behind a desk, papers and piles all around him. The man needed help organizing his stuff, but it was the dejected look on his face that tugged on her heart.

She should've brought him coffee too.

"Hey, Zuko. What's going on?"

Peter's head snapped up. "Hey. What are you doing here so early?" He obviously tried to wipe all traces of whatever he was dealing with off his face and cover it up, but his tight smile didn't come close to reaching his eyes.

So maybe she'd go easy on him. "I wanted to come in early and get started on the training schedule." She dropped her messenger bag—the closest thing she'd ever get to a purse—on the other desk in the cramped office. It was just their two desks for now, one long fluorescent light above, a scuffed-up old file cabinet, and on the other side of Peter's desk, probably the most uncomfortable plastic chair ever. But once they got a headquarters, they'd have a much better setup.

Another thing to look forward to.

"So, why do you look like your dog just ran away? Did you lose a dance off or something, Travolta?"

"Uh, not sure what you're talking about. Just going through some paperwork." He started moving stacks of paper from one pile to another, but his smile slipped even further.

Forget going easy. She did better with blunt. "Peter, I don't know if anyone has ever told you this, but you're a terrible liar." She plopped in her office chair and spun it to face him. "Spill it."

"Really, I'm fine."

So he was going to be difficult. "Did you decide on which helicopter we're getting? It's Monday. Your deadline."

It almost sounded like he groaned. But it could've been a creak from the chair.

His mouth stayed shut and he didn't look at her.

"Peter, you said you would decide—"

"I know. And I did."

"What's the problem then?"

He sighed. "It was all set. Had the chopper picked out and everything."

"Great, so which one did you pick?"

"It doesn't matter. Because at church Darek Christiansen talked to me about getting this other helo he knew from when he was a hotshot. And then at breakfast this morning at the cafe, Kyle and Pastor Dan were talking about a different one, better for remote area recovery and medical evacuations. So maybe we should get that one."

Ronnie shook her head. "At the Hagborg fire and the gravel

pit, you were decisive. You organized your crew. Made quick choices. You decide stuff all the time. Why is this any different?"

He leaned his head back and blew out a long breath. "I don't know. I thought I had it nailed down."

He really did carry the weight of the world on those magnificent shoulders, didn't he? She rolled her chair over and joined him at his desk. Maybe she didn't need to push him as much as encourage. "Okay, so which helicopter did you decide on before you talked to everyone?"

"I was thinking the Bell 429. It's got everything we need. It's a pretty common chopper for SAR teams."

"Then what's wrong with that one?"

"Nothing. It's just not as heavy-duty as the one Darek was talking about. Or as fast as the Leonardo AW119 that they use for medevac that Dan wants."

But that wasn't what was stopping him. She had to dig a little deeper. "Why are you so afraid to make this decision?"

"I'm not afraid."

She quirked an eyebrow.

He met her stare. "I'm not. I just…"

As much as she wanted to push, she held her tongue.

"I really respect Darek and Kyle and Dan. I should take what they say into consideration. And I hate the thought of disappointing one of them."

He was worried about that? Didn't the guy see that he was perfectly capable of making this choice on his own? "People are disappointed all the time. They'll get over it."

He huffed. "You make it sound easy. It's not."

"Peter, you're an intelligent guy. You've obviously spent a lot of time researching these different choppers. At this point just go with your gut."

His forehead wrinkled as he took in her words. "What if my gut is wrong?"

"Having something here is better than nothing. And until you decide, we have nothing."

"I know. Believe me, I know. But it has to be the right one. I don't want to cause any conflict."

Bingo. There was the passion in his eyes he usually kept hidden.

"What's so bad about conflict?"

"You're kidding, right? Uh, it's fighting. Fighting is bad."

"No, it's not. Not always. Conflict can often bring issues to the surface so they can be dealt with. Most of the fighters I know are fighting things like injustice, disease, illness."

"Yeah, but fighting between people? People I care about? I just can't be a part of that."

"Peter, if you think the Bell is the way to go, choose that one. I'm sure those other guys have good intentions, but *you* are the one who researched all the options and looked at it from every angle. If you were going for that one before you talked to everyone else, do that. You've got good instincts."

She could see his mind working. He flipped through the papers in his hand, schematics for choppers. He read over the top sheet. Then he set them back down on his desktop and turned to look at her again. "All right. We're getting the Bell 429."

Finally. A choice. "The Bell 429. Good job."

His stare softened. The quiet in the room grew thick as she held his gaze. "But you better watch out there, Morales," he said with a smirk.

"Why?"

His challenge, something in that smirk, did have her quaking just a bit.

"I think you just complimented me twice in one morning. You might be losing your touch."

She laughed with relief.

He smiled a real smile—the kind that made his eyes crinkle and showed off perfectly straight teeth.

And wow, did she want to see that again.

Before she could make any sense out of the little flip her stomach had just performed, Seb Brewster knocked on the doorframe of the open office door. "Just the two I wanted to see."

Peter stood to shake his hand. "Hey, Seb. What's up? Take a seat."

The mayor looked down at the orange plastic chair. "Yeah, I think I'll stand."

Peter leaned back in his chair again, relaxed, a remnant of his smile still there. "What can we do for you today?"

But Seb turned toward her. "I know we met briefly at the pit fire the other night, Ronnie, but I wanted to come and formally introduce myself. See how you were settling in." He held out a hand.

Her senses went into high-alert mode. Something was off. She shook his hand with a firm squeeze so he would know he wasn't dealing with some simpering female or weakling. "I'm settling in fine. It's a great town."

Seb nodded. "Yeah, it is." He cleared his throat, looking a little uncomfortable. "Since I'm here as mayor on official business, I also need to address a couple things."

That didn't sound good. Ronnie braced herself but stayed quiet.

"As you know, you were hired with a ninety-day probationary period. I want to make sure you're a good fit for Deep Haven and that Deep Haven is a good fit for you. If we don't see that this is mutually beneficial, we'll need to part ways."

"Yes, that was my understanding. So, what's the problem?" Ronnie lifted her chin, ready to take whatever he threw at her.

"You've been here, what, a week?"

She nodded.

"I've heard from Sheila Chase about how you saved Jordyn's life. She's talking about getting first responder certified now too. And I saw Gust in the hospital. He can't thank you enough."

Oh, so maybe it wasn't bad news?

"But—" Seb continued.

Of course. There was a but.

"I've had two written complaints come across my desk as well."

"Complaints? From who?"

"I've had formal complaints from Charlie Zimmerman and Gretchen Riggs."

Ronnie wanted to punch something. But before she could form any words on her tongue, Peter stood up. His demeanor remained calm and cool. "Seb, come on, man. Ronnie just got here. She's still learning the town, and you know Charlie. He probably has complaints filed weekly about one thing or another."

Huh?

Peter was standing up for her?

But Seb didn't look convinced. "I can't ignore these complaints. And it was pretty obvious at the pit fire that some of the parents were not comfortable having you treat their children."

Ronnie stood too. "If you mean Elton Zimmerman..." Because she knew that would come back again at some point.

Seb didn't budge. His gaze stayed fixed on her. "I mean quite a few parents."

"But they don't even know me, or what I'm capable of!"

Peter popped in again. "Seb, she saved Gust's life. She saved Jordyn's life. Jordyn wasn't breathing. If not for Ronnie—"

"Jensen and I could've administered NARCAN—"

"But you weren't there! You both left," Ronnie said. "And you didn't bother to tell me. I only knew because I watched you leave." Where was the teamwork in that?

Peter interjected again. "Let's be honest. Those parents never gave Ronnie a chance. Some are simply loyal to Kirby Hueston and wouldn't like anybody but Kirby taking the job. But Ronnie has the experience we need. You should see her training schedule. She's already updating our website and getting volunteers signed up. She deserves a fair chance."

How Peter could stay so collected was beyond her. But his steady and even voice finally seemed to be getting through to the mayor. Somehow it even seemed to soothe her nerves.

Seb held up his hands in surrender. "I'm not saying I'm firing anybody at this time. I just need to address these concerns and make sure you all understand what's at stake here."

Peter nodded in understanding. "I'll help Ronnie get to know the town better. She just needs a little time, a few introductions. And like you said, there are people that are already on her side. Like Sheila and Gust."

"That's true. And no one is going anywhere right now. Just work on it, Ronnie. I'd like to see you stay. But…"

The weight of all he implied landed squarely on her chest.

But a little pressure would not break her. Seb didn't know that now, but he would. "You have my word, I will do my best to fit in here. I want to make this Crisis Response Team the best we can."

Because somehow in a little over a week, she was falling for this town. Maybe it was just the changes she saw in Tiago, or the people like Megan and Vivien and Peter she had met. But she would give this everything she had. Tiago needed it. And yeah, she wanted it.

She wanted it more than she craved another Java Cup iced mocha with extra whipped cream—and then some.

CHAPTER 8

*P*eter stood before the shiny new-to-them Bell 429 helicopter.

"Well, what do you think?" Adrian asked. "Slick, huh?"

"Yeah." Peter lost all words. This hulking two-rotor chopper was the biggest thing he'd ever been responsible for choosing. And he still wasn't sure it was the right choice. A four-million-dollar choice. He swallowed hard, followed Adrian up to the door, and stepped inside. "You sure it's got everything? I mean, it's only been a little over a week since I signed off on it."

"We lucked out. The company had this ready for another SAR team that had to back out at the last minute. They just added our logo and the few upgrades you requested." Adrian pointed to the pilot area. "It's got the latest GPS navigation and weather reporting electronics, touchscreen controls, and an awesome communication system."

Looked like a whole lot of buttons, knobs, and gauges. How did anyone fly this thing and understand what they all did?

Adrian moved to the cabin. "There's plenty of room for equipment and the cot back here. Up to seven passengers can fit if we need to. We added a bunch of medical stuff—I don't even know what it is, but I'm sure Ronnie does. Oh, and check this out!" He jumped down out of the cabin and ran to the back of the helicopter. Peter had never seen Adrian Vassos this giddy. "You can load the cot through these clam shell doors back here. It's easy enough that one person can do it if needed. Nice, huh?"

"Yeah, that's great," Peter said through the tightening of his chest.

Adrian continued. "And we have this new tug to move the helicopter in and out of the hangar. It's really easy to use. Which is good considering how tight it is in here. Hopefully we can figure out a headquarters with more space to store this baby and we won't have to rent from the airport for long."

"Especially since it's a bit of a hike to get up here." Being situated north of the Evergreen Resort, it was still a twelve-minute drive uphill from the fire hall. He'd clocked it on the way up. In an emergency, those were precious minutes lost.

"I'm sure Cole and Seb will get that figured out soon. And they're already looking at pilots."

A black SUV pulled up outside. Ronnie. Her jaw dropped as she got out of her car and came in through the open hangar door.

"Whoa. This is our new helicopter?" The awe in her voice was nothing compared to what reflected in her eyes. "This is the big surprise, Peter?"

Peter nodded and watched as she walked up in her usual workout-inspired outfit—leggings, fitted athletic shirt, and running shoes. But today her hair hung straight. No ponytail. It softened her whole countenance, and seeing her excited made everything a little bit better.

Adrian gave her the same run-through. None of his enthu-siasm waned as he explained all the features and gadgets again. Ronnie inspected the medical equipment. Finally, something she couldn't fault about being outdated. She hopped down out of the cabin. "Now this is what I'm talking about. Look at it, Peter. Isn't it amazing?"

"It's something."

"Don't tell me you're still not sure about choosing this one. It's perfect! It's the right mix of power and speed and capacity." She looked up at the tail section, the pine tree and lake Crisis Response Team logo reflecting the sunlight that streamed in. "And it's shiny."

Yeah, she might be right. It was pretty spectacular as far as machines went. "Let's just hope it does the job."

"It will." Her grin boosted his meager confidence a bit more.

"Well, as much as I would love to stay here and admire the gorgeous Bell, I've got to go help Ella." Adrian pitched a set of keys to Peter. "Here ya go, Chief. Lock up when you're done."

As Adrian pulled away in his Porsche, Ronnie stood next to Peter and studied the chopper once more. "How can you still be floundering about your choice? Look at this thing!"

It *was* impressive. And it did have all the medical equipment Ronnie had requested, the firefighting capability to add a bucket when needed, and a rigging pully system to assist in search and rescue. Maybe she was right. "It's growing on me."

She laughed. "Well, it should, because it was a great choice."

But would she still think so when he told her what else he had done? He pushed his hair back and clasped his hands behind his neck. He just had to keep a casual vibe going. "I invited someone else to come see the new chopper."

"Gonna show it off some more, huh?"

"Well, actually it's more of an olive branch."

"Olive branch?" Her eyes glinted with suspicion.

Oh, this was harder to sell than he'd anticipated.

She fisted her hands on her hips. "Peter, what did you do?"

The woman caught on fast.

"I, uh, told Seb I would help you fit in. So that's what I'm doing."

Her eyes narrowed. "Who is coming?"

"This is the perfect opportunity to smooth things over."

"Peter!"

"My uncle is coming."

"Which uncle? You've got a few."

"Charlie."

"You invited Charlie Zimmerman here? Why in the world would you do that?"

Now that he'd gotten that off his chest, he couldn't help but notice that she was kinda cute when she was riled up. But Peter smothered his grin. "You said we need all the help we can get on our team. Uncle Charlie won't come back to the first responders until you apologize."

"But Charlie? Charlie Zimmerman?"

"We're getting a lot of new recruits, but can we really afford to turn down volunteers? Any volunteer?"

She shook her head. Adamantly. "No. I'm not apologizing to that man. Instead of talking with me, he went behind my back with a complaint to the mayor. I have no time for people like that. And as a volunteer, he was more of a detriment than a help on the scene."

"When we were shorthanded, he showed up. I know he's not the easiest to get along with, and I know he has a lot to learn still. But if you can win him over, it would be huge in showing that the town is on your side."

"No."

"He's the self-appointed spokesperson for all the Zimmermans. He could persuade others to step up and volunteer too."

"I won't."

"Ronnie, come on. We need this. We need to make sure Seb sees you getting along, fitting in. He'll be at the training session tonight. Think of how impressed he would be to see Charlie there. See you two getting along."

The stubborn lift to her jaw dropped the slightest bit.

Peter edged a little closer to her. "Charlie doesn't know you like I do. It was a stressful situation at the Hagborg fire—"

"And I stand by my decision. I wasn't going to let him drive or assist when I saw how little he knew in treating a patient as critical as Gust."

"Okay, yeah, but you were a little..."

"What? Pushy? Direct?"

"Rude, Ronnie. You came across as rude."

She looked as if she'd been slapped. She stared down at the cement floor. Her voice dropped. "I wasn't trying to be rude. I was trying to protect my patient and save his life."

There was hurt in her voice, and he hated that he had caused it. But he was willing to push a little if it got her to see how important this was. "I know that *now*. If you just explain that you were focused on getting Gust to the hospital as quickly as possible, maybe Charlie will understand too."

"Hmph." She folded her arms across her chest and stared out the door. When she looked back at Peter, a new determination was there in her posture. "You really think that man will listen to anything I have to say?"

"If he's smart, he will."

She rolled her eyes, but one side of her lips also curled up. "You're just trying to butter me up."

"But it's true." He moved to face Ronnie. "I don't know what Uncle Charlie will do, but it takes a pretty strong person to be humble enough to apologize."

Her slim shoulders relaxed, but she lifted her chin back to the same stubborn angle as before. "Fine, I'll do it. But only because my job depends on it."

Peter sighed in relief. This would hopefully go a long way in gaining some much-needed Deep Haven support for his new partner.

He wasn't ready to see Ronnie go just yet.

And it looked like he'd convinced her just in time. Uncle

Charlie's truck rolled into the airport. At first, he only had eyes for the chopper. "Now this is a thing of beauty," he said as he walked into the hangar and took off his sunglasses.

"Thanks for coming, Uncle Charlie. I thought you'd like to see the Bell, and, uh, Ronnie is here too."

Ronnie stepped out of the shadow of the chopper. She gave Charlie a curt nod.

"What's she doing here?" Charlie asked.

Since her lips were still tightly closed, Peter guessed it was up to him to get this going. "She has something she wants to say to you."

"Why should I care what *she* has to say?"

Ronnie stiffened.

He couldn't make this easy, could he? "Uncle Chuck, just listen. Please." *Come on, Ronnie.*

She closed her eyes for a split second and let out a quick breath before coming to stand next to Peter. "Charlie, I want to apologize."

Clearly it killed her to spit that word out. Peter's chest swelled a bit watching her conquer her own pride. Now it was up to his uncle.

The apology seemed to confuse Uncle Charlie. Then he puffed out his chest. "Well, it's about time."

Ronnie's nostrils flared. Peter could've smacked the man. Instead he lightly nudged Ronnie's elbow. *Please hold it together.*

She gritted her teeth. "I understand I might have come across as rude at the Hagborg incident. I'm sorry."

Thata girl! And with her coming so far, Peter wanted to help ease the way. "We were hoping you'd come back to the first responders. There's a training meeting later tonight. What do you say?"

Uncle Charlie seemed to chew on those words for a bit. "Apology accepted. Guess I could come to a training session or two. Help out a little."

Ronnie opened her mouth as if to set him straight, but Peter cut in instead. "Great! Let me show you the helicopter." And he led the older man around the new chopper.

As soon as Charlie left, Ronnie laid into him. "I hope you're happy. That was humiliating!"

"Yeah, but you did it. And you know what, I *am* happy. This means you'll be sticking around."

All her hard lines, her shoulders, her back, her lips went slack. "That's why you wanted me to apologize?"

He shrugged. "Yes." Wasn't it obvious?

A sweet smile bloomed on her face. "Okay."

And for the first time today, it did seem okay—like things would work out just fine.

Who knew a near catastrophe would have such positive ramifications? An influx of volunteers showed up for the first responders training session. Volunteers who didn't sign up, but she wouldn't complain. The town was waking up to the need in the two weeks since Ronnie had moved in, and she would do her part to help them. But they might need to find a bigger space for the next meeting—something other than the Community Center warming house.

And she should probably start concentrating on training them instead of sneaking glances at her partner. Her gorgeous, charming, hazel-eyed partner.

So she was physically attracted to Peter Dahlquist. What woman wouldn't be? He was built like one of those Italian marble statues, all hard muscle and strength.

But then again, it wasn't his strength that impressed her. Frankly, the way he'd danced for that little girl at the tryouts had done a number on her heart. Sure, he was a complete dork, but somehow it only enhanced his big heart. It didn't help that he'd also hung out with Tiago and Josh, teaching them how to throw the perfect spiral. And then there was the fact he'd gotten hurt rescuing stubborn teenagers who set themselves on fire. The way he'd stood up for her with Seb and even convinced her to apologize to Charlie Zimmerman.

Okay, so the man was a saint. And sure, she admired him. But nothing could ever come of it. Even if by some miracle he liked her, she wasn't the kind of girl people stuck around for.

Besides, she would never let any man have that much control over her. Look what it had done to her mother. Plus she had Tiago to think of. A job to do. And even though Peter wasn't her boss, they *were* colleagues. Didn't everyone say people shouldn't get romantically involved with coworkers?

She walked around, inspecting each group as they practiced CPR on dummies.

"Charlie, your elbows should be locked when you do compressions."

He glared at her.

If it was supposed to intimidate her, fat chance. She wouldn't pass him if he couldn't master these basics, even if she'd swallowed her pride and apologized to him in order to talk him into attending. She'd only done it for Peter's sake.

Okay, maybe Peter was right and she *was* a little brusque during their first emergency event. But from here on out, Charlie had a lot to prove if he was going to stay on the team.

She called them all back to their seats. "In a moment you'll break into groups of three or four again and practice on each other how to check for airway and breathing. One of you will be the unconscious victim in each group." Her gaze landed on Peter holding up the warming house wall with his shoulder, his arms folded. "Peter, why don't you come up here and be my victim?"

Snickers sounded across the room as Peter walked over and lay on the floor at her feet. "As you wish."

Ronnie knelt down and shook the image out of her head—the one of Westley using that line on Buttercup in the classic movie *The Princess Bride*. "Quiet, Farm Boy. You're supposed to be unconscious."

Get your head in the game, Morales.

"How can we check to see if the airway is clear and the victim is breathing? Dean?"

Dean Wilson sat up straight, a panicked look frozen on his face. He searched his notes and finally sputtered, "Uh, we look, listen, and feel."

"That's right."

Maybe there was hope for him after all.

"Like Dean said, first we look. Watch for chest movement."

Ronnie switched her gaze to Peter and watched his broad chest rise and fall. *Aye mamma mia*, he was buff. She could look at him all day long.

She should've picked a different volunteer because her mind was going places it shouldn't.

"What about the head tilt?"

Of course, Charlie had to be the one to remind her.

"Yes, why don't you show us how that's done, Charlie?" Someone else please take over so she didn't have to have skin-to-skin contact with this man lying at her feet.

Charlie leaned back in his chair and folded his arms. "I'm just a first responder. What do I know? You're the *paramedic*."

"Ronnie, you need to show them the breathing barriers too," Peter said, pointing to the various masks on the table.

She plastered on a fake smile and wished for the millionth time tonight that she hadn't forgotten the gloves. Because, of course, every time she touched Peter, her stupid heart raced, and her brain stopped working.

"Sometimes when a victim is unconscious, their tongue falls to the back of the throat, cutting off their airway. If there's no trauma or injury to the head, neck, or spine, use a simple head tilt." Ronnie placed her left hand on Peter's forehead and with her right she used her pointer and middle fingers to lift the bony part of his chin. "Like this."

Peter's hair curled on the floor, his skin warm on her hand.

Suddenly, she had the swift and clear memory of being in his arms—albeit for a mere three seconds a couple weeks ago at Megan's. And now she had the overwhelming desire to run her fingers through his long hair, over his strong jawline.

Oh boy. If he really needed CPR, he'd be dead by now.

"When you say, 'feel for breath,' what do you mean?" a woman from the back asked. "Do you put a hand on their chest?"

She gulped. "So, uh, when we say 'feel' we mean turn your face near the victim's nose and mouth to see if you can feel their breath on your cheek. You'll also be listening to their breathing from there. Is it rattled? Quick? Shallow? Pretty straight forward."

She started to rise when a voice from the side of the room called, "I didn't hear that so well. Can you show us?"

Others nodded, wanting the same.

Ronnie was a professional. She could totally do this. "Certainly." She held her ponytail back so it wouldn't fall in Peter's face and leaned over him, her cheek hovering right over his lips. Ronnie fixed her eyes on his toes peeking out from his hiking sandals, but they didn't distract her from the lips she was just inches from. Instead, Peter's piney scent rose up, teasing her, and his breath on her skin lit it on fire.

And right in front of all of Deep Haven. Please, let her not be blushing.

"And that's how you check airway and breathing." She stood and checked it off on her clipboard. "All right, let's take a quick break and when we come back, you can practice all this in your groups, including the correct use of breathing barriers." She grabbed her water bottle and chugged the remainder of it down.

Peter's bass voice sounded in her ear, just a whisper, but with the power to turn her weak. "Great job, partner."

"Thanks." She sidled away, trying to find her bearings. "I'm, uh, going to call Tiago. Make sure he's where he's supposed to be." She stepped outside and let the evening breeze wash over her. She leaned against the log wall and fanned her cheeks with the clipboard she still carried.

What was wrong with her? All she wanted to do was train and teach these volunteers how to save lives. She'd done these procedures a million times. But suddenly she was in need of oxygen and her own first aid with the way her pulse rocketed out of control when she was around her partner.

She groaned. This was not what she needed right now. Or ever. She had a job to do. A brother to take care of. There was no time or place in her life for romance.

The rest of the class she kept her distance and had Peter take half the group while she taught the others. When they were done, she dismissed the class and gathered up her equipment.

She closed the CPR case and lifted it.

"Hey. I'll get that." Peter strode over and reached down to take the heavy case from her grasp, but she held on and tugged it back toward her.

"I don't need help. I've got it."

He could just yank the case away from her. He was certainly strong enough to. Instead, he kept a steady pressure, a gentle tug. "Ronnie, I know you can. But would you let me help? You look tired."

His concern shouldn't surprise her, but it still shocked her enough that she let go of the handle. "What do you mean I look tired?"

"You seemed a little off tonight, flushed, or something. Are you feeling okay?"

She couldn't look at him and think coherent thoughts. "I'm great. Just distracted. It's nothing."

Shoot, but the kindness in his gaze was more dangerous than the touching. She spun back to the other bags and slung the straps over her shoulders, marched out the door and back to —that's right. They'd taken his truck. Ridden together.

Another dumb decision she wouldn't make again, even if the equipment fit better in the back of his Chevy.

She plopped the bags down in the bed, and Peter followed her out.

He stood in her path. "Got a lot on your mind? I know a good thinking spot."

"What?"

"You said you were distracted. I know a good place to help clear your head. Artist's Point. Come on."

He stepped back, opened the door for her, and she got in.

She doubted that spending any more time with him would clear her mind, but whatever.

He got in, drove them down to the harbor boat launch, and parked. When they got out, he led her past the Coast Guard station.

And her stupid feet followed.

But only because the wide-open space of Deep Haven was a safer bet for her traitorous heart than the cozy cab of his truck.

Peter followed the trail between the small bushes, hopped up the small rocky incline and down the path. A large expanse of basalt lay before her with Lake Superior crashing against the foot of stone in a happy rhythm. The lemony swath of sky above them hinted of a brilliant sunset to come.

They didn't have this in Minneapolis.

The water had an immediate calming effect. She lowered herself to sit on a small ledge over the lake. The tightness in her back eased.

Peter sat next to her. "Anything you want to talk about? I'm a decent listener."

He probably was, but she couldn't afford to let him any

further inside her heart than she already had. She kept her sights on the water in front of them. "Just a lot on my mind, a lot to do. I've got to get Tiago registered for school, work on the training classes, and apply for those grants to upgrade the equipment. And we have those sets for the play we have to build."

"Yeah, I'm a little worried. I can build the structures Vivien wants, but I'm not sure about that backdrop. The cityscape one? It's pretty elaborate. Can you paint?"

"Paint? Last time I painted..." The memory rose, dragging with it too much emotion before she could grab it and shove it away again.

"Ronnie?"

"Sorry, uh, the last time I painted walls I was seven. My dad let me pick out any color I wanted for my bedroom before he deployed. So I picked the deepest, brightest pink I could find. Berry Kiss. Mom was worried it would be too bright, so we did the walls in a pale pink, but Papa taped off a big heart right over my bed. We colored it in with that bright Berry Kiss paint, listening to the radio and singing along. When we finished, he told me that the heart was there to remind me that he always carried me close to *his* heart and he was always watching over me, even when he was far away." She didn't know where all that had come from, but saying it now brought her almost back to that moment—the smell of the cotton of her father's shirt, his husky laughter that still embedded her bones. Wow, she missed him.

"Sounds like a great guy. You said he died, though?"

"He was in the Army too. Died in Iraq. And after—" Her voice caught. "Um, after that place, we rented. Most landlords don't let you pick out a wall color." Even if they were your own grandmother, because of course, she had to share the room with two of her older cousins and they had been there longer. The Army never let her choose her wall color either.

"Will you keep renting here?"

She looked out across the lake, wondering if she dared let hope swell. "I'd love to find a place to own, but I need to save up a bit for that."

"A place you could paint however you want?"

She looked back at him. Way too much...something in his eyes. Something kind. Something intimate.

Like the man could see inside her.

And crazy enough, he didn't flinch, didn't look away. Just kept looking.

"Yeah." She tore her gaze away before his hazel eyes drew her in any more. "What about you?"

He took a breath, looked back out to the lake. "I have a house in town. A little cottage not too far from the skate park. Nothing fancy, but it's home. And I had no clue when it came to paint color, so I let my mom and sister pick it all out."

She shook her head, asking herself the same question for the millionth time.

"What?"

"I just don't get it. How are you still single? I mean, you've got your own house, you have a steady job, you're, uh..." She cleared her throat. "Good-looking—"

"Just good-looking? Before you said I was hot."

Ronnie laughed. "Don't let it go to your head, Farm Boy. But seriously, why aren't you married?"

He leaned back on his hands. "It's kind of hard to date when you're related to everyone in town."

"Oh, yeah, I suppose."

The light breeze blew through his hair, and he turned his dangerous eyes toward her. "But...*you're* not related to me, Buttercup."

Oh, her stupidity had no limits, her lips no restraint as they broke into a coy smile. "No. No, I'm not."

CHAPTER 9

*P*eter rolled primer onto one of the tall backdrops spread out on a table outside the workshop at Evergreen Resort, their makeshift stage construction headquarters. A matching cityscape of lower Manhattan had already been dropped off backstage down at the school theater.

To his surprise, they weren't half bad. Not his talents, but Ronnie's, as she turned out to have a knack for this kind of thing.

He'd thought of the Evergreen Resort after their first attempts at painting were interrupted by the vast nobody-left-out ensemble of the Jets and the Sharks.

And it got them away from the prying eyes of Deep Haven.

But after nearly a week of work, his brilliant plan to get to know Ronnie one-on-one was a flop. So far he couldn't determine if that moment they'd shared at Artist's Point was a fluke or the start of something serious. Since then, she'd been friendly but not personal or even flirty.

He sneaked a glance over to her, toned arms lithe and strong as she brushed paint onto a base of one of the false building fronts. Her hips swayed to the Latin beat from her phone. Dust swirled through the air inside the workshop.

She caught him looking and frowned. "You're making a mess."

Huh? Sure enough, primer dripped down his roller onto his arm. She laughed, laid down her own brush, and took the tray and roller from his hands while he scrambled for the paper towels.

Real smooth, Dahlquist.

She held his hand as she wiped his arm, stood close enough to tease him with her tropical scent. One touch from her sent his pulse racing. "Well, maybe if you'd stop distracting me…"

"I distract you?" Her voice was soft, playful, but her gaze bold, almost daring.

Put him out of his misery and just drown him in her cinnamon eyes already. "Very distracting." And then, without realizing it, he wiped a small drop of white primer off her cheek. Her skin was incredibly soft.

Oh.

Neither of them moved.

His gaze went to her mouth, and a weird rushing filled his ears. He wondered what her lips tasted like…

The sudden roar from a chainsaw outside the shop sent him jerking back. He cleared his throat. "Better get to work if we want to take that canoe ride I promised you on the way here." Because the point was to get to know *her*. Something a little more personal than which flavor lip gloss she wore.

She went back to her project, but a shade of pink lingered across her cheeks.

So obviously they had some chemistry. But every time he tried to ask about her family or her past, she shut down the conversation faster than he could stomp out a spark in the middle of a dry field.

This time he didn't let his focus leave the roller as he covered the backdrops in primer.

"That should do it for now," he said when he finished. "We need to let this dry before we do the base coats."

She too had finished the false front. "Good. I'm starving."

She'd painted a copy of the Empire State Building.

"That's really good, Ronnie."

She grinned at him, and warmth filled his entire body.

They rinsed out their rollers and sat at one of the Christiansens' picnic tables, watching a pair of loons on the lake while they ate the ham-and-swiss sandwiches Peter had packed them. Ronnie had brought Cheetos.

"For all your healthy eating, egg-white omelets and all, you know those things are gonna kill you, right?"

She licked the cheesy powder from her fingers. "Everyone has a vice. Look at what you're drinking."

"Hey now, don't mess with the Dew." He took a long drink from his soda.

She shoved him playfully.

"Better watch—"

A feminine voice called from the trail. "Hello!"

Ronnie scooted away, stiffened. Aw, he should've known he wouldn't have privacy for long.

Ingrid Christiansen came with a plate of fresh-from-the-oven cookies. "I saw you got everything built and primed. Looks great."

Peter introduced Ronnie. "Thanks for letting us use your workshop. We'll finish these pieces in the next few days and get them out of the way."

"Oh, Peter, you know you're not in the way. The boys are working on cutting wood this week anyway. They have the chainsaws going nonstop. Well, except for Casper. Raina had her baby last week. He hasn't left her side since."

"What does Layla think of her new brother?"

Ingrid glowed with grandmotherly pride. "She adores him. We're all just smitten with Baby Rhett. He's got Casper's blue eyes and lots of dark hair."

Ingrid stayed and chatted for a while, getting to know Ronnie, but Peter didn't learn anything he didn't already know. Eventually Ingrid looked down at her watch. "I'd better go check on the spaghetti sauce I have going. Ronnie, I'm glad to meet you. You two should take a break, enjoy the water. And I hope we'll see you at church tomorrow."

She was off with a wave goodbye.

"She seems nice," Ronnie said as they packed away their leftovers and dug into the plate of cookies. "How are you related to these guys?"

"I'm not." He stuffed the last bite of cookie in his mouth and led Ronnie down to the canoe rack on the lakeshore. Better to be out on the water. No one could bother them there, and maybe he could make some progress on understanding this captivating yet confusing woman.

"A Deep Haven family you're not related to? Did they not have any girls?" She took the stern end of the canoe he pointed to and lifted.

"What's that have to do with anything?" He flipped it over, carefully dropped the bow into the water, and grabbed the oars and lifejackets. "Get in and I'll push us off."

"Look who's bossy now." She grinned as she stepped into the canoe and sat. "But I still need an answer. Does Ingrid have any daughters?"

He pushed them off and hopped in, picking up his paddle. "Yeah, three of them. Eden, Grace, and Amelia. I'm closer in age to Grace but hung out more with Amelia. Vivien and Ree are her best friends. Why?" he asked as they paddled away from shore.

"There's three available girls you're not related to. Why don't you date them?"

He laughed. "First, they're all married or engaged now. And before that, they weren't related, but they *were* the competition. At least as far as the Zimmermans were concerned. Besides, the Christiansen girls almost felt like family growing up together like we all did." Sure, they were nice, but had never held much appeal as far as romance went.

Now the woman sitting in front of him, on the other hand... she was a different story. A light breeze played with the loose tendrils of her hair. Their paddles whooshed through the clear water in perfect rhythm.

"Seems like everyone in Deep Haven has big families. And are they all so nice? I mean, these guys let you use their workshop. Ingrid brought us cookies." She shook her head a little. "It's strange."

Finally, a segue into something a little more personal than food preferences. "I guess it just seems normal to me. You didn't have neighbors or family that would do that for you?"

"Tiago and I actually have a pretty big extended family, but it's nothing like this."

Now they were getting somewhere.

She stopped paddling and turned on the seat to face him. Studied him. The rigidness in her posture relaxed the slightest bit, as if she found something in him she'd been searching for and wasn't disappointed.

"My cousins are wrecks. Gangs, drugs, addictions, unwanted pregnancies. You name it and they are neck deep in it. And they're only following in my uncles' and aunts' footsteps. I don't know where my mother is. Last I knew she was in jail. But I think she's out now, and obviously she doesn't care enough to let us know where she is."

Peter had no words.

"We came to Deep Haven because Tiago was in foster care, on the verge of getting sucked into all the same trouble. My *abuela* isn't a bad woman, but she's too trusting. She lets everyone walk all over her. She tried to keep an eye on Tiago after Mom left and while I was overseas, but she works two jobs. She just can't do it. That's why I left the Army and came back. Now I have guardianship of Tiago, and I will make sure he has a better life. He deserves it."

Peter didn't know what to say. His admiration grew, but his heart hurt to think of what Tiago and Ronnie had been through. "That...that had to be rough."

She shrugged it off and tried to smile, but it fell flat. "My mom...she wasn't always such a wreck. With my dad, she was healthy. Strong. We had our little family and moved to wherever the Army sent us. The house with the heart on the wall was the last home we ever had. The last time I saw her happy." Ronnie leaned over, dipped her hand in the water. The late afternoon sun reflected off the lake surface and shined in her sad eyes. "When my father died, she didn't get out of bed for weeks. Maybe months. I tried. I begged so hard to get her to eat, to get dressed, anything. She just...fell apart. Stopped living. For a year, I took care of her. Even stole food at the grocery store so we could eat."

"Ronnie...how old were you? You couldn't have been more than a kid."

"I was eight, nine. It was what it was. But eventually she started going out a little and this guy came into the picture. I didn't like him, but at least my mom was among the living again, you know? Then she let him move in. And—" She shook the water off her hand with a jerk. "He took over. *Everything.* Suddenly he was the one deciding what we ate, where we went. What my mom would wear. He took over the money, and she let him. Then he sold the house and took us away from our home too."

Peter lost all words as a fist bore through his chest. He fought a fierce and crazy desire to rip the arms off the guy who had torn Ronnie's world apart.

It got worse when tears shimmered in her eyes. "That was just the beginning. That jerk left, and Mom let another one take his place. We moved back to Minneapolis to be near my mom's family, and I got my first taste of why my father never wanted to spend much time with them. Eventually Tiago came along. He was the one bright spot, but I was seventeen when he was born. Mom did okay with him initially, but she didn't work. I needed an income, so someone could take care of him. I joined the Army as soon as I graduated and sent most of my pay to Mom. But she would run off, come back, find a new guy, and the whole cycle would start over again. Tiago was left in the dust to fend for himself."

She looked up at him, so much of her past in her expression. Finally.

And in that moment he wanted nothing more than to be a safe place for her.

But a steel laced her voice as her chin lifted. "So you see, Peter...I can't...I can't let someone take over my life. I have my brother to take care of. He needs me, and I don't have room for anything else."

"Who takes care of you, Ronnie?" he said softly.

Her chin dropped slightly. "What?"

"Veronica, you are the strongest woman I know. But everyone needs help sometimes. You don't have to do this alone." He put his paddle into the canoe and leaned forward, elbows on his knees. "Who takes care of you?"

She blinked at him. Swallowed, and a defiance filled her eyes. "I do."

Oh, Ronnie.

"Ronnie, God cares deeply for you. You know that, right?"

Her jaw tightened. "Then where was He when my father died? Where was He when I begged Him to help my mom? Where was He when every other man that was supposed to take care of me instead ravaged us, took away our home, our money, our choices? Where was God then, Peter?"

He opened his mouth but shut it again.

He had nothing.

But words whispered through his soul. "I...I think He *was* there, Ronnie. Hurting right along with you. He felt it all. Heard every prayer. He wants to be your safe place when everything is falling apart."

And they weren't just words. He believed them, right down to his core.

"Then why didn't He do anything?" A single tear rolled down her cheek.

Peter fought the urge to reach out and wipe it away. "I don't know. He tells us we'll have trouble and hardship, but He also promises to be our Rock. To weather every storm with us. He promised that in the end, all wrong things would be made right." He took a breath, softened his voice. "I know what happened to you was wrong. And I know He hates that our brokenness hurts others. But He's still here. And now, so am I. I want to be someone you can count on."

She stared at him so long in silence he wondered if she'd heard him.

Then, "You won't try to control me?"

He frowned at her. What—?

"Because as much as I like you, Peter, I won't have anyone holding me back. I won't let anybody come between me and my ability to take care of my brother."

"Ronnie, I have no desire to control you or hold you back. I just want to be there for you. Maybe help shoulder that load you carry." And maybe show her she mattered too.

Because now that he saw into her heart, there was no going back.

There had to be a way to put the brakes on this thing before it rolled out of control with her heart.

How did Ronnie get to the point of baring her soul to Peter in the middle of Evergreen Lake? It might've been the ripples pattering against the side of the canoe or the slight rocking that had lulled them to a comfortable silence. A loon couple gliding on the water, tricking her into letting down her guard.

Ronnie stared at the paddle in her hand. Why wasn't she using it to get as far away from Peter as possible? End this little lake time confessional?

Why? Because she believed him. Believed him worthy of trust.

Maybe God—the God her papa had taught her about as he'd read to her from her children's Bible—maybe He wasn't as absent as she thought. Peter spoke with such quiet conviction, unwavering and yet gentle in its prodding.

God caring? About her? Surely, He had better things to do. She'd been fine on her own.

She needed no proof of sin and depravity. That was everywhere. But if God was here, if He was as good and powerful as Peter said or as her papa had taught her, she could use some proof of that.

And maybe the man across the canoe from her was just the one to show her—this man who jumped through fire to save others. Who spent his free time with a children's theater production, playing video games with Tiago, and even now showed more concern for her well-being and feelings than she'd ever known from her own family.

Of course, they hadn't known each other long. A few weeks. But she could try. See if he was who he seemed to be. Maybe she didn't have to resist the way she was drawn to him quite so much. Didn't have to hate herself for allowing him in through the back door of her heart.

She'd never wanted to follow in her mother's steps, but Peter was nothing like the men her mother followed around. Peter had shown her kindness and integrity. Like Papa. It made a girl think she could drop her guard just a tad. His strength tempered with tenderness was like nothing she'd ever witnessed. No wonder she was intrigued by him.

Okay, so more than intrigued. But she still needed to take it slow.

"Let's head back." Ronnie spun in her seat and faced forward once again, digging her paddle into the clear green water. Peter must have sensed her need to change to lighter subjects. He pointed out the other residences and resorts on the lake, Pine Acres which Jensen owned and ran, and other neighbors of the Christiansens. He told her funny stories of growing up in Deep Haven. She couldn't help but wish she had grown up here too.

Though her arms burned, the exercise felt good, gave her something to focus on. It would be worth the sore muscles tomorrow. She had a feeling it was a day she wouldn't ever forget.

They soon reached the sandy beach near the canoe racks and disembarked.

"When is Tiago done with rehearsal?" Peter asked as he pulled the canoe farther up on the shore.

Ronnie picked up her end and tried not to get lost in his gorgeous eyes at the stern. "Not until later tonight. We still have time to put another coat of paint on."

"Or maybe I could go grab some dinner and bring it over."

Slow. Remember to take it slow.

He watched her. Waiting. Not pressuring. A little quirk to his smile made her go a bit weak at the knees.

Well, a girl *did* need to eat. "Any good Mexican food in this town? I'm craving tacos."

Before he answered her question, something slithered over her toes. Ronnie screamed and dropped the canoe, lifting one foot after the other off the ground as high as she could.

"What?" Peter rushed to her side. She grabbed his arm, hanging on as she ran in place.

"What's wrong?"

"Snake!" she finally screamed and pushed off Peter, backing away from the place she'd last seen the reptile slither through the grass and pine needles. "Kill it! Chop it up into pieces and... and...kill it!" Her back hit a tree.

In a moment, Peter's expression turned from worry to—laughter? Shoulders shaking, he emitted a full-on belly laugh. It rumbled through the surrounding woods. "You're afraid of snakes?"

"What are you doing? Kill it! You said if I ever needed help to let you help, so here I am. Help me. Stop laughing and kill that evil reptile."

The snake, not more than a foot long and the width of her pinky, curled near the base of a log.

Peter bent down and actually picked up the vile thing.

"Put it down!" She jumped away, the tree between her and the snake as he held it up.

"It's a garter snake. Completely harmless. Just a baby."

"Peter Dahlquist, get rid of that thing right now! Don't you dare come near me with it."

With a quick flick of his wrist, he tossed it in the woods. "They aren't poisonous. Don't worry."

"You didn't kill it!" She slid back around the tree trunk, trying to gain some control over her panic, but she wouldn't leave the safety of the towering pine.

He held up his hands, almost in surrender. "Ronnie, there's no need. It can't hurt you." He moved closer, and his voice calmed her racing heartbeat.

But still. "You...you don't know that. I mean, the devil himself came as a snake."

He held out a hand for her to take. "You're safe. I promise."

Hardly, but... Ronnie stepped away from the tree and cried out, grabbing her head. "Ow!"

"Wait." Peter leaned in close. "Your hair is caught in one of the branches."

"Well, get it out."

He smirked. "Bossy, bossy. Just hang on a second."

He reached behind her, his hands in her hair.

Oh. Wow.

His touch sent delicious tingles all over her scalp. The musk and evergreen scent of him made her mouth go dry. Her eyes slid closed as she breathed it in deeper. "Did...did you get it?" Her voice was barely a whisper.

Oh, for Pete's sake, her knees even went soft, like she might be some dumb damsel in distress. Next she'd probably throw herself into Peter's very capable and buff arms.

"Almost." The deep bass rumbled right in her ear, his breath tickling the nape of her neck. He stood in front of her, one arm on either side of her head. If she tilted her chin up just a notch, she could—

"There. You're free."

His smile froze as he looked down at her. His gaze fell to her lips.

And call it relief from him freeing her hair or protecting her from the snake or whatever it was—there was so much she wanted to say and couldn't—but she plowed right in and pressed her lips to his.

She shocked herself just as much as she did him, probably, because he didn't move for the first few seconds. But then his lips responded. He released a quiet moan and took over, his hands in her hair again. He kissed her back, giving her all she wanted and yet not enough. His touch and the taste of chocolate on her tongue sent delight and pleasure through every tingling nerve in her body. Her own hands slid up his chest, the pounding of his heart under her palms traveling through her.

He burned a trail of kisses down her neck, his beard tickling her skin.

"Yo, Peter," someone called from the trail.

He stepped back, breathing hard, but his gaze fell to hers, something almost dark and smoldering inside.

Oh. My.

So much for taking it slow.

A kid, older than Tiago, jogged up to them. His Blue Ox hockey shirt was smeared with dirt and sawdust coated his hair.

Peter cleared his throat and turned away. "Yeah, Tiger, what's up?"

"Grandma wanted to know if you guys could stay for dinner. We're having spaghetti and she said there was plenty for you too."

"Uh, we..." And suddenly, he sounded flustered. Or still breathless.

Yeah, well her too. But that's what she did—stepped into the messes to heal the traumatized. Or at least the people whose world had turned upside down.

She slid her hand into his. "We have plans."

And just like that, Peter found his voice. "But thank her for thinking of us."

"Okay." Tiger turned back up the trail.

Peter wove his fingers into hers, his thumb rubbing little circles on the back of her hand. He turned to her, a heat still in his eyes. "We have plans?"

She nodded. "You were going to find me Mexican food. Remember?"

"Oh, right." Then he smiled. A dazed, shy, goofy smile that melted that constant niggling in her head to silence.

They walked to his truck hand in hand. He opened the door for her.

Opened the door for her.

It wasn't the first time he'd done that, but it still baffled her.

This man was sweet.

This man was dangerous.

But at this moment she didn't care.

They didn't say anything until he parked his truck in Cole's driveway. "I'll go get food. Later we can pick up Tiago."

She got out and watched him drive down the hill, wondering just how long it would take before he was back. She was hungry.

And yes, her craving was for more than just good tacos.

"Ronnie, you okay?"

Ronnie spun around and faced Megan, a worried look in her friend's eyes.

"Yeah. I'm great."

Megan threw a handful of weeds into a wheelbarrow next to her. "Oh, good. You were just standing there staring off into space, so I wanted to make sure." She walked up to Ronnie. "I wondered if you..." Stopping mid-step, Megan squinted. "Oh my gosh, you kissed him!"

She stared back at Megan. "What—how—how did you know?"

Megan tilted her head and giggled. "Well, what do you know? Thanks for confirming my hunch! You and Peter might just make a match of it yet." She tugged Ronnie over to the porch steps. "Now, tell me all about it."

Deep Haven was changing her more than she realized, because she found herself spilling her guts to Megan like she was at a girly slumber party. Not that she'd ever been to one— she didn't have those kinds of friends. But maybe Megan was different.

A real friend. The kind who could help her understand this whole crazy situation.

"I don't know how it happened. I mean, one minute there's this snake on my foot and then my hair got caught in a tree, and then...we were kissing."

"Did he kiss you first?" Megan had taken off her garden gloves and was wearing a silly grin.

"I guess I was the one who made the first move. I was just so glad to get away from that snake, and then he was there. And…I don't know…"

Megan sighed. "Your first kiss."

"Well, it's not my *first* kiss, but I certainly have never been kissed like that before."

With other guys there were sparks, heat, but eventually it fizzled out. It always did. She'd get bored or realize they wanted more than she would give them either physically or emotionally. Their kisses were more about what they could get from her.

But this kiss, Peter's kiss, didn't take or demand. It was as if he was giving her a gift. Himself, maybe. And it sure wasn't a few measly sparks that lit inside. More like a volcano of molten lava. The kind that, if spilled, would consume…well, her.

The man may look calm, cool, and collected on the outside, but inside he was full of passion and fire.

"But that might've been *Peter's* first kiss."

She stilled. "What? No way that was his first kiss. It was too good to be his first." And she didn't mean for all that to spill out, but *really*?

"Well, I can't be sure, but he never dated in high school. He was even the homecoming king his senior year, but he didn't have a date because everyone—"

"Let me guess. Everyone is his cousin."

"Yeah. And in college, he was home every weekend working at a family restaurant or one of the resorts, trying to pay his own way. He always said he didn't have time to date. So…yeah, Ronnie. You could be Peter's first real kiss."

Oh boy. Because if that *was* his first, Ronnie couldn't imagine what his second or third would be like.

"Oh, you've got it bad," Megan whispered. "Is he coming back tonight?"

"Yeah, he went to get some food."

"Good. Then you have enough time to go shower and fix your hair."

"Huh?" Ronnie touched the back of her head, felt the tangles and snarls falling out of her braid. Her bandana hung limp around her neck. "Oh my goodness. I must look like a wreck. I've gotta go!"

"Tell me everything tomorrow!" Megan called over her shoulder.

Ronnie rushed into the apartment and banged into her bathroom. She started stripping off her sweaty clothes but paused to look in the mirror.

What in the world was she thinking?

Her hair was worse than she thought. White flecks of primer dotted her nose and smeared across her cheeks. She even had paint on her chin.

She hopped in the shower.

As she scrubbed her face and washed her hair, she wondered how she'd fallen so quickly for a small-town fire chief.

Worse, she had to figure out how to put out the blaze before he completely wrecked her. Could she really afford to lose control over her heart?

But, given the way she could still feel his kiss on her lips, yeah...it was probably too late.

CHAPTER 10

*R*onnie had kissed him.

Peter could've shouted it to the world from right there on top of the hill overlooking Deep Haven.

And what a kiss. The kind that made a guy feel alive and like he could hold the world in his hand. Like when he was a kid diving off the rocky ledge into Lake Superior, the frigid water stealing his breath until a heat would surge through him and he'd push through to the surface, breaking free.

He'd held that beautiful, vibrant woman in his arms, and the memory of the feel of her lips, her hands splayed across his chest, could still skyrocket his pulse.

Not that he had a lot of experience kissing women. In fact, zero. Zilch. That truth he would be keeping to himself. But man, Ronnie was worth the wait.

If she wanted Mexican food, he would get it for her even if he had to drive all the way to Mexico to get it. Thankfully, Taco Fiesta was right in Deep Haven. It was one of the few restaurants the Dahlquists didn't have their hands in, so he wouldn't have to worry about seeing anyone there.

He walked in and breathed deep of the smell of taco meat

and salsa. Probably not as authentic as Ronnie's *abuela* could make, but for the North Shore of Minnesota, these tacos were the best around.

Apparently, everyone else in town knew it also. He took his place in the long line behind the order window.

Vivien walked in right behind him, wearing aviator sunglasses, a summer dress, and a bright white smile like the little diva she was.

"Hey, Viv. Why aren't you at rehearsal?"

"They're going over choreography right now with my dance leaders while I do the dinner run."

"So, how's Tiago doing?"

Vivien's smile fell. "He's a natural on the stage, and with Josh he does great. But he's trying to prove himself with some of the older boys and they're getting into trouble."

"What kind of trouble?"

"Just dumb pranks and goofing off when they're supposed to be running lines. I constantly have to keep them busy and well supervised during our practices. He's a good kid. I think he's just trying hard to fit in."

That didn't sound good.

Viv wagged her eyebrows. "So, speaking of Tiago...what's with you and Ronnie? You two an item now?"

He froze, deer-in-the-headlight, and his answer came out without a thought. "What? No! Of course not."

"What do you mean 'of course not'? Every time I see you, she's with you or nearby. And she's fun. Gorgeous. Not related to you in any way, shape, or form. So why not?"

Right. He swallowed hard. Why was he fighting this? He had just kissed the woman.

But still, it was too new. He didn't know where they stood enough to inform Vivie, aka, the Deep Haven hotline. "We're... just friends."

Vivien shook her head and laughed. "Oh, Peter. You have the worst poker face."

"What?"

"It's so obvious you like her."

He shoved his hands into his pockets. "Yeah, she's pretty and she's got grit, but she's also pushy and bossy and doesn't know when to back down from a fight."

"So?"

"She's opinionated and stubborn."

Vivien shrugged. "She knows what she wants and gets things done. She's basically everything you're not."

"Hey! I...I do things. In fact, I've had to smooth things over with Uncle Charlie and Dean and quite a few others just so they'll stay with the first responders, thanks to her way of 'getting things done.'"

"And yet she's got the biggest group of responders volunteering that we've had in years, from what Seth and even Kirby Hueston said at trivia the other night. And that was after Kirby admitted she was the better person for the job."

There was that. "Maybe."

"It's true and you know it." Vivien pointed to the gap in front of him as the tourists had moved up in line.

He took a few more steps and closed the gap. "Fine. She does get a lot accomplished. But like you said, she's everything I'm not. We're...combustible. Not exactly dating material."

Vivien rolled her eyes and huffed. "Peter, you *need* someone like Ronnie in your life, someone to give you that nudge. Shove you when you get really indecisive. And she could use a calming influence. A strong and steady man. You're just the guy."

Just the guy. "You...you really think so?"

"I know so. Ronnie is a strong woman. Strong women like us need men who aren't intimidated. Men who will accept us for who we are, encourage our dreams, and...and be a solid place to land when we've gone a little too far."

Something in the way Vivien's gaze dropped to the floor made Peter wonder what had happened in New York. But the thought of really making something work with Ronnie...it sparked hope beyond the memory of the kiss.

He took another step forward. "So, say I'm interested. Not saying I am, but if I was, what do you think I should do?"

She chuckled. Probably saw right through his flimsy fabrication to his infatuated heart. "Dive in. Get involved in her life and don't wait by the sidelines, Peter."

"How?"

"Start with Tiago. Maybe you can talk to her about him, spend some time with them. Show her you're invested."

He nodded, taking in her words.

She pushed him from behind up to the order window and whispered in his ear, "For once in your life, you know what you want. Go after it."

It sounded good. But was it too good? He'd have to think about—

His alarm went off. "Deep Haven Fire Department respond to fire alarm at Arrowood Auditorium in the high school. No sign of smoke or fire—"

"That's the theater!" Vivien grabbed his arm and they raced to his truck. As she hopped into his passenger seat, Seth and Cole responded over the system that they were already at the station and bringing the trucks. Peter zipped through town, up the hill, and drove directly to the school.

They ran through the stage entrance door, now propped open. Beth Strauss stood at the entrance with some of the older teens, watching over the younger kids. They'd beaten the fire department to the scene.

He didn't see Tiago among the kids.

"Where's the fire?" Peter shouted, and Beth shook her head.

"I don't know—we just evacuated!"

Peter and Vivien ran onto the stage as the fire alarm blared.

No smell of smoke or heat from flames at first glance. But two sprinklers poured water from the high auditorium ceiling, soaking the seats in the middle section, water pooling on the cement floor and running down the incline, collecting at the bottom by the stage.

"The theater—it's ruined!" Vivien said, standing on the stage and looking at the destruction.

Seth and Kyle rushed in with some of the other firefighters. Peter sent them to do a sweep and then moved toward raised voices backstage behind the curtain. Ben, Tiago, and a few other boys were yelling. Josh stood to the side. He looked up with something of fear on his face when Peter stalked over to them.

"What's going on here?"

"Good thing you're here, Uncle Peter," Ben said. "If you want to know who to blame for this mess, it's this guy." He pointed to Tiago. "He pulled the alarm."

Tiago stared at Ben, his mouth dropping open. He was soaking wet, his red T-shirt plastered to his body.

"Tiago!" Ronnie burst in, wet hair, clean clothes. She ran over to him and pulled the kid into her arms. "Are you okay?"

"Apparently, he's the one who pulled the alarm."

"Good job, kiddo." She leaned away, looked at Peter. "Where's the fire?"

Silence.

And by the expression on her face, she got it. "Oh." She turned to her brother. "Tiago, you pulled a fake alarm? Why?" She grabbed his arm.

"No! I didn't!" He shook his head.

"I swear, Tiago. The only thing I asked of you is to stay out of trouble and yet I keep finding you smack in the middle of it." Her raised voice echoed off the dark walls.

Ben and the other boys smirked, not bothering to hide their amusement.

Peter stepped closer. "Hey, Ronnie, let's just calm down and hear his side of things." No time like the present to dive into her life and family and show her he was in this.

She looked up at him and shot him a frown.

Or not.

Hopefully her brother had a good excuse. "Uh, Tiago, why don't you tell us what happened," Peter said.

The kid tried to jerk away from Ronnie's hold but couldn't. "I didn't do anything! I was practicing my lines." He stopped struggling long enough to point back to Ben. "It was those guys. They were throwing the football around even though Vivien told us not to earlier. The alarm just went off. It's their fault."

Ben's friends jumped to his defense. They called Tiago a liar.

Ronnie turned to Josh. "What did you see? Did Tiago do this?"

The kid looked scared. Tiago's eyes begged his friend for confirmation.

"I...I don't know. I didn't see anything," Josh said.

Tiago wrenched his arm away from Ronnie with a yell. "I hate this place! I hate all of you!"

He ran out the door as Seth walked up, a broken sprinkler head in his hand. "Not sure how this broke, but it set off the system. No fire here. Cole is trying to reset the alarm and turn off the sprinklers in that zone."

Ronnie looked from the sprinkler head to the door. "Tiago!"

Peter reached out to stop her. "Hey, Ronnie, maybe just give him a little space right now. It was probably just an accident."

She pulled away from him. "Accident? Yeah, right."

"I can go talk to him. We can figure this out."

She rounded on him. "I don't need your help. This is my problem. Stay out of it." She pushed him aside and ran after her brother.

Kyle led Ben and the other boys outside and left Peter alone.

Suddenly the sprinkler right above him sputtered and released a deluge, soaking him to the bone.

And with it went their one finished backdrop, wet paint dripping down it, multicolored streaks turning the cityscape into a formless, chaotic mess.

Perfect.

Her brother should be on a track team. If she decided to let him live.

He'd made it out of the school and down an entire block before she spotted him running hard for the beach. She took off after him and headed for the clutter of the tourists on shore.

"Coming through!" she shouted, hoping to avoid one of the tourist couples strolling down the sidewalk blocking her path. She barely dodged them and ignored the guy's loud protest as she leaped off the cement walk.

Tiago was already down the beach, heading into the disappearing daylight. Her shoes sank into the pebbled shore. She kicked up rocks as she chased him through the marina and past the campground. He climbed onto the breakwater, the long line of haphazardly placed boulders stretching into the quiet bay.

Good. He couldn't go any farther unless he jumped into the water, not something he was likely to do since he wasn't a strong swimmer. But in his state of mind and the dark night approaching, who knew what could happen.

He scrambled over the last hunk of rock and stood there, breathing hard.

Then he sat and wrapped his arms around his skinny knees. His back convulsed as he sobbed.

She stopped before she reached his rock. Caught her breath.

She wanted to shake some sense into him or tell him to get with the plan and settle into this town because it was growing on her. He was ruining everything.

And crying didn't change anything.

But she sort of wanted to cry too. Because she'd just blown the best thing to ever happen to her.

Peter.

So what if she'd freaked a little about Tiago getting into trouble again? How could she be so cruel to the guy who had shown nothing but kindness to her? She hated that he'd seen her in that weak moment. Panicked. Scared.

And yeah, maybe he wasn't wrong in his words about listening to Tiago's side of the story. Ben Zimmerman wasn't exactly a model citizen, as evidenced by his behavior at the pit fire. How could she have listened to that punk over her own brother?

Ronnie took a couple of slow breaths and pushed back inside the drive to demand and conquer. If she was ever going to get Tiago to like it here, she had to go easy. What was it Megan had said at the pit party? *Don't forget to listen... He needs to know you still care even when you don't approve of his behavior.*

So much easier said than done.

She approached slowly. "T, be careful."

His head snapped up. "Leave me alone."

"I can't do that."

He shook his head. "I hate it here."

She sat down on the boulder next to him.

"Look, T, I should've listened to you. I'm sorry. Why don't you tell me what happened?"

"Like you care!"

"I do." She scooched closer. "I'm ready to hear you out."

He glanced up, scowling, but then his lower lip trembled slightly. "I didn't do it."

So many years she'd spent on the other side of the world. Did she even know her brother? Her gut said he was right. But more than anything, he needed her to believe in him. He needed her to see him.

"I believe you." She spoke softly.

He lifted his head off his knees, looked at her. His face was tear stained. "You're not just saying that?"

"Not just saying it. I really believe you. And I'm sorry I didn't listen earlier. I just…I just really want you to like it here. It's a cool little town, and there are some great people."

He rolled his eyes. "You're delusional."

"No, really. Peter is a good guy. You like him, right?"

"Maybe."

"And Josh? You guys were getting along—"

"Until he stabbed me in the back."

"T, that's not fair. He didn't see what happened."

"But those other guys *lied* for Ben. If Josh was a real friend, he would've lied for me too."

"That's not being a good friend. It took a lot of guts for Josh to tell the truth. I know he really wanted to help you. But lying isn't the answer."

"Whatever." The scowl returned and Tiago turned his back to her.

She was losing him.

A memory pierced clear and bright. Ronnie caught her breath and closed her eyelids against the sting of tears.

She couldn't go there. She didn't want to go there.

But it might be the only way to help Tiago.

"Did you know for all the birthdays I could remember when I was a little girl, I wished for a baby brother?"

Tiago didn't respond.

"When I was five years old, Papa asked me what my wish was when I blew out my candles, and I told him. He said, 'Veronica, wishes are fine, but if it's truly the desire of your heart, you should ask God. He's the One who can do anything. And He's your Heavenly Papa.' So from then on, instead of wishing, I prayed for a little brother. Every night for a long time. Years."

Tiago's voice carried over his shoulder, small, unbelieving. "You *prayed* for me?"

Yes. And how she remembered the fierce love pulsing through her the minute the nurse placed the newborn wrapped in a blue blanket in her arms. Remembered her promise to him, that she would take care of her baby brother no matter what.

Guess even when she'd stopped believing, God still had answered her prayer.

"Yes, Tiago, I really wanted you. I still do."

His silence echoed inside her.

Yes, she got it. She too wanted to matter to someone.

To her mother. To Tiago.

Maybe even to Peter.

Tiago turned, then took her completely by surprise and lunged into her arms. There was still a lot of little kid in him, a child who desperately wanted to be loved. She squeezed him tight and planted a kiss on his forehead, like her father used to do to her. "I know I'm not your mom or dad, T, but I do love you. And I'm trying. I screw up. A lot. But please know that I love you. 'Kay?"

"Okay."

"What do you think? Can you give Deep Haven another chance?"

He blew out a deep sigh. "I don't know."

"Remember our deal?" She almost hated to remind him, but he needed to know he came first. "Let's get through this summer, and if you still hate it, we'll...we'll leave."

"You would still do that?"

She looked him in the eye, seeing only him, and said, "I give you my word."

"But you like it here. I can tell."

"We left everything behind before. We can do it again. But you have to give it a fair shot."

He thought for a moment. "Fine. I'll try. But I'm telling you now, nobody wants us here." He started the climb back toward shore. Ronnie turned to follow.

A towering shadow of a man stood halfway down the breakwater.

Peter.

Shoot. How much had he heard?

His deep voice carried over the water as Tiago approached him. "Hey, little man, you okay?"

Tiago shrugged but gave him a fist bump when Peter offered it and then continued to shore.

Ronnie took a different route, jumping from rock to rock along the edge of the water. She stopped on a smaller boulder, looking for the next step. She hadn't realized that Peter had angled to meet her until he offered his hand to pull her up to his rock, a much bigger and steadier boulder than the wobbly one she was standing on.

Yes, she could make the jump to the next rock from her precarious position. Or she could take the guy's hand and follow the easier path he used down the spine of the breakwater. Part of her longed to prove she didn't need any help. But another part, the weaker part, wanted nothing more than to touch him again, to hold that big, capable hand and never let go.

And that was the danger.

If she couldn't get Tiago to fit into this town, she would keep her promise and they would leave. So it really wasn't fair to Peter to give him the wrong impression, was it?

Still, she couldn't stop herself from taking his hand. The warmth of his grip spread inside as they climbed the rest of the way to the edge of the water.

"Can I walk you guys home?" Peter asked as they joined Tiago.

He still held her hand as she looked out at the dying sunlight glowing and bouncing off the gentle ripples of the bay. "Yes."

The block and a half walk to the apartment was quiet. And frankly, over too soon.

Tiago said good night to Peter and went inside. Ronnie lingered by the garage.

Peter squeezed her hand and let go, giving her space like the thoughtful guy he was. "Just so you know, you *are* wanted here. *I'm* glad you and Tiago are here."

So he had heard them. He gazed down at her, strong and so sweet, his desire evident.

She didn't deserve him. Not one bit. "Look, Peter, I'm sorry. I didn't handle things very well back at the theater. I shouldn't have pushed you away. I know you were only trying to help. I just…I've just been on my own so long I don't know how to do this."

"Ronnie, you know I'm here for you, right? All I want is to help."

"I know." But her words to Tiago echoed inside her. Maybe she should end this now before it burned out of control. Before everyone got hurt.

Before she found herself needing him and he was ripped out of her life like every other person she'd loved.

"Peter, Tiago is my first priority. If Deep Haven doesn't work out for him, I need to go. We need to find a place he belongs, where he's safe." She swallowed hard and lifted her chin. He had to understand. "Maybe it's not the best idea for us to get involved."

She waited for his reaction. A flinch in his eyes. A flash of anger.

But instead he moved closer. "Maybe you should take your own advice."

"Huh?"

He leaned, whispered in her ear. "Give Deep Haven a chance. Give us a chance." His lips hovered over her cheek, landed a soft kiss, and glided away. "Sweet dreams."

He walked away into the night—his long hair lifting in the breeze, broad shoulders pulled back, hands in his pockets as he headed uphill.

Shoot. Because maybe it was too late.

The man was already walking away with her heart.

CHAPTER 11

*P*eter knew how to put fires out. He'd never thought about starting one—or keeping it going. But he liked Ronnie—really liked her.

The thought of her leaving put a knot in his gut.

With another swing of his ax, he split the pine log, releasing the scent of fresh-cut wood in the air. A woodpecker knocked on a tree trunk nearby. Young morning light filtered through spruce, birch, and pine trees. The faint sound of Nick's dogs barking carried on the wind.

The calm surroundings of his cousin's cabin in the woods did nothing to calm the storm inside.

"What are you doing here this early?" Nick yawned as he walked down the mulched trail between the trees with two steaming mugs. He still wore Superman pajama pants and a University of Minnesota Duluth T-shirt. Bed head had his dark hair flat on one side of his head and sticking out over his ear on the other.

Thwack. Two more pieces fell. "Aren't you the one always grumbling about having to chop wood for the winter? You should be thanking me." Peter sank the ax into the chopping block and took the mug from his cousin.

"Sheesh, how long have you been here? Looks like you cut enough for two winters."

The scalding hot brew burned Peter's tongue. He said nothing.

"Okay, what's on your mind?" Nick sat down on a log.

"Nothing. Just had some energy to burn."

"You really gotta work on that face if you want people to believe you when you're lying through your teeth."

"You sound like Vivien."

Nick shook his head. "Uh-uh. Not gonna work this time. Bringing her up won't deter me. Spit it out."

"Why don't you show me the latest batch of puppies? I'm thinking of getting one."

Nick never needed much encouragement to show off his animals. He rolled his eyes but stood up and moved toward his state-of-the-art eighteen-foot Quonset kennel. During the summer months, the dogs slept outside—well, they did also in winter, which begged the question as to why Nick had built the kennel. But he used the facility to breed his beautiful Alaskan huskies and board dogs as a side business. "Since when do you want a dog? You don't sled."

"You're always telling me dogs are more reliable than people. Maybe I just want a dog for companionship."

The barks of Nick's pack grew louder as soon as he opened the gate to the kennel.

"Well, I did have a runt in this litter. She's too small to mush. And Alaskan huskies do make good pets. You sure you're ready for the commitment?"

"Let's see her."

Nick led the way through the outdoor fenced area to the large shed. The bigger pups all came up and sniffed, barked their hellos and followed Peter and Nick to another enclosed area where Nick kept his youngest puppies. With one hand he picked up a dark gray and white little furball with big blue eyes. "Here she is." He set her in Peter's arms. "This one needs a home."

Peter set his mug down and sat in the straw. He soon had puppies climbing all over him. The one in his arms licked his face.

Nick slurped his coffee. "She likes you."

She *was* pretty cute. Peter set her down and watched her with the litter. The other pups jumped and wrestled with each other, rolled around in the straw, but the runt sniffed Peter's boots and whined, pawing at his leg to be picked up again.

He obliged.

"Dude, how are you single? I swear I could take one picture of you right now surrounded by puppies, you in all your brawny flannel and long hair, and you'd have to go into hiding from the women wanting to marry you."

"I could ask you the same thing."

Nick shrugged. "For one, I don't have the hair. I'll probably go bald early like my dad. And besides, who wants to live in a dinky cabin in the middle of the woods where it's winter half the year?"

"Please. What is your follower count now on your Instagram? Sixty thousand? And it's ninety percent women. Not to mention your vlog. How many subscribers do you have?"

"A hundred twenty-four thousand, but they love the dogs, not me. Besides, we're talking about you. What's holding *you* back?"

Peter shrugged. "Just never found the right girl."

"Uh, I think you found the right girl."

Guess there was no use pretending he didn't understand. "So, you heard about Ronnie."

"Who hasn't? I might live in the middle of the woods, but

this is Deep Haven. Word gets around. And word is, she's hanging out with you quite a bit. That's a good start."

"Yeah, but Ronnie...she's got her brother to take care of. They don't think they belong here. And, well, to be honest, they come with a lot of baggage." The puppy curled up in his lap, her soft fur brushing against his arm. "And then this vote on the Westerman place... It's a lot."

"So that's what got you chopping cords of wood and considering dog adoption in the early morning hours, interrupting my beauty sleep." Nick set down his mug. "Okay, one thing at a time. The Westerman. Forget what everyone else wants. What do you think is the best option?"

Forget what everyone else wanted? It took a while, but the answer rose up once Peter quieted all the other voices in his head. "The youth center."

"Why?"

"Vivien's right. I've been working with the kids and teens and they need a place to hang out, things to do in town. Kids like Tiago and Josh would love it. It would help the school, community sports leagues, Vivie's theater, and we could still rent it out for large events. It could benefit a lot of families. Our dads don't want to hear it and I have no idea how to pay for it, but I think it's the best choice."

"So, go for it. Make it happen."

"How am I supposed to tell *both* families that I'm not voting for them?"

"Afraid you'll have a repeat of your grad party?"

His cousin knew him well. "That's *exactly* what I'm afraid of. I'll never erase the image of sweet little Grandma Doris throwing her apple pie at Uncle Charlie."

"Best day of my life," Nick said, laughing as he picked up one of the other puppies and checked its teeth. "But who knew they'd all go to war over your future plans? And then you showed them. You became a firefighter."

The puppy nibbled on Nick's finger. "At least by voting for the youth center you'll tick both families off. The town can't claim nepotism."

"Gee, that's helpful."

"What can I say? I'm full of good advice." He let the puppy down and it scampered off with the rest of the litter.

"You're full of something, for sure."

"Back to Ronnie—and for the record, I knew you liked her the very first time you mentioned her. So what's the problem there?"

Peter looked down at the runt asleep in his arms. "Okay, so yeah, I like her. A lot. But we work together."

"So? People meet at work all the time. Are there any rules about not dating a coworker?"

"Well, no. But she's also made it clear her brother is her priority. And I get that. It's one of the things I admire about her. But she basically said, if Tiago doesn't like it here, she's moving. So, there's that."

"So, you help Tiago like Deep Haven. Help the kid make some friends. Look at where we live. Take him fishing. Kayaking. Climbing. Show him how awesome it is on the North Shore."

"It is awesome up here."

"It is. And you gotta show him that. Even if you have to sacrifice something else, like…I don't know…your pride?"

He looked at Nick. "What?"

"Put your heart out there, man. Show the girl—and her brother—that you like her."

He made a face. "You sound like Vivie. And I did. I do, but…I don't know. There's a part of me that thinks if I get into this thing too far, it could backfire on me."

"Dude, I've watched you sacrifice things you've wanted for the sake of someone else our whole lives, regardless of your feelings about it."

"What are you talking about?"

"When you knew money was tight, you gave up that football camp so your sister could take dance classes. You gave up summer ball to watch your brothers and sister for your parents so they wouldn't have to hire a nanny. You picked UMD for college so you could help me pass my classes, so I could play ball and you would be close enough to keep working for both the Zimmermans and the Dahlquists during the weekends."

"I didn't want to leave them in the lurch."

"You had no social life in college because you were always here in Deep Haven."

"I like it here in Deep Haven."

Nick sighed. "When you get down to it, what is it you want, cuz?"

"I just want everyone to be happy."

"Yeah, but what do *you* want? What would make you happy?"

The puppy awoke, perked her ears, and climbed up Peter's chest. She licked his beard and cheek, slathering him with puppy kisses.

"Never mind." Nick chuckled.

"What?"

"Oh, I know what you want." He squeezed his eyes shut and made kissy noises.

An idea came to mind. Peter stood up with the puppy still in his arms. "How much for the dog?"

Nick opened his eyes. "Save your money. She's yours."

"Really?"

"Yes. And we'd better get going. One thing about Deep Haven—you can't escape your mom. And ours will pitch fits if we show up to church late." He made a face. "You can use my shower."

∽

Ronnie stopped in the middle of the sidewalk and watched her brother. Seagulls above them leaned over the edge of the bank building, looking for scraps dropped by the people out enjoying the glorious morning. Tiago took another bite of his skizzle.

The sugary pastry smelled amazing. She waited for his eyes to light. A smile. A thumbs-up. Any sign of enjoyment would be an improvement to the quiet and gloomy kid her brother had become since the fire alarm fiasco last night. "So, what do you think?"

"It's okay, I guess."

"Just okay? They're from the World's *Best* Donuts."

He didn't say anything.

"Try this. It's incredible." Ronnie handed him a chunk of her roly-poly, a lemon-filled croissant covered in powdered sugar. Not the greatest choice with a black T-shirt and dark gray jeans, but it was so worth the mess.

Tiago popped it in his mouth. He shrugged and walked down the sidewalk, took another bite of his skizzle, still sullen and quiet.

Looked like it would take more than World's Best Donuts to convince Tiago that Deep Haven was worth sticking around for. Ronnie scrambled for another idea, anything to shake the somber mood.

"How about a hike after church? I heard there's lots of rivers around here, some cool waterfalls too."

If possible, the kid's shoulders slumped even more. "Are you really going to make us go to *church*?"

Yes, she was. Because sometime in the middle of the night when she'd pressed pause on the memory of kissing Peter rewinding through her head, she'd decided Tiago needed some more positive influences in his life. Like church. Especially if donuts weren't cutting it.

She held the passenger door to her SUV open for him. "We're going. Get over it."

Tiago groaned as he sat down. "Why?"

"People have invited us. It'll be good. Help us figure some things out."

She hoped. The only church experiences she'd had in the last twenty years were funerals, weddings, and a few services she'd attended with Abuela on holidays as a kid. After Papa died, Mom stopped going.

But she would do whatever it took to get Tiago to like it here, to find friends he could connect with. The kind who wouldn't get him in trouble.

And if she was being honest with herself, church wasn't just for her little brother. And it wasn't just Peter's kisses keeping her awake. The things he'd said about God...they kinda made sense. Or maybe she just wanted to *believe* they were true. If God really cared like Peter said He did, maybe she needed to give Him a chance too.

She'd asked Tiago to give Deep Haven a shot. She should do the same.

She parked in the almost-full lot of Deep Haven Community Church. A couple families with young kids, the parents loaded down with diaper bags and baby carriers, moved from minivans to the church entrance. An elderly man with a cane held the door for them. Everyone looked so...clean-cut. So good.

She so didn't belong.

"Are we going in?" Tiago asked.

"Uh, let's wait a few minutes. I want to finish my coffee." She took another sip and tried not to call herself a coward.

She jumped at a knock on her window. Megan.

Josh appeared at Tiago's door.

Tiago didn't move.

"Open it, T."

He shrugged and opened the door. Josh stuck his head in. "Hey."

A pause. "Hey."

"Um…my Sunday school class has this hockey pro talking to us today. He lives around here and—"

"Cool," Tiago said.

Ronnie glanced at him, but he was already sliding out of the seat. He closed the door and ran inside.

She might as well follow him. Ronnie took one last gulp of her coffee and got out.

Megan hugged her. "You're here. I didn't think you'd come, but I'm so glad you did. Come on. I'll introduce you to Pastor Dan."

They went inside. After a whirlwind of introductions—so many names Ronnie could never remember, but a few familiar faces in the crowd too—Ronnie sat next to Megan and Cole in the third row from the front of the sanctuary. So much for sitting inconspicuously in the back and sneaking out before the last song.

But by the time they were done, Ronnie was glad to be sitting by someone who knew what they were doing. They actually took out the Bible and read from it with the pastor. In fact, a lot of people brought their *own* Bibles. Megan shared hers as Pastor Dan talked about Jesus knocking on the door of their hearts.

"He wants us to experience life with Him inside us. He wants to carry us through the hardships. Join in our celebrations. Hold us when we're hurting. But He won't force Himself on you. He'll wait. He will nudge, prod, and knock at the door, remind you that He's there. But it's your choice to let Him in. And if you look, I bet you'll see ways He's acted on your behalf, even while you pushed Him away. He's that persistent."

The words might have been written for her alone, the way they pierced. And the music was nothing Ronnie was used to, but people really seemed to be feeling it. Some closed their eyes as they sang. Others even raised their hands.

Weird.

But kinda neat too. These people prayed out loud and sang like they believed God listened to them. And the way the pastor talked, He *did* seem close. Real.

After the service, Ingrid Christiansen found her. "Ronnie, I'm so glad you made it."

The older woman's smile seemed genuine, making it easier for Ronnie to admit she was glad too. "It's been a long time since I've been to church, so a lot of it is kinda new."

She looked around at the clusters of people scattered throughout the sanctuary, talking, laughing. Two little girls in matching dresses ran down the aisle squealing and giggling. When Ronnie went to church with her *abuela*, everyone left as soon as the last blessing was uttered. But here, everyone acted reluctant to leave, herself included. "Is it always like this? So... happy?" Was that the word for it?

Ingrid nodded. She must've understood. "Even in the hard times, coming together on Sunday mornings to worship brings me joy and comfort. It's like a weekly family reunion. We share the good things and support each other through the difficult things. It reminds us that we're not alone."

Something in Ingrid's gentle eyes spurred Ronnie on to ask the question that had been burning inside since the sermon. "How do you do it? Let God in, I mean? When I was a kid, I believed. But after certain things happened, I just sort of forgot."

"That's a great question, dear. And believe me, it's not hard at all. Just talk to God."

"Like in the prayer time?" Ronnie's heart sank. She shook her head. "I can't pray like that."

"You don't need fancy words or a special language. Just talk to God like you're talking to me right now. He knows what's on your heart. He can translate."

But before Ronnie could ask any more questions, Tiago rushed up to her and practically dragged her out of the building. "Let's go."

"Hey, wait a minute. I wasn't quite ready. And what about Josh? I was going to ask if you wanted to invite him on our hike."

"I don't care about him and I don't want to go on that stupid hike."

The stormy look in his eyes, those furrowed brows...something was wrong. Her discussion with Ingrid would have to be saved for another time.

Ronnie said a quick goodbye and followed Tiago out the front door. She waited until they were back home and finished with lunch to approach the subject. "You gonna tell me what happened at church?"

"Nothing happened."

"Tiago—"

"Look, they don't want us here. I told you that!" He ran into his room and slammed the door.

Something had definitely happened.

She flopped down on the dining room chair. She should've kept a closer eye on him, but she had thought he'd be fine with Josh. And she'd been really intrigued with what Pastor Dan and Ingrid had to say.

But it seemed like everything that drew her in pushed her brother away. Just when she was starting to find a place and people she liked, Tiago was further than ever. And she was running out of ideas on how to bridge that chasm. Hopelessness sat like a heavy weight in her chest.

A knock sounded. She opened the door.

Peter.

Of *course* it was Peter.

She couldn't get him out of her head. And now he was standing in her doorway with those jade green eyes shot with bursts of gold, his T-shirt pulling taut against his muscular shoulders and biceps.

He had such nice arms.

And, yeah, she just wanted to crawl right into those strong arms, rest her head against his chest to hear his steady heartbeat, and forget the world for a little bit. "Come in."

A little bark sounded from somewhere behind him. "What is that?"

"Saw you at church today, but you left before I could talk to you." He moved to the side and she spotted a pet carrier.

"Peter, what is in the carrier?"

"Patience, Buttercup. It's a surprise. And I promise, it's not a snake." He crouched, opened the door, reached in, and pulled out a fluffy, white and gray puppy.

Now this hot man stood in her living room holding a *puppy*. Oh, heaven help her. Slap this picture on a fireman fundraiser calendar and the station would be swimming in cash for all of eternity.

"I know Tiago is having a rough time fitting in. My cousin had a litter of puppies and one needed a home. Tiago needs a friend. It's a win-win." He held out the blue-eyed pup to her. "What do you think?"

She could hardly swallow as she ran her fingers through the puppy's soft fur and held it in her arms.

"It's an Alaskan husky. My cousin raises them as sled dogs, but she's too small for his team. And I bought everything you need." He picked up a bag and walked to the kitchen table. He pulled out puppy food, a bright magenta collar and leash, food and water dishes, a little doggy bed, and an adorable moose chew toy.

This man. He kept showing up. He kept taking her by surprise and touching her in ways that brought emotions she'd thought she'd long outgrown to the surface.

Those emotions clogged her throat and blurred her vision.

"Ronnie, it's okay. If you don't want to take on the responsibility of a puppy, I'll take her—"

"No!" She cuddled the dog closer. "No, I'm sorry I didn't say anything. You just...took me by surprise. I love this idea. It's perfect."

His worried expression melted away. "You sure? I can keep her at my place if it's too much."

She shook her head. "What ten-year-old boy wouldn't want a puppy? It's genius. Tiago will love her."

"I hope so." Peter stepped closer, petting the dog in her arms. "Ronnie, I really want you to stay."

She looked up at him—and the truth that had rooted deep inside her but stayed below the surface now bloomed. "I...I do too."

Her words registered on his face with a smile and a nod. And a look of desire.

Between them, the puppy let out a little bark.

Right.

She stepped back. "One peek and Tiago will be in love. He's always wanted a dog. I can't wait to see his face."

"Where is he?"

"In his room. I think something happened at church. But just wait until he gets a load of this cuteness. He'll forget all about it." She held the puppy up to her face and let it lick her. "Here, you should be the one to tell him." She placed the puppy back in Peter's arms and called out. "Tiago. Come out here."

Nothing.

She knocked on Tiago's door. "T, come on out. Peter's here. He's got something you'll want to see."

"I don't care. Leave me alone."

Why did he have to make things so difficult? She opened the door and pursed her lips to keep from yelling. Tiago lay on his bed, staring at the ceiling.

"Peter is here and he'd like to see you. Don't be rude."

"Fine." He rolled his eyes as he got up and pushed past her to the living room.

Ronnie tamped down her ire and watched his face, waited

for his scowl to fade away and the joy to set in. The skizzle didn't cut it. But, hello, this was a *puppy*. How could he not melt at those big blue puppy dog eyes?

"Hey, Tiago, I'd like you meet someone." Peter held the puppy out to her brother.

Tiago drew in a breath, then folded his arms. "Why should I care about a dumb dog?"

CHAPTER 12

Oh, it might be harder to get Tiago on his side than Peter thought.

Any other kid would be ecstatic to get a brand-new puppy. But hardened dark eyes, folded arms, and the frown on Tiago's face didn't exactly speak of gratitude or delight.

"You want to hold her?"

"Fine." The hardness and scowl melted into a general coolness as Tiago reached out for her. He petted her once and tried handing her back.

"Don't you like her?" Ronnie asked.

The boy shrugged. "She's fine, I guess." He held the puppy out for Peter to take. The animal was squirming in his grip, aiming licks at his face.

Maybe Tiago didn't understand. "She's *yours*."

Tiago frowned at him, and for a second, a softness entered his expression.

Then, a tinkle sounded on the hardwood floor. "What?" Tiago dropped the puppy who yelped and ran under the table. Tiago glared at Peter. "I hope you can get your money back because I don't want it. Stupid thing peed all over me. And I should've known you'd be just like the rest trying to buy me off." He fled out the apartment door.

Ronnie's shocked face swung from puppy to door. "Tiago! Get back here!"

What in the world had just happened?

Ronnie moved to the kitchen, ripped paper towels off the roll on the counter, and wiped up the mess on the floor. "I should've remembered." She threw away the soiled paper towels and sank onto one of the dining room chairs.

"What did I do?" Peter scooped the dog up and sat down across from her. "Who was Tiago talking about, *like everyone else?*"

Ronnie pinched the bridge of her nose, eyes closed, and took in a deep breath. "It's not your fault." She reached over and put her hands on the puppy's head, but she looked defeated, tears clinging to wet eyelashes.

"Tell me how to fix this. I want to help."

She pulled away from the puppy. Shook her head. "You can't fix this, Peter. It's not your problem anyway. It's mine." She sighed. "I knew this was a bad idea."

"What are you talking about?"

She looked away from him, out the window. "Look, Peter, I know what you're trying to do. It won't work. You...you're good. *Too* good. How in the world can you understand people like us? Tiago and I didn't grow up with happy families and homemade cookies and small-town festivals. We grew up needing to protect ourselves from our own family—or from the men my mother brought into our lives." She looked back at him, met his eyes. "Like the guy who would hand Tiago twenty bucks and tell him to scram so he could have privacy with Mom. And heaven forbid if Tiago came back too early. I was old enough to know how to stay out of the way with these guys, but I missed a lot of his growing up. I wasn't there to protect Tiago."

He had nothing, everything inside him going hollow at her words. He looked at the puppy and felt a little sick.

Yeah, he could see how Tiago thought he might be buying him off to get time with his sister. Not exactly what he was doing, but in a way…

"Tiago just wanted some attention," Ronnie said softly. "Instead he was kicked to the curb with money to blow. To him, you're just another guy trying to buy him off, to get what you…want."

But she was wrong about one thing. The most important thing. "Ronnie, I'm not looking for some…fling. Do you want to know what I really want?"

She looked up at him, and behind the anger and the sparks of indignation, he saw it—that scared little girl, like Tiago, afraid to want something that would be soon ripped away.

"I want *you*. I want *Tiago*. I want to be a part of your lives. I want to be there to celebrate when he nails his role in the musical. I want to be there when you save the next patient's life. And I want to be there on the hard days too. When things fall apart. When he flunks a test, or when you have to kick my hotheaded uncle off the first responders team. What will it take to prove to the both of you that I'm in this for good?"

A few beats of nothing.

The puppy barked as if echoing the question.

Slowly, a smile slid across her lips. "How did you know I kicked Charlie off the team? You weren't at our last training session."

He met her smile with one of his own. "Small town, remember?"

She made a huffing sound but took the puppy out of his arms and looked at him with a small shake of her head. "Good thing it's a small town. Can't be too many places we'll find my brother. Are you sure you want to give this a shot?"

"I'm in this. Let's find Tiago."

They clipped the collar and leash on to the dog. Peter pocketed a few of the treats and they walked toward the school. He had a hunch…

And it paid off. They found Tiago at the skate park. Alone. The cooler temps and gray skies that had moved in after the sunny morning must've kept others away.

The puppy didn't want anything to do with the boy on the skateboard, scrambling away and pulling on the leash.

Peter handed Ronnie the leash. "Do you mind if I talk to him first?"

"Good luck." She took the dog to the grassy area at the edge of the park.

He approached the boy, standing on the edge as Tiago tried a board flip. "Tiago, can we talk?"

"Leave me alone." He set the board at the top of a ramp.

Peter took a cue from Ronnie and ran down into the pit, planting himself in Tiago's path. "That's not going to happen. In fact, I'm gonna bug you until you realize I'm here to stay. I can wait all day."

"What's there to say? You like my sister. You wanted me gone. Bam. You got what you wanted." He turned on his skateboard to avoid hitting Peter and rode the board back and forth between one of the ramps and the quarter pipe.

"That's not why I got you the puppy. I brought her to you because I thought you would be the perfect person to care for her. I thought you would understand."

"Understand what?"

"Think about it. She's alone for the first time, away from everything she knows. She needs a lot of patience and care. And I've seen the way you and Ronnie take care of each other. I thought you guys would be the perfect home for her."

Tiago stopped, kicked up his board. Looked at him. "She doesn't even like me. Peed all over me."

"Because she's scared. She's been taken away from her mom

and her family. I peed my pants for a month when my mom remarried and we moved into a new house."

Tiago made a face. "Gross. TMI, dude."

"I was six."

"So what does this have to do with me?"

"This puppy doesn't know you. You'll have to earn her trust. Be gentle with her. And if you do, you'll have a friend for life."

Tiago didn't say anything, but his gaze followed Ronnie walking the puppy around the playground equipment. A young mother and a preschooler walking by stopped and oohed and aahed over the puppy.

Peter walked over to Tiago. "You're right. I do like your sister. But no matter what, you are Ronnie's first priority. She already told me that if you don't like it here, you're going somewhere else, until you find a place you do like. And if you guys go, the puppy is still yours. She needs someone to love her. Train her. Take care of her. You in?"

Tiago was silent for a few beats. "Don't think that this means I'm going to like it here."

"That's fair."

Another beat. Finally, Tiago shrugged. "Okay."

They walked to the edge of the skate park. "So, what are you going to name her?"

Tiago glanced at him, grinned. "How about Killer?"

"Your sister might have something to say about that."

Tiago smirked. "Probably."

Peter handed him a dog treat as they approached the puppy and Ronnie. "Try giving her this."

The boy held out the treat. The puppy gave a sniff but stayed wrapped around Ronnie's ankle.

"Here, Blue," Tiago said with a gentle voice and squatted down.

The dog considered him, then finally trotted over and took

the treat. Tiago picked her up and tried not to smile as Blue licked his neck.

Peter met Ronnie's eyes and matched her smile. Then, easily, as if the earth hadn't just moved, "You guys up for some pizza?"

"What do you say, T?" Ronnie said, still looking at Peter. Still smiling.

"I only like pepperoni. None of those gross peppers or mushrooms or anything."

Peter reached out his hand for Ronnie. She took it. Squeezed.

"I think we can work with that."

If this is what it took to get ready for an actual date, no wonder it had been awhile since Ronnie had gone on one.

It wasn't so bad earlier in the morning. She'd still been floating high on a cloud of anticipation since Peter had asked her out after the whole puppy fiasco last weekend. But at this point, in the sweltering heat of the crowded store, the small-town shopping experience had lost all its charm. The lack of caffeine and the smell of the candles and incense sticks on display were giving her a headache. Her feet hurt from standing in the new wedge sandals she bought, and she would kill for a bag of Cheetos.

"Will one of you remind me again why we're doing this?" Ronnie asked as she stood in front of the full-length mirror in her twelfth outfit for this store alone.

Ella and Megan eyed her critically from head to toe. Megan motioned for her to spin. "I like the color. That gold in the shirt looks amazing with your skin tone. But I'm not sure about the cut."

Ella's scrunched up nose said she didn't like it either. "Try the purple one, Ronnie."

And maybe it was a little childish, but she'd had enough. "No. I can't try on one more thing until I get some sustenance."

"Ronnie, you can't go on a date with Peter tonight in yoga pants and a T-shirt. We need to find a few more things that are a little more feminine," Megan said.

"And flirty," Ella added. "Even if you don't know where he's taking you."

"But I'm hungry." And frustrated. And tired. All she'd wanted was to find a nice pair of jeans, but when she asked Megan where she could find some, she'd insisted on calling Ella and making a girls' day of it. And what had started out as fun was now quickly escalating into a new form of torture and starvation. "And for the record, I have more than yoga pants and T-shirts."

"Football jerseys don't count." Megan pushed Ronnie back into the dressing room. "Especially a Green Bay Packers jersey. Now go try one more top on, that cute lacy one in orchid, and after that we'll go get you an iced mocha."

Finally! A reward in sight. "With one of those Java Cup scones too?"

"Yup. We'll get you a scone too. But first one more shirt." Megan used her soothing but firm mom voice very effectively.

Ronnie threw the black and gold sleeveless top on the floor. It landed in a heap on top of her jersey as she wriggled into the lacy shirt Megan insisted on seeing. The white skinny jeans she still had on were highly impractical, especially for a girl who lived in black and gray because they hid so much. But Megan and Ella had way more experience with guys and fashion, so she'd give this one last try.

She popped back out of the dressing room. Immediately both friends shook their heads. "Maybe that red—" Ella started to say.

"No. No more. I need coffee." She had to put her foot down at some point. "Please."

"Fine. At least we found the dress and shoes and a couple of things to add to your wardrobe. Let's go get your mocha," Megan said as she picked up her purse.

Ronnie had never changed so fast in her life. Ella hung the clothes back on the rack and they left the store. Heat radiated off the sidewalk. Before they took five steps, they ran into Izzy Knight, the football coach's wife. And while she was tempted to run the couple of blocks over to the Java Cup and leave Megan and Ella to discuss the weather and latest news with the sweet lady, Ronnie couldn't abandon her friends after all they'd tried to do for her today.

Besides, she needed all the town support she could get.

But her mouth watered at the thought of that first sip of ice-cold mocha.

Sweat pooled down Ronnie's back and she was ready to gnaw her own hand off by the time they started walking again. Where was the lake breeze today?

"I still can't believe Peter got you a puppy," Ella said after they waved goodbye to Izzy.

Megan stepped around a light pole. "I can. Let's be honest. Cole always had my heart. But for as long as I've known Peter Dahlquist, I've wanted a good woman to see the hidden gem he is."

Ronnie wasn't sure she qualified as a good woman, but she couldn't argue that he was a great guy. "Yeah, he's amazing." She sighed. "But don't you think it's fast? I mean, we've known each other a month. Maybe I shouldn't be dating right now. I should focus on my job. I still have to prove Deep Haven and I are 'mutually beneficial' as Seb put it."

And even though he loved Blue and was taking such good care of her, Tiago still wasn't convinced about the place.

But the place was sure growing on her, and she was falling hard for Peter. Maybe too hard. Certainly, too fast.

"Ronnie, you're just hungry. A scone and iced mocha will set you right up." Megan led the way to the Java Cup entrance.

Ella fanned her face with one hand as she held the door for them with the other. "Besides, look at how many new trainees you have and how many people you knew at church. At this point, everyone has gotten over the fact that you're not Kirby Hueston. You *are* showing this town that you belong,"

Ronnie drank in the words. They were right. She *was* fitting in. Everything would be fine once she had her scone and an ice-cold drink. She joined the long line inside the Java Cup. Coffee and chocolate should wake her up and knock some sense into her. She had a date to get ready for.

Megan stepped away to talk to someone she knew, and Ella went to save a table for them in the little room off to the side. Finally, there was only one more person in front of Ronnie in line.

He ordered seven drinks, the last five scones, and he scooped up the lone donut in the basket by the cash register.

No! No more scones?

By the time Ronnie reached the counter she wanted to cry. Or scream. It was a toss-up. Either way, she used all her strength to hold it together. "Please tell me you have some more scones hidden somewhere."

Kathy—Ronnie's usual barista—shook her head. "Sorry, that was the last of them. And I know you like your iced mochas, but with this heat our ice maker isn't keeping up. I used what we had on the last order. I can only serve hot drinks at the moment."

Oh, that was just it. "You're kidding, right? Can't someone run to the gas station and grab a bag of ice?" Or maybe tackle the guy who'd just left and wrestle the frothy iced-caramel frap out of his greedy hands?

"No, we can't. Especially for someone wearing *that*." Kathy smirked.

Ronnie looked down at her green-and-gold Aaron Rodgers jersey. "This?"

"We don't serve Packers fans here." Kathy winked at the other girl behind the bar. "Right, Sarah?"

The other customers snickered.

Maybe Kathy meant it as a joke. But this was not the time to mess with Veronica Morales. If Kathy wanted to withhold a caffeine addict's coffee, she'd better be prepared for battle.

Ronnie slapped her hands down on the counter and leaned in. "I'm a paying customer. I'll wear whatever I want. One large mocha. Please. I'll go to the gas station myself and buy a cup of ice for it."

"Oh, really?" Kathy fisted her hands on her hips and lost the amused expression on her face. The humor in the room died. "If you want the coffee, you'd better find a different shirt. And an apology."

Why did everyone feel the need to critique her wardrobe today? "You can't tell me what to wear."

"I own the place. I can refuse service to whomever I choose. Says so right there." She pointed to a printed sign on the wall behind the counter. "So until you come in with a different set of colors and a nicer attitude, don't bother coming back."

Was she seriously refusing service because of a football jersey?

Megan ran over. "Kathy, please. Ronnie's just a little hypoglycemic at the moment. A little cranky, but a shot of coffee and sugar and she'll be—"

Kathy pointed to the door. "I have zero patience for rude customers. Out."

With mouth clamped tight, Ronnie allowed Megan to lead her out of the Java Cup.

Ella ran out after them. "I heard what happened. I'm sure Kathy will calm down in a day or two. Why don't we grab some ice cream?"

Ronnie turned to them both. "No, thank you. I think I need to just go back—" She'd almost said "home." But that wasn't the case, was it? "I'm going to go back to the apartment." A place she probably shouldn't get used to just yet, but where she could at least have a little meltdown, gorge on some Cheetos and a sports drink, and try to pull herself together before her date. "I'll see you both later." She grabbed her shopping bags and what dignity she could scrape up and left.

Guess she still had a long way to go to fitting in.

It was amazing what a little food, a cold shower, and a twenty-minute power nap could do for a person. Ronnie woke up with a clearer head and ready for a fun, romantic outing. The swirling sensation in her middle had nothing to do with hunger this time as she checked the clock on her nightstand. One last swipe of the lip gloss Megan had picked out for her and she was ready. The off-the-shoulder fuchsia top paired with studded jean capris was cute and comfortable. She'd taken Ella's suggestion and left her hair down to display the natural wave she usually hid. It was a glammed-up version of Ronnie staring back at her in the mirror, but still her.

A knock sounded at the door. Of course Mr. Keep His Word was right on time. A strange nervousness tickled Ronnie's belly. She brushed it aside and opened the door. "Hey."

"Hi—" The look on Peter's face made the whole shopping torture worth every second. He stood in her doorway and stared. "Wow."

Yeah, she owed the girls big time.

She'd had men comment on her looks, heard catcalls while jogging, and had the occasional compliment from the opposite sex. But Peter's obvious admiration was so much more. He wasn't just looking at her body or noticing her curves. He was looking at her. And crazy enough, he seemed to like what he saw.

And so did she, even if he was in another T-shirt with cargo shorts. The man wore it so well, and the moss green and warm gold in the shirt perfectly set off his eyes.

It was safe to say her day had completely turned around. "So where are you taking me, hot stuff?"

"Hot stuff, huh? I like that."

"Don't let it go to your head. It's only because you're a fireman."

"You sure about that?"

The tease in his eyes exposed her as a liar. She laughed as she grabbed her brand-new purse—another purchase Megan and Ella had insisted on—and they headed down the stairs and to his truck. "So are you going to tell me where we're going?"

"It's a surprise." He opened the door for her and kissed her cheek before she settled into the cab.

Okay then. So far, she liked surprises.

"Where's Tiago?" Peter started the engine.

"He's staying with Josh tonight."

"Is he doing okay since the sprinkler episode?"

"Not really, but at least Vivien is keeping the play going."

"Yeah, she already has me on call to help install new seats when the replacements arrive." Peter drove downhill and turned onto Highway 61.

Was he taking her out to an early dinner? She was kind of hoping for a more intimate setting, a place where she could have him to herself and not have all the Deep Haven old-timers watching their every move. But they would've stayed on the highway if he were taking her out of town. Instead, he turned after only a couple blocks.

"We're here." Peter parked in front of a rundown three-story hotel that perched on the edge of the shore overlooking Lake Superior. Some of the windows were boarded up. Graffiti marked the walls. Weeds choked the scraggly landscaping and reached the first story windowsills. He ran around to her side of the truck and opened the door for her. "I want to show you a piece of Deep Haven history. Welcome to the Westerman."

Not that she was an expert in romance by any means, but a dilapidated hotel leaning up against the eastern shore of the bay didn't exactly seem like a first date kind of place. "Are you sure it's…safe?" And had she totally misread him? Maybe this wasn't a date. Maybe it was a work thing. Either way, her spirits sank.

"Structurally, it's sound, but let's just say I'll be glad when it's all renovated and the fire safety systems are in place. One spark and this place could go up in flames."

Okay, so not a date at all. A work project. She'd gotten all dolled up for nothing. Wow, had she read *that* wrong.

He unlocked the chain across the front doors and led her inside. "This main entrance to the building is a hundred years old. The original Westerman Hotel was built even earlier, 1901, but it burned down. In fact, most of this downtown area burned at one point or another."

Ronnie tried to shake off the disappointment and adjust back to work mode. "Deep Haven has tragedies? I thought it was always fairy-tale happy endings."

"Nope. For instance—" He cleared his throat and did a snooty tour guide accent. "Otto and Maria Westerman moved from Illinois to Deep Haven with their two daughters, Elise and Greta, in the late 1800s. They built their hotel here, right down shore from the Eversons, who ran a big boarding house."

She laughed at his silly accent even though it took more effort than usual. "Let me guess, the two families were business rivals?"

"You guessed correctly. But the animosity went even further.

Otto and Maria were rich, and rumor was they had ties to the Chicago mafia. The Eversons, like many of the other townspeople, didn't trust them. But it didn't stop Caleb Everson from falling in love and marrying Elise Westerman."

"Ah, Romeo and Juliet, Deep Haven version." A story with a tragic ending.

A lot like this so-called date.

She probably shouldn't have bothered with the cute black wedges she'd just bought as she stepped over piles of old brochures spilled out on the floor and around the random mattress in the middle of what used to be a lobby.

"Yup. Both families shunned the couple. But blood ties were still strong. When Caleb's brother died suspiciously, he blamed the Westermans and their mafia connections. He vowed revenge and planned to burn down their hotel. But his wife discovered his plan and went to warn her parents. She was in the building when Caleb started the fire. She died."

Ronnie looked up from the staircase she leaned against as she plucked a stray newspaper stuck to the bottom of her shoe. "No!"

Peter nodded. "Not only did Caleb lose Elise, the Everson boarding house and three other businesses caught fire and burned to the ground. The Eversons were never able to recover."

"Wow, that *is* tragic. What happened to the Westermans?"

"They survived. And they had the money to rebuild. Their other daughter, Greta, married Walter Zimmerman and they took over the family business, bought up another hotel, and that's how the Zimmermans got started in the hospitality business."

"Then why don't the Zimmermans own this place anymore?"

"Well, we don't talk about it much, but my great-great-uncle Stephen who managed this hotel in the '60s had a gambling problem. Got so bad the family sold this property to pay off his debts. The hotel passed hands a few different times, but by the late '90s it went bankrupt and has been sitting here ever since."

"Why didn't the Zimmermans buy it then?"

"I think my great-grandpa was still embarrassed about losing it. Not to mention a huge permit cost for an environmental impact study because the property includes shoreline. We're talking a hundred grand for that one permit. But once Adrian Vassos came talking about rebuilding—and conveniently paid for that testing—all of a sudden, the Zimmermans wanted to stake their claim and the Dahlquists didn't want some outsider taking the prime location. But both families *did* allow the Vassos corporation to sort through all the expensive legal tangle to free it up. Adrian released the permit to the city when he decided not to buy."

Ronnie moved to the next room. The high ceilings and what was once probably a glossy wooden floor gave the room a lot of potential, even though at the moment the long wall was lined with stacks of broken chairs and tables.

If they cleaned out all the junk in here, there was a lot of usable space. A vision started forming, one of Tiago and Josh dribbling a basketball down the length of the room.

"You know, this big ballroom would make a great gym. We could add a little snack bar or concession stand over there in that alcove."

"Vivien wants a theater too, but I'm not sure."

"Why not? We could fit it in that other wing off the lobby. There's plenty of space."

Peter moved closer to her. "What about an arcade?"

She walked down the hall and skirted around overturned tables in what might've been a breakfast room. There were no windows, but they could add some cool black lights and neon signs to give an arcade feel to the room. "I think we should put it here."

Peter didn't follow. Just stood in the doorway and watched her.

She fought the urge to squirm. "What?"

"You said it again." He stepped into the room.

"Said what?"

He came closer, slipped one of his strong arms around her. His other hand traced her jaw.

Now this was starting to feel more like a date.

"You said 'we.'"

She had? She was having trouble recalling anything she'd said in the last ten minutes.

"And I have to admit, I like the sound of it." The green in his eyes drew her in like a warm spring day after the bitter winter. More evidence that, like it or not, she was already invested. But if one little word was all it took to show him she really was on his side, then... "We should really—"

He lowered his mouth and kissed her. And she forgot everything she was going to say, especially when he pulled her closer. Her hands slid over his shoulders and around his neck and she lost herself in his woodsy scent and the taste of cinnamon.

Yes, most definitely a date.

He finally moved away and rested his forehead on hers. "So does 'we' mean you're gonna help me?"

"Yeah." And it wasn't as hard as she thought to add, "We're a team."

"You really like this idea?"

"Peter, you're right. This town has plenty of hotels and restaurants. It needs a youth center. A place kids can hang out, maybe even learn skills. We could use that small kitchen to teach cooking classes. There's so much potential right here."

He sighed. "It's gonna be a battle."

"Your family?"

"Neither side is going to like it."

"Why does that matter so much?"

He let out a long breath. "Let's just say I don't want a repeat of my graduation party."

"What happened?"

He let her go and moved away, then picked up a broken lamp and set it on a table. "During my senior year, there were a few times my work schedule at the restaurant conflicted with the Zimmerman resort. It was causing problems, so my mom tried to talk me into doing two parties. But I didn't want my parents to go through all that expense and work twice, and I was kind of excited to have all the people I care most about in one place. I thought they could put away the rivalry and arguments for a day."

"Makes sense."

"But it was tense from the start. Mom and I ran back and forth with the Zimmermans. Dad kept the Dahlquist side happy. But at one point my Grandpa Zimmerman made a big show of giving me my present. He wanted me to open it up in front of everyone."

"What was it?"

"A plaque that read *Peter Zimmerman, Moose Ridge Resort Assistant Manager.* Said I was going to train under my Uncle Charlie while I was in college and then take over once I got my degree."

"He didn't even put the right last name on it?"

"Nope. Said now that I was an adult, I should legally change it back to my *real* name. Dad went ballistic. Apparently, he was planning on me taking a management position in *his* restaurant after college. He and Grandpa got into a shoving match. It wasn't pretty, and practically everyone in town was there to see it. It spiraled out from there, and food got involved…"

"So they both thought you would work for them? Didn't they bother asking you?"

Peter shrugged. "No. I worked at all the resorts, filled in at all the restaurants whenever they needed people. I was going to study business at the University of Minnesota Duluth. Everyone assumed I would work for *their* business. Part of it is my fault, I guess. I always wanted to learn how to do a good job whatever I did. I think they saw that interest and mistook it for something more."

Yeah, that sounded like typical Peter, always striving to do the right thing.

He kicked at a pile of old magazines. "Do you know what it's like to have these two men I've looked up to all my life at each other's throats? They've never been able to speak civilly to each other since then. And it was my fault. I made a choice...and everyone suffered for it."

Oh, Peter. "Which is why you haven't been able to vote."

"Yeah."

She nodded. "Well, no wonder you feel stuck. But, Peter, you do know that the fight at your graduation party was not your fault, right?"

"Whose fault would it be? I was the one who chose to bring everyone together—"

"But that's what you do, Peter. And you're good at it. You bring people together. You help us to see potential in others and try to help people get along. But they were so busy thinking about what they wanted, they didn't even bother to ask what *you* wanted! That's what caused the fight. Not your choice. Besides, lots of other people believe in the youth center idea. You've got some of your family on board already, right? Vivien and Ree?"

"And Nick. He'll always back me up. I just hate the thought of disappointing everyone else. Causing more fighting."

"Peter, if they weren't so full of themselves, they could see that all you ever wanted is what is best for Deep Haven. If they can't see that, they're idiots."

"Maybe. But they're still my family."

And she, better than anyone, understood the pull of family. "True. But there are others who care about you too."

He touched her face, running his thumb down her cheek. "Others? Others...like you?"

He was so unaware of how rare a man he was. Strong, but the kind of man who used that strength to serve others. The kind of man who sacrificed his wants for somebody else. The kind of man who reached out to her brother and who made her feel like part of something good.

He made her feel like she belonged.

"Yes, like me. I said 'we,' remember?"

He slid his hand around her neck. "Would you like to meet my family? I mean, after that history, I wouldn't blame you if you said no, but..."

"I have met your family—Uncle Charlie, Elton Zimmerman, Ben—"

"No. Those are the troublemakers. I'm talking my Grandma Zee and my father. My mother."

Oh. He wanted her to meet his *family*. That was a big deal, right?

"We could start small. Go to the Fourth of July fish fry at my folks' house next week. Just my immediate family, but something low-key to get to know everyone."

She pushed past the unease in her belly. If he was willing to go out on a limb, so would she. "I'd love to meet them."

"We could watch the town fireworks afterward from the breakwater." He leaned in, his mouth near her ear. "Maybe set off some of our own."

She laughed and stepped back. He waggled his eyebrows.

"You dork. You've never had a girlfriend, have you? Especially if this is what you plan for a first date."

"For the record, this is not the date. I have a gourmet dinner and a projector set up in my backyard. Thought we could watch

West Side Story since neither of us has seen it." He pulled her to himself. "Now shut up and kiss me."

"Whoever said you don't know what you want never saw you like this."

"Oh, honey. I know exactly what I want." And then he kissed her.

Best. Date. Ever.

CHAPTER 13

*P*eter wasn't sure which he was more nervous about as he took the kitchen trash out for his mom— Ronnie meeting his family or telling them that he had cast his vote for the youth center tonight. He needed to get it over with before they heard from someone else.

Hopefully having Ronnie by his side would make it a little easier.

Then again, it might not put her in the best light for his parents. He dropped the lid down on the garbage can.

He should've thought this out better.

Because, really, what was he thinking dragging Ronnie into family drama this early in their relationship?

But when he'd held her in his arms and she'd said things that had made him believe he was doing the right thing, that he could weather the disapproval of the two clans he cared about, for some crazy reason, he'd wanted her to be a part of it.

He wanted her involved in his life, even the hard parts.

And, yeah, he hoped that she and Tiago would feel welcome here, like they belonged. Because the thought of them leaving gutted him.

So probably better to just focus on Ronnie and Tiago coming to meet the fam, making sure these two parts of his world meshed. He could tell his parents about the vote tomorrow. And hopefully by the end of the night, they would be as crazy about Ronnie and Tiago as he was.

Armed with a plan, Peter walked back to the kitchen and was met with the yeasty scent of freshly baked bread. The white quartz countertops were spotless as always even in the middle of his mother's efforts to finish her last batch of dinner rolls.

"Thanks, dear. I don't know why it's so hard for your brothers to keep up with the garbage. It's not like I ask a lot of them." Mom shook her head and rolled the last bit of her dough into a ball. "So back to you... this is the woman who saved Gust, right?"

"Yeah, Mom. Ronnie."

"She's the paramedic. The one your uncle Charlie was worried about? Didn't she get kicked out of the Java Cup?"

"News travels fast," he said under his breath as he brought his glass to the fridge ice dispenser.

"Don't mumble, dear. And besides, can I help it if Brenda Baker happened to be sitting there with her book club and saw the whole thing? She called Deb who told your aunt Connie who was worried about you and wanted me to know."

"Then you should know it was all a big misunderstanding."

The quirk of her eyebrow as she brushed the rolls with butter said she wasn't convinced.

Peter paused with the ice maker. "Mom, give her a chance."

"Oh, Peter, you know I will. If she's important to you, I'll give her every benefit of the doubt. At least I can't fault her taste in men." She patted his cheek and moved past him to put her homemade rolls in the oven. "I just hope she's good enough to deserve you."

Yup. He should've just met Ronnie in town for fireworks and skipped this whole fish-fry-meet-my-family business. He started up the ice dispenser again. Cubes clattered onto the tile floor just as the doorbell rang.

Too late now.

It figured she'd be early. He left his glass in the kitchen and rushed to open the front door. Ronnie stood there, Tiago by her side holding Blue. The sight of her swept away his mother's words. Her chin was lifted high and her smile looked confident and sure. She even wore a *dress*—a dress that showed off her slim shoulders and tan arms and made it hard to keep his head on straight.

She could totally win over his parents. What was he worried about?

"Hey, come in. Glad you guys could make it."

"Like I had a choice." Tiago stepped into the entry.

"Shush!" Ronnie elbowed him then hissed in his ear, "This is a big deal. Remember."

Okay, so maybe she wasn't as confident as he'd thought.

Ronnie held a covered pan. "I made brownies."

"Brownies? No Cheetos?" Peter bent over to kiss her cheek.

"Yeah, I watched her bake. You're gonna wish she brought Cheetos," Tiago said.

Peter steered them to the kitchen where Mom pulled a pitcher of iced tea out of the fridge and set it on the counter. Carrying an empty tray, Dad walked in from the porch wearing his Hands Off My Buns apron.

Mom really needed to stop buying him aprons.

Here went nothing. "Mom, Dad, I want you to meet Ronnie Morales and her brother, Tiago. These are my parents, Gary and Barb." The puppy barked. "Oh, and this little thing is Blue."

Ronnie handed his mother the pan. "Nice to meet you."

"What do we have here?" She took the foil off the pan to reveal the—

Those black lumpy things were brownies? And apparently his mother had a worse poker face than he did. "Oh. Uh, you shouldn't have. I'll just cover these back up until dessert." She placed the offending pan in the back corner of the counter and wiped her hands.

Perfect. *Thanks, Mom.*

Before he could smooth things over, Johnny and Michael barged into the room wrestling each other for the Nerf football tucked in Jonathan's arms. Both boys were tall and slim like their father, but Johnny had inherited the Dalquist blond hair while Michael looked more like their mother's side of the family with dark brown.

"These guys are my brothers. Michael is studying computer programming in the Cities, and Johnny will be a senior this year at the high school."

"Hey, is this one of Nick's puppies?" Johnny released the ball, letting Michael snatch it, and reached for Blue.

"Mind your own business." Tiago backed away and sheltered the puppy in his arms.

"T! Manners." A blush spread across Ronnie's cheeks. "Sorry. He's really protective of her."

Johnny backed away, hands up in surrender. "I'm not gonna hurt her. I love dogs."

"Why don't I show you where she can play outside, Tiago? She can meet our dog, Shep." Dad tried to lay a hand on Tiago's shoulder, but the boy cringed and pulled away.

"She stays with me."

"Tiago!"

Peter felt Ronnie's embarrassment from across the room. And Dad was only trying to protect Mom's beige carpeting and oriental rugs. Tiago glared at everyone.

Yeah, this was off to a great start.

His mother knelt near Tiago but gave him space.

"She's a lucky dog to have you looking out for her. Why don't we all go outside? It's so nice out and Blue can play in the yard."

Tiago took a breath, then nodded. Finally, progress.

Mom led them out the French dining room doors to the backyard where the long table was set with red, white, and blue paper plates and decorations. Edison lights were strung across the patio. Blue barked, wriggling in Tiago's arms.

"T, why don't you set her down? Let her run," Peter suggested.

"There's no fence and I forgot her leash. What if she runs away?"

"She'll be okay. Besides, she might need to do her business, and you don't want that on you."

Tiago set her down. Blue started exploring, trotting off the cement pad to the grass. The boy stuck close by her, and Peter stayed with them as they wandered out to the middle of the yard. Ronnie was capable. She could handle herself with his parents for a while. Tiago, on the other hand, was like a cornered animal. He just needed to feel safe enough to relax.

"So, T, what part did you get in the play again?"

He didn't look at Peter, his gaze on Blue. "I'm just one of the Sharks."

"Yeah, but aren't you the second in command? That's a big deal."

"I guess so."

"You're still going fishing with me on Saturday, right?"

Tiago hesitated, then looked up at him. "You're really gonna take me? I've never gone fishing before."

Peter met his eyes. So much like Ronnie's, including the wariness. "Of course I'm going to take you."

T glanced at Blue. "I suppose you're bringing Ronnie too."

"Nope. Just you and me. I'll teach you how to catch a boatload of sunnies and crappies, fillet them, and then we'll eat them. And if you prove yourself worthy, I might let you in on my secret ingredient for the best homemade tartar sauce you've ever had. I learned from my mom."

Tiago shoved his hands in his pockets. "That might be cool."

Abby came into the backyard with Shep. "Hey, everyone!"

Shep, their yellow lab mix, bounded over for introductions. Blue gave a happy bark as the two dogs sniffed each other. Tiago reached down for her, but Peter stopped him.

"This is how dogs meet each other. She's okay."

"But he's so much bigger. He'll hurt her."

"We've had Shep for a long time. He's a good dog. Just let them play. She'll actually learn from him."

Peter counted it as a victory when Tiago held back and watched, worry on his face as the animals rolled on the grass, wrestled playfully, and barked.

Abby laughed at the dogs, then came over to Peter. "So who do we have here?"

"Tiago, meet my sister, Abby. She works with a youth group down in the Cities." Abby, in typical Dahlquist casual style, had left her long blonde hair in a braid and dressed in athletic shorts and a running shirt.

"That is the cutest puppy I've ever seen. You must be taking great care of her."

Like his mother, his sister was received better than his brothers, maybe because she was used to working with kids. Or maybe Tiago was leery of men in general. Either way, Peter breathed easier watching Tiago eventually relax while Abby showed him all of Shep's tricks.

Now to make sure Ronnie was enjoying herself too. He walked back over to the patio where Ronnie regaled his brothers and parents with stories from her military career by the sounds of it. Her *medical* military career.

Johnny and Michael listened rapturously while a look of horror froze on Mom's face. "That's quite...graphic."

Apparently, Ronnie didn't notice the green tinge to his mom's skin and was about to launch into another tale of gore and dark missions.

Peter jumped in. "Mom, do you need help with anything? Should I bring out drinks for us?"

But his brothers didn't get the hint.

"Wow. I didn't know you could do all that as a medic in the Army. Maybe I should look at the military after I graduate next year," Johnny said.

A shade of red blotched Dad's face. Before he could get a word out though, Ronnie continued enthusiastically.

"The military is a great option. I went in right after graduation. There was a lot more I could do as a medic than I can as a paramedic here. The benefits are great. I would've stayed in longer if I could've and retired at thirty-eight with full pay. Still plenty of time for a second career."

"That sounds awesome," Johnny said.

"Johnny, you're practically a shoo-in for the U of M. You don't want to lose that football scholarship," his father said.

"Yeah, but if I joined up, I could still take over the restaurant when I'm older and—"

"We'll talk about this later." There was no mistaking Dad's tone.

That shut the boys up.

Ronnie didn't know, but she could not have picked a more volatile topic. Mom set a veggie tray and platter down on the table in front of them. "Why don't we enjoy some appetizers? This brie and artichoke dip is Gary's special recipe, Ronnie." Her strategy to keep the peace hadn't changed much in Peter's lifetime—shut people up by feeding them.

Ronnie picked up a triangle of flatbread and dunked it in Dad's famous dip. "So what do you think about Peter's idea for the youth center?"

Oh. No.

She was like a rabbit in a minefield for her ability to find the one topic more volatile than Johnny's college choice and football career. His mother went pale, mouth gaping open.

Dad looked at Peter. "Son? Is there something you want to tell us?"

Ronnie's hand covered her mouth, her amber eyes wide. Yup. She may have been late to the game, but she got it now. And it was his fault.

He should have told them before she arrived. But, no. Selfishly he'd put it off to have one more evening without conflict.

But like it or not, his worlds were colliding.

Peter swallowed hard. "I decided about the Westerman Hotel. I'm voting for the youth center. I think it's the best option for Deep Haven."

"I thought we had an understanding." The hardness and disappointment in his father's voice cut straight to Peter's heart.

This. *This* was why he hated conflict—because he was always the bad guy. "Dad, I have to vote for what's best for everyone. Not just our family."

"Peter, do you know how many people we could help with that restaurant? How many people went out of work when Pierre's burned down? Not to mention the housing those rental units can provide. I thought it was pretty obvious. It *is* the best choice for Deep Haven."

Ronnie tensed but stayed quiet. Johnny and Mike sneaked away to the other side of the yard with Abby and Tiago. Peter wanted to flee with them. Instead. he met his dad's eyes.

"Dad, I know Pierre's could help. But think about kids like Johnny. Or Tiago. A youth center, a safe place where kids can hang out and have fun, meet positive role models, learn some skills—that can be a huge influence on their lives. It can provide jobs too."

"You did just fine without a youth center. Abby, Michael, and Johnny have been fine without it. You know what helped you? Working. A *job*. And where is the revenue going to come from to staff this center? Not that I agree with much of anything

Charlie Zimmerman has to say, but on this I might. Who is going to pay for a youth center?"

Mom cut in before Peter could answer. "Let's leave this business talk for another time. We should get that fish going, Gary."

Ronnie stood. "I'm sorry, but I disagree. You're right, Mr. Dahlquist, that Peter did great without the help of a youth center. But Peter also has you two, as invested and healthy parents. Not everyone does. I didn't have that. My brother doesn't have that. Do you know what that center could do for kids like him? You should be proud of your son. Nobody has a bigger heart for people, for this town, than Peter. And nobody could love his family more. If you don't see that, you're a blind fool."

Mom gasped. Dad stood, lips in a tight line.

Oh no. Apparently, the fireworks had started early.

But he wasn't about to let Ronnie hang out to dry. He took her hand. "Mom, Dad, you know I love you guys, but I made my decision. There's nothing else we need to discuss."

He said the words out loud, but he knew this wasn't going to be the end of it.

Ronnie squeezed his hand.

And he knew...if he had to choose between them, he chose her.

With Tiago at play practice, Ronnie could finally catch up on laundry and cleaning the apartment. She switched the clean wet clothes into the dryer and folded the warm load while her mind relived the romance under the fireworks she'd shared with Peter last night.

Every kiss, every touch, every look into those gorgeous hazel-green and gold eyes had knit him into her heart a little more.

Made the thought of leaving a little more devastating.

And Tiago was asking every day to do just that.

She sorted out the darks for the next load and sighed. Any day now Peter would realize what being with her would cost him and decide she wasn't worth it.

She wasn't stupid. Meeting his family was a disaster. His mom hated her. His father blamed her. His brothers and sister were cool, but they wouldn't take a stand with Peter.

It was obvious from the first day that Peter valued relationships above all, and here she was standing between him and the people he cared most about. The only thing she brought to the mix was her own family drama.

Tiago relied solely on her. If this move had taught her anything, it was how deep Tiago's wounds ran, thanks to being at the mercy of their mother. Ronnie had to do whatever it took to help him—and that meant keeping her promises.

No matter what the cost.

And boy, the cost was growing exponentially with every kiss she shared with Peter and every day they spent in this quaint little bay town she wanted to call home.

She folded the last of the whites. Of course, Tiago was missing one sock.

She dropped the laundry basket, ran up to Tiago's closet, and dug through the shoes at the bottom. There. She picked up the sock balled into his tennis shoe and started to close the door. Blue barked and plunged into the closet for a shoe to chew on.

"Oh no you don't, pup." Ronnie pulled Tiago's flip-flop out of the dog's mouth and threw it into the closet.

What was that?

A small brown paper bag was stuffed into the corner of the shelf. She opened it. Fireworks and a lighter tumbled into her hand.

Her heart sank. Why couldn't he just stay out of trouble?

The front door opened and slammed shut.

Stay calm. Listen. Ronnie jammed the fireworks and lighter back into the paper sack. Then she met her brother in the living area holding out the bag. Blue followed, barking. "What's this, Tiago?"

Momentary shock lit his face, quickly replaced by indignant anger. "What were you doing in my room?"

"Answer my question."

"You have no right to go through my stuff!"

"I have *every* right, but that isn't the issue. Do you know what happens if you get caught with this? If you get in trouble with the law again? They'll take you away from me!" Her voice was anything but calm as the thought of them yanking Tiago back into foster care took root.

His jaw hardened. "I told you I didn't set that fire!"

"Then what is this?"

Tiago picked up the puppy and dropped his gaze. His breath washboarded out, as if he might be trying not to cry.

Her voice softened just a little as she got a hold of the panic that set in. "Tiago, where did you get these?"

"If I tell you, will you drop it? I don't want...I don't want someone to get in trouble." He looked up at her, held her gaze. "But it's not mine. I swear."

She didn't know why, but she believed him. Or maybe she just *wanted* to, so very much.

"I can't promise anything. But if this isn't yours, then you need to tell me whose it is and why you have it."

Please tell me it's all some mistake.

He held Blue closer. His gaze shifted to the window, the view of Cole and Megan's place.

Josh. What—?

"Are these Josh's?"

Tiago froze and then slowly nodded.

"Come with me. We need to settle this right now." She walked over to the door.

"Ronnie, please. Can't you just get rid of it and pretend like it didn't happen? I don't want Josh to get into trouble."

"If Josh is causing trouble, Megan needs to know. And you won't be hanging out with him anymore."

Because she would not lose her brother again.

She marched next door but heard voices in the backyard so went around the house.

Cole and Josh were tossing a baseball. Megan waved from where she read a magazine in her Adirondack chair. "Hey, guys. What's going on?"

Ronnie stopped in front of her. Took a breath. Megan was her friend, and probably she'd be just as upset as Ronnie was. "I found this in Tiago's closet. It's Josh's." She held out the bag.

Megan stared at her with a frown, then opened the bag. Silence as she pulled out the fireworks and lighter.

Cole and Josh had stopped their game. She looked up at them. "Josh, is this yours?"

Josh came over, shook his head. "No. That's not mine."

Megan stood up and handed the bag back to Ronnie. "You heard him. Sorry. It's not his."

And Ronnie had nothing. Megan simply *believed* him? "How can you be sure?"

Megan put her arm around Josh. "If my son says it's not his, it isn't."

Ronnie shook her head, trying to keep her voice even. "Are you saying this was Tiago's?"

Cole put a hand on Josh's other shoulder. "Ronnie, you need to calm down. Megan's right. Josh isn't the kind of kid to lie or hide things from us."

"And yet both these boys were at that pit party. You can't tell me he never gets into trouble." And yes, she'd raised her voice, her heart banging.

"Ronnie, I think you need to calm down here—"

"I'm not going to calm down! Your son got in trouble just like Tiago and we need to get to the bottom of this."

"Trouble that didn't start until Josh *met* Tiago," Megan said quietly but with a hard edge to her voice, the same one she'd used that night at the pit fire. "If anyone is influencing for the worse here, I think we know who it is."

Right. Ronnie's mouth tightened. So that's how it was going to be. "I don't think the boys should hang out anymore."

"Maybe that's for the best," Megan said, meeting her gaze.

In a split second, memories of laughter and conversations she'd shared with Megan slammed at Ronnie's heart. All those times of gushing over Peter, the camaraderie they'd shared with raising boys...over.

Ronnie spun and stormed back to the apartment. Tiago rushed into his room with Blue and slammed the door.

In the silence, Ronnie slumped onto the couch and dropped her head into her hands. This wasn't how it was supposed to go. She'd thought Josh was a good kid, a good person to befriend Tiago. Of course, Cole took Megan's side. And if she lost Megan's friendship, she probably would lose Ella's and the rest of the town's too.

She should start packing now.

Everything inside her hurt.

Someone knocked on the door. She almost didn't answer it, but a part of her hoped it might be Megan on her doorstep to apologize.

Nope. Peter stood there, wearing jeans and a flannel shirt, a frown on his face. How did he always seem to know when she needed him?

And shoot, she did need him.

"Hey, what's going on?"

"Oh, Peter—"

He pulled her against him. And yes, she should be stronger. Push him away and deal with this on her own like she always did. She'd most likely be leaving him soon anyway.

But heaven help her, she sank into his arms like a drowning person clinging to a buoy in the storm. She breathed him in. His woodsy scent and warmth wrapped around her.

It felt so good just to be held.

"What's wrong, Veronica?"

Oh how she loved the way her name sounded when he said it. She'd moved to the more masculine Ronnie in middle school. Something to make her sound more intimidating, more like someone who couldn't be pushed around. But the way Peter said "Veronica" made her feel...soft.

Even treasured. Like she mattered to him.

"It's just..." Then she leaned back and told him the entire story. He came inside and listened, no comment, his expression set on worry, even compassion.

Finally, "How is Tiago?"

"He's upset. The boys hung out a lot. Josh is probably his closest friend. But if he's having Tiago hide stuff that could get him in trouble, I can't have that."

Peter took the bag from the coffee table, pulled out the lighter and studied it. "Ronnie, something's going on here. I know who this lighter belongs to, and it's not Josh. We need to talk to your brother."

Peter knocked on Tiago's door and went in. Tiago was curled up in a small ball on top of his bed, petting Blue, his face chapped with tears.

Ronnie waited in the doorway while Peter approached him. "Hey, T. Can I talk to you?"

"What do you want? You gonna blame me too?"

"No, especially since I know this isn't yours."

Tiago sat up slowly. "You believe me?"

"Yeah, I do. But I don't understand why you blamed your best friend."

Tiago looked down. "I...didn't actually say it was Josh's."

Ronnie stepped inside. "Yes, you did."

"No. *You* assumed it was Josh's. And I...went along with it."

"Why?"

He shrugged. "Because...it was better than telling you the truth."

"So who does this stuff belong to and why do you have it?"

Tiago looked away.

"We care about the truth, Tiago, and we care about you." Peter's voice stayed steady. "We believe you when you say this isn't yours. Help us understand why you have it, though."

"Because I didn't want to get beat up, all right?" He looked at Peter. "I tried. I tried to make friends. And Josh is cool, but these other guys, much bigger guys, don't want me here. And one of them said if I didn't hide that stash for him and keep quiet, he would—"

"He would what?"

Tiago shrugged again, but she saw the fear. "He said he'd get rid of us"—he pointed to Ronnie and himself—"once and for all."

No way! A soft hand on Ronnie's back stilled her mouth, Peter's silent warning to tamp down the reaction and stay calm.

But oh, she wanted to punch something. Hard. And the way Peter's nostrils flared, he was furious too.

"Oh no. If this punk is threatening your life, then we need to know who it is," Peter said quietly.

"No! That will make it worse. Do you know what these guys will do to me?"

No wonder he'd been acting so strange lately. *Oh, Tiago.*

She sat on the bed and reached for Tiago's hand. "You shouldn't have to shoulder all that. We can help. Why didn't you tell me what was going on?"

He sat up and let go of Blue, who scampered onto the floor and over to Peter.

"I know you like it here, sis. You want us to stay. But these kids...they don't. And—"

"Who threatened you?"

Tiago didn't say anything.

Peter sat next to Ronnie, holding the puppy. "I think I know, but I'd like to hear it from you."

Tiago clenched his jaw. She knew that look well. She'd *lived* it. That I-can-handle-it-on-my-own determination. But often it was fueled by anger, or fear that it might not be true. That she might just do everything she could and would still be betrayed. Or the fear that she couldn't handle it and there was no one else to lean on.

Maybe she could show Tiago a different way.

"Bro, let us help. You don't have to do this by yourself."

Tiago said nothing for a long moment. "It was Ben and his friends."

"Just to clarify, we're talking about Ben Zimmerman, right?" Peter asked.

Tiago nodded.

Ronnie looked at Peter. "Is that who you thought the lighter belonged to?"

"Yeah. It's Elton's. He's had it my whole life."

"So how long has this been going on, T?" she asked.

"Since the pit party. He'd make me do stuff at play practice. Made fun of me at church. He gave me that bag and said when he needed it, he'd get it from me."

"Let me guess, he broke the sprinkler in the auditorium too?"

He nodded.

"And you were more afraid of him than losing your friendship with Josh."

Oh. Josh. *Megan.*

Ronnie groaned. "All right, Tiago, Peter and I will take care of Ben. But there will still be consequences for you. You need to come to me with this kind of stuff. And you may not have said

Josh's name, but you let me believe he was to blame. For now, you're grounded. You do play practice and come home. That's it." She softened her voice. Because more than anything, this next truth had to sink in. "But most of all, you need to know I'm on your side. Whatever you face, we face together."

He turned to her. "I'm sorry. I was just trying to be tough like you. Handle it on my own. But I'm not strong enough."

Ronnie knelt in front of her brother, framed his sweet face with her hands. "You are *so* strong, Santiago Morales. Stronger than you know. Stronger than you should have to be. But if there's one thing I'm learning here, it's that sometimes strength means asking for help when we need it. That takes real courage. To trust people. To let them in." She kissed his forehead. "I'm here for you. You can let me in."

He looked at her, his brown eyes so hungry. "You mean it?"

"Yeah. I do." And for the first time since coming home from the Army, she saw a lightness in him she hadn't seen since... well, she didn't remember the last time.

Maybe she hadn't seen it in herself either.

She smiled at him. "We'll figure this out. But for now, why don't you take Blue on a little walk around the block, and we'll go talk to Josh and Megan later."

Tiago nodded and grabbed Blue. A few moments later, she heard the front door close.

Peter plopped next to Ronnie on the bed. "So...what was that groan about earlier?"

"Megan."

"Right."

"Yeah. She probably hates me now."

"Doubt that. She might be angry, but it doesn't have to be the end of the friendship. Go apologize."

Before Deep Haven, she'd never cared. If someone was angry with her, she walked away and didn't look back.

She didn't want to be that kind of person anymore. Maybe

apologizing didn't have to be the sign of weakness she'd always attributed it to. It sure seemed like this took a lot more guts than walking away.

And she didn't really want to lose Megan.

Peter nudged her shoulder. "Do you want me to come with you?" He held out his hand.

She should go by herself, but her own words to Tiago echoed back.

Sometimes strength means asking for help when we need it.

And she needed it. More, she needed *him*.

She looked at him, so much kindness in his eyes, the way he held out his hand, and she took it. "Yes, Peter. I want you to come with me."

CHAPTER 14

"They have some kind of catastrophe happening in the kitchen," Peter said as he put down the burger. "This is terrible." The dark lighting of the VFW, mostly provided from the neon signs on the walls and dimmed fixtures hanging from the ceiling, couldn't mask the burnt flavor and bitter aftertaste of the meat. Peter leaned back in the blue plastic chair and chugged his fountain pop.

"I think the cook quit," Nick said, stirring a tot around in ketchup. "So she really yelled at your father?"

Peter still couldn't believe the disaster of Ronnie meeting his parents. "Yes." He pushed his plate away, his appetite gone.

"That's one way to introduce her to the family." Nick shook his head. "I wish I could've been there to see Uncle Gary's face when she brought up the military career to your brothers. He's been counting on Johnny to get a football scholarship and take the U of M Gophers to the Rose Bowl since forever."

"You mean since I failed to do so when I chose UMD over the U of M."

"It wasn't just you. Michael quit as a freshman."

"Yeah, apparently he has more guts than I do because he told

Dad that football took away from his time with girls and video games."

"Yeah, that's gutsy. And ever since, your dad's been pinning all those hopes and dreams on Johnny-boy. His last chance."

Peter sighed and threw down his napkin. "And Ronnie plowed right into 'em."

"Your dad must've been livid." Nick laughed.

"It's not funny. You know how he is. He's not like Uncle Gordy losing his temper and spouting stuff off. He held it together in front of everyone, but I saw the look on his face. And he talked to me the next day. He was not impressed. He's afraid she's *brainwashing* me."

Nick was still smiling, but he shook his head. "Brainwashing? Like the KGB or something?"

"I don't know." He motioned to Melissa Ogden, another third cousin on the Zimmerman side, over for a refill of Coke.

"What about your mom? She liked Ronnie, right? She likes everyone."

"She was insulted by her brownies, grossed out by her stories of medical procedures, and when Ronnie called my dad a blind fool, I think her fate was sealed as far as Barb Dahlquist was concerned."

"She really called your dad a blind fool?"

"Well, it was something more along the lines of sticking up for me, saying if they couldn't see how much I cared about this town and our family, yada, yada, yada, then he was a blind fool."

"Ahhh." Nick nodded like everything made perfect sense.

"What?"

"Peter, you are so far gone over this girl."

Melissa came over. "Hey, Peter. Whatchya need?"

"I could use another." He lifted his glass and she took it back to the bar to be refilled.

"So what are you going to do?" Nick asked.

"About what?"

"Well, about your vote and your family. You and Ronnie gonna leave Deep Haven and ride off into the sunset together or stay and join me as the black sheep of the family?"

"Oh, Nick. That honor is all yours." But probably Peter would be close to it. "No, my life is here. I'd need to finish out my term on the city council at the very least before I can move. That's over three years away. And I want to see this youth center through. How hypocritical would it be if I fought for it and then left town?"

"So you're going to have to convince your family or live forever with their disapproval."

"That's the gist of it, but I think they'll come around. Eventually. Don't you?"

"To Ronnie or the youth center idea?"

"Both."

"The Dahlquists know three things—football, cooking, and how to hold a grudge."

Peter sighed. "That's what I was afraid of."

Melissa returned. Set his drink in front of him. Glanced at Nick. "I saw your latest vlog. I like your puppies."

Nick seemed to turn a little red. "Thanks, Mel."

Peter chuckled. "You're so famous."

"Leave me alone."

Peter picked up the drink.

"Listen, Pete. You know I'll support you any way I can. I'm used to their disappointment. And who knows? Maybe Ronnie will win them over in the end."

"I hope so." It was hard to remember, but yes, they'd had their own rocky beginning, and she'd won *him* over. "In the meantime, I just hope their disapproval doesn't push her away."

"I know family is everything for you, but don't let go of this woman, Peter. She's your champion. Most guys would kill for a woman to believe in them like that."

"But what if she doesn't stay? What then?"

"Stop thinking about the what-ifs. That's your problem. You get all tangled up in things that may—or may not—happen. Enjoy the ride, dude. And have a little faith that it'll all work out."

Faith. Huh.

Nick stood. "I've gotta run. You're meeting Seb here?"

"Yup. He wants to know more about the youth center before he leaves for his vacation. The town meeting will be right after he gets back."

"Why isn't Vivie meeting him?"

"This is the only time Seb had free and she has practice." And since Nick had brought her up, maybe his cousin needed a bit of prodding too. "And speaking of Vivie, gonna take your own advice, stop worrying about the what-ifs, and go for it? She's been back for over a month now."

Nick said nothing as he waved, maybe a little bit of heartbreak in his eyes. Probably he'd heard the question and simply chose to ignore it. Like always. One of these days though, maybe Nick would fess up or do something about the girl he'd pined for since second grade.

Peter organized the folder with all the youth center plans and ordered a slice of pie and coffee just as Seb came in.

"Thanks for meeting with me before I go, Pete. Lucy's already packed the car, so you've got an hour to convince me." He settled into the booth and gave his order to Melissa. "Tell me about this youth center Vivien Calhoun came up with."

Peter went over the rough plans for transforming the abandoned hotel into the Deep Haven Youth Center. Seb listened attentively, asked good questions. By the time Peter was on his third mug of coffee, they had gone through the whole proposal.

"Sounds like this project is important to you."

"It is. We've seen an increase in kids who need this kind of escape. The town can use the space, indoor playground, theater, two big gyms. It would help ease some of the overcrowding with community sports and the school."

"I see the social benefit, believe me. Wish it had been around when I was a kid. But I also have to see the money side of things too. The hotel and restaurant proposals would be bringing in revenue and have more people spending money in Deep Haven. Plus, the owners would foot the cost for the demolition and rebuilding. Who is going to pay for the youth center?"

"Thankfully the bones of the hotel structure are still good. It needs to be gutted and revamped, but we wouldn't have to start from scratch. We can do the remodeling in phases. But no, we haven't figured out all the funding. Obviously, we would be asking the town and people for help. Seth Turnquist's family and the Christiansens have already agreed to help with labor and donating some of the materials. If we have more people like them on board, we can cut a lot of costs."

"And the revenue?"

"Think of how many times people have wanted to rent facilities like these. We could host sports tournaments with the gyms, use a big meeting space and auditorium for special events. All those would bring people to Deep Haven as well as provide our youth with positive activities. And maybe we can turn the rooms on the second and third floors into offices and rent out the space. The possibilities are there."

"And you think there's enough town support for this?"

"I think the need is here."

"That's not necessarily the same thi—"

"There you are!" Elton thundered into the building and stormed toward them. "You're a liar, Peter, and you've betrayed your own family."

Peter leaned back and put up a hand to push Elton's meaty finger out of his face. "What are you talking about?"

"You said the Westerman belonged to us! It was going to be our next hotel!"

Ready or not, the fight was on. Peter took a deep breath. Leveled his gaze at his cousin. "I never said I was voting for the hotel."

"Yes, you did. At the campfire at the Memorial Day hot dog roast. You said we could count on you."

Peter blew out a breath. "No, Uncle Al said that."

Elton leaned over the table. "You calling me a liar?"

"I'm saying you made assumptions. I didn't say which way I was voting."

"It's tourism that drives our economy. We need more hotels. Who needs a *youth center?*"

Peter bit his tongue but hello, how about *Ben?* He and Ronnie hadn't had a chance to talk to Elton about what his son was doing, and clearly Elton was in no frame of mind to have that discussion now. Not that Peter wanted to do so in public anyway. "There are lots of kids in the community who could utilize a place like this."

"You mean like that little Hispanic kid? He's been causing trouble since he arrived. And this"—Elton made a circle over the youth center proposal papers—"is all her fault. Isn't it?"

"What are you talking about?"

"It's that woman. That *paramedic.* She came in, kicked my father off the first responders team, accused my son of being a drug addict, and it's only a matter of time before she destroys this whole town."

Peter kept his fist restrained at his side and bit hard, grinding his molars, trying to get a leash on everything pounding through him. "I think it's time you left. We can discuss this later."

"You're choosing her over your own family!"

And that was just...*enough.* Peter stood up, met his cousin's gaze straight on. "I'm choosing what's best for our whole town. *Including* our family."

Elton's eyes narrowed. "She's going to be your ruin, Pete."

"You don't know anything about her."

"Yeah? Well I'll tell you now, this youth center is not going to pass the vote."

Peter crossed his arms over his chest. "We'll see about that."

Elton shook his head as he stomped out. Peter's pulse roared as he watched him go.

Seb cleared his throat. "Uh, as I was saying, as much as I love the idea of this youth center, need and support are two different things. If we have a lot of people like Elton, who don't support it, we can't pass it. I'll need to see a lot more people who want it before we can move forward."

"We'll get you your support. I promise."

Seb nodded, then stood and held out his hand. Peter met it across the table.

"You've got two weeks before the vote. Let's see what you can come up with."

Last week was quiet. Not one call went off. But apparently it was the lull before the storm because so far this week Ronnie's alarm had gone off multiple times a day—and this one might be the worst call yet just to get to the patient. Especially with the rain soaking everyone and everything.

Ronnie leaned over the edge of the Superior Hiking Trail and looked down into the forest ravine where a hiker had fallen. The thick trunks of pine, maple, and spruce trees blocked the view of the creek or river that was down there according to the map. A streak of mud in the carpet of pine needles and leaves showed where the forty-six-year-old man had slid down.

Someone tugged on her jacket sleeve. A little girl with soggy brown braids and teary blue eyes looked up at her. "Are you going to save my daddy?"

Ronnie knelt down by her. "Yup. We're going to go down

and get him. But I need you to be really brave. Can you wait here with my friend Peter?"

The little girl nodded. "You promise you'll save him?"

"I promise we're going to do everything we can for your daddy."

Now it was time to see if this team had learned anything from all the training they'd been doing over the last six weeks—and she'd have to rely heavily on the rookies with Seb and Pastor Dan gone.

Cole helped Peter finish setting up a belay system and turned to her. "Ronnie, who's going down with you?"

Ronnie brought the little girl to Peter and scanned the members who had shown up. Dean Wilson stood tall, the desire unmistakable in his posture. The man had come a long way since the Hagborg fire. He'd even lost some weight and started exercising. She met him on her runs in the morning as he biked. He was now the first to raise his hand in the classes and always had a good answer.

He'd earned the chance to prove himself. Charlie Zimmerman could take some lessons from him.

"Dean, strap in and you'll go down with me. Jensen and Seth, we're probably going to need the basket stretcher. Have it ready and I'll let you know what else we'll need when I'm down there. We'll have you come down when it's time to load the patient and bring him up."

Everyone got to work. Other first responders were already working with the hiker's teenage son who had gone down into the ravine after his father and scraped his hands and knees pretty good and twisted an ankle. Peter held the little girl. Ronnie strapped the jump bag onto her back and hooked onto the belay. She and Dean carefully climbed down the slick ravine, using the rope for balance. The incline was rather steep, but not a straight drop. As they approached the bottom, they heard moaning over the rushing of the nearby river.

They skirted around brush and knelt by the man on the ground. His dark brown hair was plastered down his face, a contusion already forming on his forehead.

"What's your name?" Ronnie asked, leaning in to listen to his breathing.

"Jason. Jason McCray."

"I'm Ronnie and this is Dean. We're with the Crisis Response Team. Can you tell us what happened, Jason?"

"I tripped. I don't even know how it happened. I just remember—" He grunted and tried to sit up. "I just remember falling."

Breathing was fine, a little fast, but understandable with the pain he was experiencing. "Lie back down. Tell me where it hurts."

Dean pulled on gloves and started taking his pulse and then blood pressure. "Pulse stable. BP is 108/70."

The numbers were normal. But when asked, he ranked his pain at a level nine out of ten.

The hiker grunted again, sweat and rain pouring down his forehead and his eyes pinched shut. "It's my leg. I hurt my leg. I can't move it."

"We're going to cut away your pants so I can see it. Dean, why don't you get some oxygen for Mr. McCray? Maybe a blanket too."

Dean got the oxygen ready while Ronnie cut the light fabric of the hiking pants. The large bump in the middle of Jason's thigh was not good. She felt the skin around the bulge as softly as she could. Jason screamed. The thigh was hard to the touch. She checked his hip and the rest of the leg and had him wiggle his toes, but didn't like that his toes were starting to feel cold.

"Jason, you broke your leg when you fell. Not just any bone either. Your femur. Looks like your hips and lower leg are fine, but we need to get you to a hospital. And I promised your daughter up there we would do everything we can for you."

He opened his eyes for a second. "Emily. Is she okay? And Bryce?"

"The rest of the team is watching over them. Just try to stay calm."

"Do what you need to."

"We're looking at a femur fracture, Dean. Keep him as comfortable as possible and take a pedal pulse. I'm going to radio up for help." She laid a gentle hand on Jason's arm. "We're going to get you out of here as soon as we can."

She moved away a few paces and radioed up to the rest of the team. "Jensen, Kirby, I'm going to need you to bring down a Sager traction splint with the basket stretcher. We have a femur fracture, possible compartment syndrome. Radio for the chopper."

Within minutes, Jensen, Kirby, and two more first responders—Sheila Chase and her husband—descended. They were all dripping wet, but the light drizzle couldn't dampen their determination. Everyone helped board the patient, but with Jason's symptoms time was critical. Even once he was loaded, they'd have a thirty-minute ride to the hospital. They needed to splint his leg here before moving him to the chopper. Dean and Ronnie set up the traction splint just like they had in practice.

"Now, Jason, I need you to take a deep breath. This is going to hurt, but we're going to get those bones lined back up. You should feel some relief when that happens."

Sheila held Jason's hand as he gritted his teeth. "Do it," he said.

Ronnie applied the necessary pressure to the splint. Jason's back stiffened. He bit down on his lips, grunted through clamped teeth, but then sagged in relief. She stopped. The bones were realigned. They finished securing the splint and strapped Jason to the basket stretcher.

Dean checked pedal pulse and circulation. "Ronnie, his pulse is racing. Signs of shock."

"Take his blood pressure again."

Cole radioed down that the helicopter was on its way and would land at a nearby campsite on the trail.

"BP has dropped. Pulse is 150."

Not good. "Let's get this man up to the trail, folks. He's got a daughter, son, and a chopper ride waiting for him." And probably emergency surgery as soon as they got him to Duluth. Shock indicated internal bleeding. He needed to get out of here fast.

Together, with help from the team above and the ropes, they carried Jason up the incline to the trail. That's when the poor guy passed out. Ronnie pushed what meds she could, but his blood pressure stayed dangerously low.

They loaded him onto an off-road vehicle and drove him to the new chopper just as the sun came out. After loading Jason into the chopper through the aft clam doors, Ronnie chose Kirby to assist the temporary flight medic Cole had hired. A crying Emily and limping Bryce crawled in after him.

The rest of the crew watched the helicopter lift up into the sky and fly away. There was a patch of blue sky that broke through the clouds. Chirping birds hopped around the campsite, but a somber mood permeated the group. They worked quietly as they cleaned up the scene, then drove back to the fire hall to restock.

Even though Ronnie was the one to write the report, the others lingered, claiming they were waiting for their jackets to dry out. There was nothing more they could do, but they waited around. Hoping. The Chases were about to leave when the call came in to Cole. He turned to the team. "That was Kirby. Jason arrived at the hospital and is in surgery. Looks like he'll be all right."

Seth whooped. Everyone cheered and clapped. Ronnie breathed a sigh of relief as Peter pulled her into his chest and squeezed. They'd done it.

Dean walked over and shook Ronnie's hand. "Thanks for giving me a chance out there. It's an honor to work with you."

Ronnie smiled through the tears that hovered on her lashes. "It's an honor to be here, Dean."

Even if she had to leave, she could go knowing she would leave behind a well-equipped rescue crew. They had certainly proven themselves today.

~

Peter moved the folding chairs from the sanctuary of Deep Haven Community Church to their original spot in the Sunday school rooms. Aunt Bea and Uncle Al were the last ones to leave, and they did so in a huff.

His two-week countdown was almost up. Seb came back tomorrow, just in time for the city council meeting, and Peter hadn't come close to convincing his family about the youth center.

Or anyone else for that matter. He'd been so busy meeting with first the Dahlquists and then the Zimmermans that he hadn't had time to talk to anyone else. He'd hoped meeting with the clans in smaller groups here at the church would make it easier to keep the peace. But no.

So much for thinking the location might inspire some open-minded discussion.

Now he was out of time.

Peter moved the last chair and returned to the sanctuary.

"How did your meetings go?" Pastor Dan asked as he walked down the aisle.

"You really have to ask? I thought you'd be able to hear the yelling all the way from your office." Peter tried to inject a little humor into his voice but failed. "But thanks for letting me use the church for all these meetings. It was helpful to have them all in one place."

"I take it they didn't go well then." It wasn't a question.

"Not really. I had hoped..." Peter shrugged. "But that's okay."

Dan's direct gaze showed a mix of empathy and invitation to go further. He sat in the last pew, ready to listen. And something about the quiet surroundings made it seem like it was okay to be honest.

Peter sank into the seat next to him and stared at the cross on the back wall of the altar. "I had hoped being here we could avoid the fighting. You know, have an actual discussion where people listen to each other and come to a peaceful resolution. But that's not what happened."

"If you thought coming to a church building would remove the element of conflict, you were bound to be disappointed, Peter."

"But church is supposed to be about peace and love. There shouldn't be conflict and fighting here."

"True, we want the church to be a place where people come together. But conflict is part of life, even in the church. To struggle, to wrestle is not always bad. Look at Jacob in the Bible. He wrestled with God and received a blessing for it."

"And he limped for the rest of his life too. I'd like to avoid that if I can."

"True." Pastor Dan smiled. "Gust taught you well."

"He was a good teacher." Peter remembered how he would bribe their class of squirrely third- through sixth-grade boys with Smarties to learn their memory verses. And when they had a hard time sitting still for too long, he would keep them busy with little fix-it projects around the church. "He always told us that to be a believer was to be a servant of Christ."

"And Gust owes you his life because you have a servant's heart. But, Peter, there's a warrior inside you too. And that's a good thing, because sometimes we have to take a stand. Some-times we have to fight."

"I thought we were supposed to live at peace with one another."

"Jesus Himself is called both the Lamb of God *and* the Lion of Judah. He was gentle enough to have children seek Him. Humble enough to wash the feet of his disciples. But He also rebuked the Pharisees and had some pretty strong words for those same disciples when needed."

"So how do I know when to wash feet and when to roar?"

"Roar when you find something worth fighting for." Dan stood and placed a fatherly hand on Peter's shoulder. "I think you'll know when the time is right." He left the sanctuary, and Peter sat in the silence for a minute more.

Pastor Dan made it sound simple.

But there was nothing simple about engaging in battle. People got hurt that way. Still, maybe...

Lord, if there's a time I need to take a stand, show me.

Peter's phone beeped.

Uh oh. He was late. He was supposed to be helping Ronnie with the last of the sets.

He sent her a quick text saying he was running a little late as he left the church parking lot. He had one more stop before seeing her.

Peter picked up his order and drove to the school. The auditorium was empty for the moment, but Ronnie's music could be heard from the backstage area. He slipped behind the curtain and watched her from the shadows.

She wore a light pink top and running shorts as she stood on a stepstool. Her slender fingers held a small paintbrush. Among the dark curtains and shadows, she was the bright spot as she painted reflections of light in the city backdrop.

But her ponytail didn't sway to the beat of the music. She didn't hum or even smile like she usually did when she painted.

She must still be disappointed to see that little bungalow on 2nd Avenue East sold. She'd had her eye on it as soon as they'd driven past it last week. Even though she knew she couldn't buy or make an offer on it, she'd talked about how nice the exterior would look painted a dark gray and the peaks of the gables a lighter shade of gray. She wanted a bright yellow door too, which sounded a bit out there. But what did he know about colors?

Not that it mattered. Nathan Dekker already had a buyer. She'd sent a picture of it with the sold sign in the yard and a sad face emoji during one of the Zimmerman meetings today. Peter loved that she wanted to stay, even to the point of daydreaming about how she would buy and remodel a house, but he hated that she was disappointed. Hopefully, he could cheer her up with his surprise.

He set it down and quietly sneaked behind her. He cleared his throat.

Ronnie screamed and spun around, falling off the stool right into his arms just as he'd hoped.

But his brilliant plan didn't account for the brush in her hands and the paint that now dripped down the front of his shirt.

The look of shock on her face switched to laughter. "That's what you get for scaring me."

He set her down on her feet and grabbed a wide brush resting in a can of blue paint. "Oh really?" He wielded the brush like a sword, lunged, and painted a swath of aqua blue down her whole arm.

"Peter!" She dashed behind a backdrop and came out on the other side to face him double handed with the small brush of yellow and a roller of pink paint. She parried with a soldier's yell.

He advanced and deflected her stroke. "*Skol!*"

Ronnie lunged again, streaking pink paint across his chest. "Give it up, Dahlquist. You are going down."

"Never!" His wet brush lightly swiped her cheek before she batted it away.

"What's going on back here—" Vivien pushed aside the curtains and stuck her head through. "Oh. It's you two." She grinned. "Carry on with the flirtation, but don't ruin my stage. I need those backdrops done for dress rehearsals next week." She winked before disappearing again behind the curtain.

"Truce?" Peter smiled and slowly crouched down to drop his brush back in the can.

Ronnie dropped her brush and roller too. "I guess. Since you concede."

"I concede nothing!" He rushed at her, swung her around in a big circle, and planted a soft kiss on her lips. She melted against him and kissed him back with a passion that was all Ronnie.

Now that was more like it.

She could probably feel his wild heartbeat beneath her hands, his pulse racing out of control. She had a way of undoing him. Whether it was the scent of her shampoo, the softness of her full lips, or the silkiness of her hair that did it, he didn't know, but he wanted to spend a lifetime trying to figure it out.

The chatter and laughter of the kids in the auditorium broke the enchantment and Ronnie pulled away. Gripped his shirt. "We should get back to work."

"First, I have something for you." Peter pulled her over to the side of the stage. "It might've melted a little. I got distracted for a bit there by a beautiful woman. But I brought you some contraband." He handed her a Java Cup iced mocha.

She smiled, her amber eyes shining. "Is there anybody in town who *doesn't* know about that?"

"Honey, *everybody* heard about you getting kicked out of the Java Cup. Word to the wise, go apologize and keep your Packers Cheesehead at home. You smoothed things over with Megan, so we know you can kiss and make up when you want to."

"I tried a few times, but Kathy wasn't there. Or maybe she just didn't want to talk to me. I hope she forgives me someday." Ronnie took a sip and sighed. "I can't make coffee taste this good. I'd take this over money any day. But don't tell Seb that. I still want him to sign my paycheck."

"Seb won't have anything to hold against you when he hears about the call yesterday."

"The team did well with that hiker, didn't they?"

"Ronnie, you *led* the team and *taught* them how to do well. Jason McCray's wife sent a huge gift basket to the fire hall and her note with it is singing your praises. The card included a picture that Emily drew. She wants to be a paramedic just like you when she grows up. Wait until Seb reads that."

"It feels good to make a difference somewhere." Ronnie's smile faltered as she set down her drink and picked up the brush again.

"What are you talking about?"

"Sure, I helped the McCrays, but the people I care the most about? What about them? I mean, Tiago is still saying he wants to move at the end of summer, and I've single-handedly turned your whole family against you."

"Give Tiago time. He's starting to loosen up a little bit more with me. The last fishing trip I even caught him smiling when he reeled in a bass all by himself."

"Did he now?"

"Yup. And as far as my family, well, you heard our history. This stuff has been going on long before you ever came."

"How did your last meeting go today?"

He really didn't want to recall the failure of his last attempt to bring them on board, but he couldn't lie either. "Not great." He pointed to the final backdrop to be finished. "We should probably get this done. You know what a taskmaster Vivie is. And being one of the few family members who's still talking to me, I don't want to make her mad too—even if she is only a third cousin." He tried to hide the truth behind a wink.

But Ronnie hid nothing in her narrowed eyes and tight lips. "They're still mad?"

Peter moved away, picking up a cloth to wipe his face. "Of course. I thought I could try to discuss this rationally, show them what a good thing this youth center could be, but no one will listen. The two weeks Seb gave me are up tomorrow, and I haven't won *any* of them over. All I'm trying to do is bring people together, but I feel like I've pushed them further away."

"You haven't pushed anyone away. They're being childish and unreasonable."

"True, but I'm still out of time. I have nothing to show Seb."

"Oh yes, you do. I've got a surprise too." She wiped her hands on a rag and reached into her bag.

"What do you have?"

Ronnie handed him a clipboard.

Peter ran his finger down a long list of names. He flipped to the next page. More names. She had pages and pages of names. "Ronnie, what is this?"

"I thought it was obvious. But if you need me to spell it out for you, it's a petition. You know? A list of signatures? These are all people who are in full support of the youth center."

He looked at the last signature on the numbered line. "There are almost a thousand signatures here."

"Only nine hundred twenty-one actually."

He looked at her. Her huge grin and that twinkle in her eyes were a beacon of hope once again. "You've been busy."

"There are a lot of people that believe in you. Believe in this idea."

"You did this for *me*?"

"Well, yeah, we're in this together."

"Huh." He reached out his hand. "I really love the sound of that."

"Me too." She laced her fingers through his.

"You really think this will go through?" Because somehow, having her believe in him made Pastor Dan's words resonate.

You have a servant's heart. But, Peter, there's a warrior inside you too.

"It'd better go through. It's the best option. And look at how many people support it."

"Nine hundred twenty-two."

"No, twenty-one."

He shook his head and took the pen wedged in the clipboard. He signed the next line on the last sheet. "Twenty-two."

It was time to roar.

CHAPTER 15

*R*onnie came early to the courthouse town room to find her seat for the meeting. She, Peter, and Vivien had gone over all the information that morning. The slideshow was done. The plans printed off. They were ready. And with all the signatures she'd collected over the last two weeks, she had every confidence the proposal would pass.

It was obvious. This town needed a youth center.

And everyone but the Dahlquists and Zimmermans could see that.

Vivien and Megan took seats next to her. Charlie Zimmerman glared her way as he took a front-row folding chair at the other end of the room. Elton sat next to him and didn't look too happy to see her either.

The feeling is mutual, bud.

Thankfully, there were plenty of friendly faces in the crowd too. John and Ingrid sat a few rows back. Some of the other first responders and firefighters sat in the middle, waved at her when she turned to count supporters.

Peter's parents stood along the back wall. No friendly smiles from them.

Ronnie faced forward again.

Okay, so maybe this wouldn't be the shoo-in she'd thought.

The temperature rose as bodies filled the seats. Jensen Atwood dragged a fan to the front of the room and plugged it in. Mayor Seb Brewster and the councilmen took their seats. Two microphones sat on their table, one on a stand in front of the crowd.

Seb glanced at the clock and opened the meeting. All chatter died down. Ronnie missed all the preliminary business stuff, instead going over the points she'd drilled with Peter in her head.

"And now we come to the Westerman property. We tabled the vote and discussion at the last meeting. At this time, we will hear from Councilman Peter Dahlquist, who has researched the youth center option and has a report for us."

Pride swelled within Ronnie's chest as Peter stood and presented the plan for the youth center. His voice grew in confidence as he pointed out the different features on the slideshow they'd put together. The passion shone in his eyes as he spoke. "We can open this area and fit a full-size gym, complete with locker-room facilities and a weight room. In this part of the building, we'd like to have a tutoring center, a small arcade—"

"Arcade?" Elton sputtered. "Are you serious? Like our kids need any more time with screens and video games. They have too much of that already." He crossed his arms over his chest and leaned back in his chair.

It took all of Ronnie's strength not to go over and pop one on Elton's smug face.

Peter, on the other hand, stayed cool, kept his voice even. "What about winter? We deal with six months of it here. A small arcade—think pool tables and interactive games—can offer the teens a place to socialize in a healthy environment, offer alternatives to just sitting at home in front of a screen. Plus, an indoor playground for younger children will give kids of all ages more opportunities for active play. All year long."

A few people nodded their heads.

Ha! Take that, Elton.

"What about the jobs you're taking away?"

Of course one of the Dahlquists, probably Peter's Uncle Gordy, had to have his say.

But Peter was prepared. "A youth center will need staff. We're still creating jobs here. And our plan is to build in office spaces to rent, which are hard to come by downtown."

"I still want to know who's paying!" Uncle Charlie chimed in. "How are we, the taxpayers, going to afford this? You're talking millions of dollars." His loud voice carried over the room. "As a hotel, we wouldn't be asking the town for *anything*. In fact, we'd be paying a hefty city tax, bringing people in to patronize our town's businesses. This is going to cost us. A lot!"

A few echoed his question and chatter overtook the crowd.

"Hey." A simple command from Peter and everyone quieted. It wasn't angry, but his voice was firm. Confident. He redirected attention to the plans. "Yes, this youth center will cost us. But don't you think it's a worthy investment? The healthier our kids are, the healthier society we have. And we can keep costs down as people donate labor or materials. This facility also qualifies for grants and other programs for funding. We can still bring in revenue for other businesses by hosting sports tournaments and educational programs for our region and across the state. That's bringing people in—people who will stay in Deep Haven hotels, eat in Deep Haven restaurants, and purchase goods here. It's a win for everyone. Yes, it will take an initial investment like every good business does, but we'll all reap the benefits."

Ronnie wanted to jump out of her seat and clap. Vivien grabbed her hand and squeezed. Ronnie could feel the tide turning, the crowd following their fearless leader as Peter calmly addressed each and every question and concern. She looked over the heads behind her, anxious to see how his parents were taking it. Barb had a new admiration shining in her eyes as she watched her son. Gary tilted his head to his brother, a whispered debate about something. Maybe one of them was coming around.

She hoped so.

Oh, how she hoped.

Wow.

It hit her. Just how invested *she* was. In Deep Haven, in this youth center.

In Peter.

She sat back and watched the man she loved. Yes, shoot—she *loved* Peter Dahlquist.

As he admitted the risks, he focused on the outcome, the benefits of this project. Like relationships.

The risk it took to believe in something, to have faith in a better future.

She got that, because she'd taken that risk. But she was definitely reaping benefits too. Megan, Ella, Vivien. Their friendships brightened her world in a way she'd never felt before. They added depth. It was like when she painted the shadows and light on the city backdrop. Suddenly the scene was more than a flat two-dimensional drawing. The buildings and streets took the shape of a real city.

And Peter had taught her how a gentle word often took more strength and had better results than all her bluster and muscle. He didn't force people to do what he wanted. He listened. He took the time to understand them. He was with them in the trenches, in the celebrations, in all those moments.

Just like Pastor Dan had said about God in his sermon. *He wants us to experience life with Him inside us. He wants to carry us through the hardships. Join in our celebrations. Hold us when we're hurting. But He won't force Himself on you. He'll wait.*

That was so like Peter. Yes, it was safe to say she loved him. Even needed him.

And it didn't in the least scare her.

And whether this youth center happened or not—but how could it not?—she'd found the place she wanted to call home. A haven. And she prayed—yeah, she'd started doing that somewhere along the line—that Tiago would choose to make a home here in Deep Haven too. That they wouldn't have to leave.

She sobered. But the risk to her heart was still high.

If she had to, she *would* leave. Because as much as she loved Peter, she loved Tiago too. Her brother came first. Maybe if they had to leave, she and Peter could find a way, a long-distance relationship.

But she was all Tiago had.

She refused to be the same person her mother was. She wouldn't abandon him.

Peter understood. So hopefully, God could change Tiago's mind before summer's end.

Yelling from the hallway broke her concentration and disturbed the crowd. Someone tried to push in the doorway.

"Let him in," someone else said.

Josh leaned on the door, chest heaving as he sucked in air, panic in his eyes. "Fire! The Westerman! And Tiago is caught in it!"

For a second, no one moved as the words hung in the air, as they fell and landed.

As Ronnie sorted out the words.

Fire. Tiago.

Ronnie bolted out of her chair, shoved her way to the door, and sprinted downtown.

~

Peter shot out the side door to the hall. Ronnie was in front of him, already past the security gate. He raced past the guards and out of the courthouse to the street. An ominous cloud of dark smoke billowed in the sky to the east.

"Ronnie!" He barreled downhill, Ronnie still several feet in front of him. She reached Highway 61 but didn't even look at the traffic or break her stride as she plunged into the busy road. The driver of a black pickup laid on the horn and swerved out of the way, just missing her.

Peter yelled, but she didn't pause. He held out a hand to stop the gray sedan coming from one direction and crossed the street after another SUV flew past.

He had almost caught up to her. "Ronnie!"

Her arms only pumped harder. But she looked back—

And her foot caught on something. Suddenly, she went airborne.

"Ronnie!"

She landed with a skid and a scream.

He caught up to her, reached out to help her up, but she was already back on her feet, running hard, blood on her hands, her chin.

He still barely stayed paced with her as they rushed into the parking lot and skidded to a stop, the entrance to the Westerman Hotel engulfed in flames.

"Tiago!" she screamed as she finally paused at the front doors and scanned the building.

Fire shot out of every window, writhing tongues framing the doorway.

He grabbed her back. "This way!"

They ran to the side, a boarded-up door clear of flames.

For the moment.

Ronnie lunged for it, but Peter caught her by the waist and held her fast. The smoke pouring out under the door was black.

Toxic. Even if he could break through the board, they'd be walking into a poisonous fog.

"Let me go! I have to save my brother. Tiago!" She pounded at his arms wrapped around her middle. Kicked at his shins. Her elbow caught him in the eye.

He gritted his teeth against the pain and held her tight. "Ronnie, you can't go in there."

She screamed, something feral and dark. "He needs me! Let me *go!*"

She had the will of a mother, and he almost lost his grip. "No, Ronnie—wait for the firemen!"

She whipped her head back and forth, crying out her brother's name.

But one glance told him she'd die if she went in. The fire was consuming the building, now almost an inferno. And they didn't have the slightest idea where Tiago might be.

Please, God. Please. Please.

The boards nailed across the door started glowing as they caught flame too.

Peter backed them away. Ronnie twisted in his hold to face him, dark streaks of mascara-stained tears streaming down her cheeks, blood dripping from a scrape on her chin, her eyes wild and frantic, but her body finally still, not fighting him.

"Peter. Please. I *have* to save him. If you care about me at all, let me go."

Oh, Ronnie. "Babe." He pressed his forehead to hers. "I can't."

Shoot—if he could trust her not to follow him, *he* would go look for Tiago himself. But he knew the moment he relaxed his hold on her, she'd bolt.

She would plunge into that fire and never come out.

As if he needed any more proof, something inside the building exploded, shaking the earth, and flames launched into the sky from the window right above them. Heat seared, a hot wind swallowing them.

And behind it all, a siren whined.

Help, too late.

He met her gaze. "I'm sorry, Ronnie." His voice was a whisper, but his resolve as unmovable as iron. "I won't let you go."

And she apparently knew it. She took a shaky breath. Shook her head, the fight drained from her. "You! You took him from me." Her breath caught, and suddenly she screamed. "You took him from me!"

Then she reached out, as if to slap him. He caught her arm, holding her tighter to his chest. "Stop, Ronnie."

She sagged in his arms, weeping. "Please. Let me save my brother."

He wanted to cry too. "Ronnie, the fire department is on their way. They'll look for him. But you can't go in there. It's too dangerous. You'll die."

A crowd formed in the parking lot, and the sirens grew closer. Peter took a few more steps back, dragging Ronnie away from the fire. She was nearly limp in his arms.

As if in disbelief.

Him too. The fire had chewed through the roof, the sky black and…no, there wasn't a hope that Tiago could be alive.

Cole jogged up to them. "What do we do?"

Ronnie looked up at him, her mouth open. Nothing came out.

"Tiago is in there. You gotta find a way in."

Cole's eyes widened, and he glanced at Ronnie. "Right."

"Have Seth run the crew. Tell the guys to get water on the surrounding buildings—"

But Cole was already waving his hand, running away.

The truck pulled up, and Seth Turnquist and Darek Christiansen soon called out orders to the volunteers.

And all Peter could do was watch. Pray. And not let go of Ronnie.

The roar of the fire grew. The wind shifted, blowing smoke

and sparks over them. Peter moved Ronnie farther to the side of the building, away from the watching crowd, closer to the back of the hotel.

She collapsed onto the rocky berm and he went down with her, his legs and arms around her.

She just stared at the building, unmoving.

"Ronnie."

She shook her head.

"Ronnie—"

Sheltered from some of the noise, a faint barking called to him.

He stilled.

She looked up, then at Peter. "Do you hear that?"

They heard the bark again. "Blue?" She pushed away from him, and he barely caught her hand, scrambling to his feet.

They ran around to the back side of the hotel facing the East Bay.

By the edge of the water, Blue barked over a lump lying on the ground.

Tiago.

"Oh!" Ronnie said, and Peter let go of her hand. She ran for him and he turned, waving to his crew.

Dean Wilson spotted him.

"We've got a child back here! He's hurt!" Then Peter took off after Ronnie.

She was checking Tiago's airway. He lay unmoving on the large pebbles. Eyes closed, ash smeared across his face, a burn covering most of one arm and a leg.

Peter kneeled next to her, rocks digging into his knees. "What can I do?"

Her hands shook, but her voice was steady, her eyes never leaving Tiago. "We'll need the helicopter. He has smoke inhalation and his pulse is too faint."

"We're here." Seb and Kirby nudged Peter out of the way.

They carried an oxygen kit, medical bag, and a backboard from the ambulance.

Peter stood back as they masked Tiago and put him on the backboard. Ronnie was all over him, and he saw the woman he'd met six weeks earlier.

All business.

Saving lives on the battlefield.

Tiago was in the best care. But he never opened his eyes. Didn't respond to any of the stimulus tests. *God, please save him.* Blue trotted over to Peter, whining. He held the dog close as he watched Ronnie work.

The whir of the helicopter carried over the noise of the sirens and the fire.

"The helo can't land here," Jensen ran up and told Ronnie. "They cleared the parking lot at the co-op. We'll meet them there."

By that point, they already had Tiago loaded on the backboard and a cot. They lifted him into the back of the ambulance and pulled away. Peter handed Blue off to Dean and cut across the beach in a sprint to meet them near the helo. They lifted Tiago into the Bell 429. Ronnie jumped in after them, holding a saline bag and IV line, her face a mask of concentration, no hint of the panic from before. She started to close the door, yelling over her shoulder at the pilot to get going.

She was back. But she would need all the support she could get as soon as they took Tiago out of her care. Now he could help. He could be there for her. Peter held the door fast, blocking it. "Ronnie, want me come with you or follow in my truck?"

Her face was hard, lips drawn tight, nostrils flaring. "Don't bother following. I don't want you near me ever again."

"What—"

"Stay away from me. Now get out of the way. Family. Only." She slammed the door and he staggered back.

The helicopter rose up, the blades slicing the air, whipping his hair across his face.

He'd seen plenty of disappointment in the eyes of people he cared about in the last two weeks, a lot of anger, plenty of failure and letdown. But Ronnie's amber eyes burned with a hatred that speared his very soul.

Right. Maybe he couldn't blame her. She was upset.

She'd come around. Maybe.

Please.

The sounds from the fire drew him back to the scene. He grabbed an extra jacket and helmet from the pump truck and helped aim one of the hoses at the roof.

The building was a lost cause, but they could at least keep the fire from spreading.

With the rest of the town, he fought the fire and watched the Westerman Hotel burn to the ground.

CHAPTER 16

*R*onnie paced the waiting room for the millionth time. Her nails were chewed to the quick. Shoved out of the emergency room upon arrival, she had nowhere else to go, nothing else to do.

And the beefy guy at the nurses' station had threatened to kick her out of the building if she didn't leave them alone and stop demanding updates.

But that was her baby brother in there.

How was she supposed to sit and wait?

She wanted to walk down to the vending machine to find something to drink and clear away the smoky taste in her mouth, but she'd forgotten her purse somewhere along the way.

Back in Deep Haven.

A town she never wanted to see again. She hated the place, the people. The life that might have been theirs.

An illusion.

And if Tiago didn't make it...

No. She couldn't go there.

He *had* to make it.

She resumed pacing, ignoring the glares from the middle-aged man in the corner flipping through old *Golf* magazines.

"Ronnie!" Megan and her family whooshed through the door. She engulfed her in an embrace despite Ronnie's stiff posture. "How is he?"

Ronnie couldn't look her in the eye. She fixed her gaze on Megan's shoulder instead. "I don't know. He never regained consciousness and they haven't updated me."

"He's a strong kid. He'll pull through, Morales." Cole's steady hand landed on her shoulder. The other was around Josh.

She nodded, the lump in her throat choking off words. She wanted to turn to the kid and ask him what they were doing at the hotel. Why had they gone into that fire trap? And why hadn't he gotten Tiago out?

But shouting wouldn't bring her brother back to life, would it?

Megan handed Ronnie her purse and a small duffel bag. "I hope it's okay, but I brought some things from home. Toiletries and clean clothes for you and Tiago. And we have Blue at the house too."

Ronnie turned away from them and looked out the window. She could see Lake Superior, the sun glaring off the water as it sank below the horizon. She should thank Megan. She should. But right now, she wanted to forget them all. Forget how much she'd hoped she'd fit in to the small town and how instead it had wormed its way into her heart—then destroyed it. She wanted to take her brother and drive far away from it all.

No matter what Megan called it, Ronnie had no home.

"Ronnie, can we get you anything?" Megan stood next to her.

If that meant they'd give her some space… "Yeah. I could use a coffee."

"Sure." She told Josh to sit while she and Cole went to find the cafeteria.

Ronnie stared out the window and saw nothing. This wasn't

how it was supposed to be. In a perfect world, she and Tiago would be fixing up that cute little house on the hill. He should be playing with Blue or riding his skateboard in the park.

Not fighting for his life.

She was supposed to take him away from danger. Keep him safe. But no. She'd gotten soft. Weak. She'd let Deep Haven and Peter lure her into a false sense of security.

She was such an idiot because she'd known—just *known*—this would happen.

Josh came up to the window. "Um, Ronnie?" His voice shook. "Do you think he'll be okay?"

She should probably sugarcoat it and make the kid feel better. But she wasn't doing him any favors with that. Better to know now how cruel this world was and prepare him for it. "I don't know." And then she couldn't stop herself. She rounded on him. "Wanna tell me why you two were out running around town when Tiago said you were going to be playing video games?"

Josh took a step back. "It was hot in the apartment. We went to take Blue for a walk along the lake."

"Then what?"

"We heard some popping sounds and Tiago saw some smoke coming out of the windows of the hotel. People were yelling inside, like they were in trouble. Then Blue broke away and ran into the building through a hole in one of the doors that was boarded up, but it was too small for us. Tiago and I ran around until we found another opening. A window. Tiago went in after Blue and to save those others. He told me to get help."

She stared at Josh, trying to sort out his words. He was crying softly, and deep inside, she believed him. Still, "Why would he do that? He's just a kid!"

The man in the corner looked up from his magazine with another glare. She hadn't meant to yell. But what was Tiago thinking?

"He...he wanted to save Blue and...and he said this is what you and Peter would do. You would try to save those people. He said you two always think of others first and he wanted to be like that too."

She stared at him, her eyes filling.

Oh, Tiago.

From the periphery of her vision, she saw Megan and Cole standing in the hallway with coffee and a roll.

"Josh, did you see those other people?" Cole asked, walking over.

He nodded.

Cole squatted down in front of him. "Son, you need to tell us what you saw. Who was it?"

Josh looked up at his mother, then over to Cole. "Ben Zimmerman and his friends. They were crawling out of a different door when I came around the building, and they ran away. I went to the door they came out of and yelled for Tiago. But the fire was already close. Tiago said he almost had Blue and I needed to run for help." He turned to Ronnie again. "He was supposed to be *right behind* me. I wouldn't have left him if I knew—" He started crying again, his hands over his face.

Cole drew him into his arms. Megan kneeled by them both and hugged them.

Ronnie turned away.

She was just sick of it. Just wanted them all to leave. They'd done their good deed. They should leave and let her figure out how to pick up the pieces.

If she helped them feel better, hopefully they would. "Josh, it's not your fault. It's mine."

Megan looked up. "Ronnie, what are you talking about?"

"Nothing." What was she going to say? That she'd been an idiot and given her heart to a man—just like her stupid mother —and he'd shown her exactly how much power he had over her. If Tiago hadn't been on that beach...

She couldn't trust Peter.

And she certainly couldn't trust herself when he was around.

"Ronnie, you know this wasn't your fault."

But it was. "I should've never come to Deep Haven. It was obvious from the beginning we didn't belong. Tiago knew that and I should've listened to him." She looked at Cole. "You need to find yourself another paramedic."

"Hey, let's not make any hasty decisions here—"

"No. It's over. We're done here." She turned back to the window. Maybe they'd get the hint that she needed to be alone.

But they stayed. They settled into the hospital chairs, their presence rubbing her wounds raw. Ronnie paced and sipped the coffee Megan put in her hands. She didn't taste it, just swallowed. Her hands still stung from the spill she'd taken, but at least her chin had stopped bleeding.

Minutes or hours passed, who knew. But darkness had smothered the city outside when finally a doctor came in with an update. She sank into a chair as fragments of what he said computed. Coma. Touch and go. PICU. Smoke inhalation. Second-degree burns. Head trauma.

And she was done waiting. Done asking. She stood toe to toe with the doctor. "Let me see him. Now."

Megan held out the purse and duffel bag again. "Ronnie, we'll be right here. I can stay the night if you like."

She was done begging people to stay. Done letting them into her heart. They might mean well now, but in the end, no one really stuck around.

She had no one else to blame for this tragedy but herself.

"No. Go back to your home and family, Megan. It's just me and him now."

And she needed to start getting used to that all over again.

~

Peter leaned hard on his shovel, watching the smoldering remains of the Westerman. The dark of night fell as the fire died. The scrape of shovels filled his ears as the others over-turned ash and debris. They stood watch over the pile, making sure nothing reignited.

His crew worked around him, many townspeople too, some with their own shovels. Others used their headlamps to help light the scene or held flashlights. Seb handed out bottles of water. Ingrid and Ivy Christiansen fed them with simple ham and cheese sandwiches. Everyone pitched in.

He was surrounded by people he'd known his whole life, both sides of his family finally coming together for a good cause —and yet, he'd never been more hollow or alone.

Peter's phone buzzed. Cole. *Finally.* "How is he?"

"He's in a coma, in the pediatric ICU. Doc says it's really touch and go, but all they can do now is wait."

"And…Ronnie?"

Silence.

"Cole. How is she?"

"She's hurting. What do you expect?"

"Should I come? I think I should be there—"

"No, buddy. She's…she doesn't want anyone here." Silence and Peter winced, his heart thudding.

"She told me to find a new paramedic."

Oh, Ronnie. Don't give up on us. Not when they'd come so far. "You're not going to, right?"

"She's pushing everyone away. And I get that she's trying to cope, so we're leaving. Giving her space."

They were going to leave her there? Alone? What were they—

"Peter, there's more. Josh told us what happened. He said he saw some older kids climb out of the hotel as it was burning. Tiago was trying to help put out the fire and save his dog. But these other kids? Well, I have a feeling they started the whole thing."

A fire ignited inside him. "Who was it?"

"Ben Zimmerman and his friends."

He wanted to throw the phone. "You sure?"

"Josh wouldn't make it up."

No, he wouldn't. And Ben certainly hadn't proven himself very trustworthy these days. Peter had tried approaching him last week about the fireworks and lighter and the kid had blown him off. Cussed and lied to his face. The shifty eyes and tough-guy bravado had only convinced Peter that Tiago was right. But Elton wouldn't hear it. He'd denied everything and backed up his son, lashing out at Tiago and Ronnie even more.

Cole ended the call. Peter slipped his phone back in his pocket and dug his shovel deep into another pile of glowing rubble. His gut churned. His own family was responsible for this destruction.

Conversation carried over to him.

"What a tragedy!"

"How did this start?"

"Wouldn't take much. The place was full of old curtains, mattresses, and furniture."

"I bet I know who started it." Elton's cocky smirk was visible in the spotlight of a work lamp. He stood and watched everyone else work. "I bet it was that Hispanic kid they found out back."

Peter froze.

"Who?" Aunt Carol asked. Wait, Aunt Carol? A Dahlquist voluntarily talking to a Zimmerman?

"It was that Hispanic kid. I'm telling you, he's trouble. And it's all his sister's fault for not keeping an eye on him."

Aunt Carol nodded. "Yeah, we have had a lot more problems since they moved here. I heard the boy was in trouble in the Cities too. That's why they had to leave. No wonder she wanted a youth center, so others could babysit her delinquent brother."

Uncle Charlie lumbered up to them. "I told you she'd be trouble. And now look at this mess."

Seriously? *Seriously?* Peter threw down his shovel. "You don't know *anything* about how this fire started. You don't even know what's going on in your own family. And you certainly don't know anything about Veronica and Tiago!"

Elton stepped up into his face. "I know if it weren't for that woman brainwashing you and ruining things, this building would still be standing here."

Aunt Carol and Uncle Charlie nodded in agreement. Others gathered around for the show.

Yeah, well stick around and grab the cotton candy.

"Ronnie wasn't the only person who wanted the youth center. It wasn't even her idea. But you're right in that she brainwashed me. Got all the cobwebs and lies *right out.* Showed me that you all might be the most selfish people I've ever met."

"She's been stirring up trouble from the moment she rolled into this town! She kicked my dad off the first responder team. Who does that?" Elton said, his expression lethal.

Peter met it with one of his own. "She gave him a fair shot like everyone else on the team. All she ever wanted was to make our EMS staff the best it could be, make a difference here. She wanted to make a home for herself and her brother—a place to belong. And here I kept telling her it was possible, that Deep Haven was a great place to call home. But now I'm ashamed. I'm ashamed of all of you, my own family."

"Well, that's obvious since you turned your back on your own flesh and blood! You chose her. This"—Elton pointed to the remains of the hotel—"is her fault. And I tried to warn you."

Peter shook his head and then he raised his voice loud enough for the entire county to hear him. "You wanna know who started this? Your son, Elton. Ben started this fire."

"Liar," Elton said. "You don't know what you're talking about!"

"A witness saw him climbing out of the hotel and running away after the fire already started. And can't say I'm surprised when I found out Ben bullied a younger kid to stash fireworks and *your* lighter. But you wouldn't listen to me."

He turned to Aunt Carol, whose smug look said she was enjoying Elton's humiliation a little too much. "And like your kids are any better. Tommy and Gina were out at that pit party, drunk. Making fools of themselves. Vivien's idea for a youth center was something a lot of people in this town wanted. I wanted it. And maybe if your kids had something better to do than bully others, vandalize property, get drunk, and set fires, we wouldn't be in this mess either."

Out of the corner of his eye, Peter caught movement just as Elton shoved him.

He looked at Elton. "Really?"

Elton swung at him, but Peter deflected it. "What is wrong with you?"

Someone in the crowd screamed.

Elton pulled his arm back for another swing.

Okay, buddy, let's go then.

One quick duck and jab to the chin, and Elton staggered. Peter's follow-up punch landed Elton flat on his back.

Peter stood over him and stared down the Zimmermans and Dahlquists gathered there. "Before you go pointing fingers and blaming others, why don't you shut up, take a hard look at your own lives, your own kids, and show a little compassion for others!"

Uncle Charlie and Aunt Carol stood silent, mouths open in shock.

A slow clap started behind him.

Huh?

It built, and Peter turned around to see the rest of the crowd clapping, drowning out all other noise.

Vivie was crying, grinning, and she came over and hugged

him. "Who said you don't belong on a stage? That was fantastic. You're like Hugh Jackman! Tough *and* tender."

Whatever. He set Vivie away. Elton had gotten up, swearing, but walked away.

"Let's get back to work," he said and picked up his shovel.

But as the crowd dug back into turning over the fire, Peter walked to the edge of the water.

"Feels good, huh?" Pastor Dan joined him, hands in his pockets, looking out across the moonlight on the lake.

"What?"

"Letting that warrior out. Standing up for what you believe in."

Peter breathed in deep the fresh air scented with pine and smoke, trying to calm down the rush of adrenaline still in his veins. "My whole life I tried to keep everyone happy. Tried to keep the peace. Love others. But I just couldn't…" The rest of the thought escaped him.

"Keeping others happy is not your job, Peter. We are called to love God and love our neighbor, but that looks a little different at times. There's a time when it means to keep the peace, but there's also a time to fight, to defend others. A time to build and a time to tear down. And there's a time to put a bully in his place and stand up for truth. That's when you go ahead and roar."

"I couldn't let him talk about her that way. She didn't do anything to deserve it."

"Some things are worth the fight."

"Guess it's something Ronnie showed me."

"Smart woman."

Yeah, she was. If only she didn't hate him. "I really thought… I really thought we had a future together. But she doesn't want anything to do with me now. And she's probably leaving."

Pastor Dan laid a hand on Peter's shoulder. "Like I said, some things are worth the fight."

CHAPTER 17

*A*ll Ronnie wanted to do was forget Deep Haven ever existed and move on with her life. She needed to start looking for jobs. A new place to live. Maybe Megan could even pack up her stuff and ship it somewhere so she wouldn't have to go back.

The day nurse knocked and came in to Tiago's room. "Good morning. How are you feeling today, Tiago?" She carried yet another balloon bouquet, this one purple and gold, tied with curling ribbon to a stuffed animal.

Apparently, however, Deep Haven wouldn't forget them.

Over the last four days, it seemed the town had decided to slather them with gifts.

Tiago rubbed his eyes and sat up in the hospital bed. "I'm good. Ready to bust out of here."

The nurse laughed as she set the Vikings jersey-clad teddy bear on the ledge with all the other get-well gifts. She moved to the bed and took Tiago's vitals.

Ronnie opened the card. *From Kathy and the Java Cup staff.* A gift card slid into Ronnie's hands.

Okay, so maybe she'd miss *some* things about the town.

"Vitals look good. Keep it up and we'll be saying goodbye to you tomorrow." She removed the blood pressure cuff from his arm. "Now that that's done, you feel up to a visitor?"

Tiago perked up. "Yeah."

"Great, I'll send in your friend."

Ronnie held her breath. It was probably just Megan and Josh again. But maybe…

Vivien swept in. "My favorite Shark!" She ruffled Tiago's hair and handed him a big stuffed Great White. "You, sir, need to get back to rehearsals. We only have a few days left before the big performance." She held out a tall coffee shop cup to Ronnie. "It's not a Java Cup iced mocha, but I came last night and stayed with a friend. This was the best I could do this morning."

Ronnie took a sip of the drink and tried to push back the disappointment. It definitely wasn't a Java Cup drink.

But that was okay. She needed to move on. Find a new favorite drink. A new coffee shop in a new town.

Her phone buzzed with a text.

Megan checking in on her again.

Seriously. The town had attachment issues. Why didn't they just let her go?

Starting with Peter.

He'd texted and called multiple times, and the only instance she'd responded to him was to tell him to stay away.

Apparently, he'd finally listened because she hadn't heard from him for at least twenty-four hours.

But Tiago had asked about him constantly since coming out of his coma three days ago. She couldn't put him off forever.

Vivien told them about the latest rehearsal mishaps and gave Tiago a card signed by the whole cast. By the time his lunch came around, his lids had started to droop. He still tired easily. Maybe now Vivien would leave and Ronnie could start her job search.

"Ronnie, grab some lunch with me. I'm starving and need more caffeine."

Tiago's eyes were already closed. Breathing steady.

"I should really stay here," Ronnie said.

"He'll be fine. We'll tell the nurses to call you if he wakes up." She grabbed Ronnie's arm. "Come on. He'll be asleep for a while."

Vivie had this way of not taking no for an answer. Besides, Ronnie was sick of cafeteria and vending machine food.

Vivien settled into the burgundy booth of the café across the street and didn't bother looking at a menu when the hostess handed it to her. "I'll take a Diet Coke and club sandwich with fries." Vivien was a woman who knew what she wanted. And yeah, Ronnie would miss her too. But not enough to stay.

Ronnie perused the menu. Nothing sounded good.

Vivien cleared her throat and tugged the laminated sheet out of Ronnie's hands.

Ronnie held out her hand. "Hey, I was reading that. I don't know what I want yet."

"Yes you do. You're just too chicken to admit it."

"I'm not...did you call me a *chicken*? What is this, a middle school playground?"

Vivien narrowed her eyes. Studied her. "Fine. If that's how you want to play it. But you should know what's happening in Deep Haven."

"Why should I care what happens there?"

"Because Deep Haven is your home. And you can try running away, but that town has a way of not letting you go. I should know. I ran off to New York, seeking fame and glory." Vivien got a far-off look in her eye and ran a finger down the window looking out toward the Aerial Lift Bridge. "But I also lost part of myself too. I should've come back sooner."

"Why?"

"Because in Deep Haven people know who I really am, flaws

and all. But they still care about *me*—not what I can do for them, like advance their career or play a part. I don't know...I guess it's just nice to be accepted for who I am."

"Easy for you to say. You've got a family there."

"Just my mom." She folded her arms. "But I saw all those cards, the flowers, and balloons in Tiago's room. That's Deep Haven for you. You may not have grown up there, but you're one of us."

"Not really. Cole can easily find another paramedic for the Crisis Response Team."

"What about Peter?"

"What about him?"

"He stood up to the whole town, to his own family defending you and Tiago. Told them all about how much good you've done for Deep Haven. He yelled at Elton and Charlie Zimmerman. Even his Aunt Carol. Called them out in front of the whole town. And...he got into a fist fight with Cousin Elton."

He'd gotten into a fight? Over her? She ignored the twinge of heat inside. Vivie was clearly reading way too much romance into his fight. "Elton had it coming, I can assure you. And if it was about me, then clearly, he'll be better off if I leave. Maybe his family will start talking to him again."

Drinks came and Vivien sipped her Diet Coke. "Wow. For such a tough girl, I so didn't peg you as a chicken."

"And we're back to that. Listen, I'm not *afraid*. I'm accepting reality."

"If you really think you're better off without Peter, then go, because he doesn't deserve that. It takes a lot more courage to stick around. To be vulnerable. You're just running away while Peter faced his worst fear—being the town villain—for you. Tell me again how he doesn't mean anything to you?"

Ronnie drew in a breath. A sharp pain went straight through her chest. "I never said he doesn't mean anything." Because the truth was Peter meant far too much, and that was the problem.

He took up so much room in her heart, she could hardly breathe. "But you're right. He deserves better."

Vivien just stared at her, and Ronnie stared back.

Finally, she backed down, leaned back against the booth. "Okay."

Food came and went. Vivien told her how Ben and his friends had confessed and were facing charges, how the town had held an emergency meeting and voted for a brand-new headquarters for the Crisis Response Team to be built on the Westerman site, and how the current municipal building they were about to revamp for the team would be converted into a youth center. By the time they got back to Tiago's room, Ronnie was caught up on the Deep Haven news.

And it affected her more than she wanted it to. Shoot, she still cared.

Tiago snored lightly thanks to the pain meds doing their job. Vivien left without another mention of Peter.

Ronnie sat in the chair by the window and watched her brother as he stirred under the covers. His arm bandaged, probably scarred for life.

But he was alive.

And, well, it occurred to her that if Peter hadn't held her back, she wouldn't be here to take care of him. He'd saved her from *death*. Which meant he'd also saved Tiago from going back to foster care and juvie.

Peter wasn't like any of her mother's boyfriends. He never demanded. Never barged in and took anything. Peter was trustworthy and kind. The only thing he'd stopped her from was self-destruction.

She scrolled over his multiple texts on her phone. A tear slipped and plopped on the screen.

He was there for her even when she hated him, pushed him away.

And maybe God was too. Maybe He'd always been there.

Loving her, desiring her. A gentleman not forcing Himself, but patiently waiting for her to turn back to Him with open arms. Waiting for her to see how much He cared, to let Him in.

It would be nice to have someone to hold on to. Because, yeah, if she were honest, it was pretty exhausting trying to hold everything together all by herself.

She'd always thought being vulnerable was exposing weakness. Something she needed to fight. *It takes a lot more courage to stick around. To be vulnerable.*

"Ronnie?" Tiago's small voice pulled her out of her musing.

She moved to the bed and perched on the edge. "How you doing, buddy?"

He tightened his jaw, as if trying not to cry. "Have you heard from Peter? Is he…is he mad at me or something?"

"Oh, Tiago. Of course he's not mad at you."

A hardness seeped into Tiago's voice. "So he's basically like every other creep."

She frowned. "What?"

"He's gone. Left us."

"No, T." She couldn't bear to hear Peter slandered that way. And hearing Tiago expose out loud the lies she'd secretly been telling herself made them seem so much worse. Vivien was right. She didn't deserve Peter. "No, he cares. It's…it's my fault he hasn't come."

"Why is it your fault?"

She fiddled with her phone, scanning the long line of texts she'd left unanswered. She handed it to Tiago. "He's been asking about you, begging to come. I'm the one who's put him off."

Tiago read and then looked up. "Why would you do that? I thought you liked him."

Liked him? Up until he'd refused to let her go, she'd thought she loved him.

This last week had been the worst of her life, but how much useless suffering had she caused by pushing Peter away?

Pushing God away, insisting she do it all alone? "T, I screwed up. I was so scared of losing you. So scared that liking Peter as much as I do was making me weak and dependent on him. And I lashed out. I told him to stay away."

"Then tell him you were wrong."

She looked at him. "I thought you didn't really care much about him. I thought you wanted to move."

Tiago dropped his chin. His fingers plucked at the hospital blanket. "Josh said Cole isn't his real dad, but he's the one that comes to all his games, the one who helps him with his homework and stuff. And his mom is a lot happier now. I guess...I really hoped Peter would do that for me. Not that he would be my dad, but he spent time with me. And, I don't know, it was nice. Doing guy stuff." He looked up at her, challenge in his eyes. "I know he makes you happier too. Stronger. Not weak."

With the emotion choking her up, all Ronnie could do was nod. Her brother was right. She *was* stronger with Peter in her life. Life had more color, more richness and fullness with him. She was depriving herself and Tiago by pushing everyone away.

And if that was true, she needed to win Peter back. She caught her breath and wiped away the tears. "So, what should I do?"

Tiago handed her phone back. "Call him."

Maybe it was time to stop running away and trying to forget. It was time to reach out and hold on.

She pressed the call button. Waited.

He didn't answer, and his voicemail didn't pick up.

It was probably full.

She texted.

Waited.

Delivered.

Waited.

And waited.

But just like she'd expected, she got no response.

Once again Ronnie's SUV crested the hill with the mini golf course on one side and a Welcome to Deep Haven sign next to it. Tiago was fast asleep in the passenger seat just like he'd been the first time she'd made this journey. But this time it was broad daylight, and a bright summer sun and a herd of fat lazy clouds stretched over the bay. The town wasn't strange and unfamiliar any more.

In two months, it had become a home. What was it Vivien had said yesterday?

Deep Haven is your home. And you can try running away, but that town has a way of not letting you go.

As Ronnie turned on their street, she smiled. Yeah, Vivie might be right.

Tiago woke up as she pulled into their parking spot. "Do you think Peter will come see us now?"

That was the question, wasn't it? "Um, I don't know."

"You called him, right?"

"He didn't answer. I sent a couple of texts too."

"Then he'll come. You'll see."

If he did, it'd be another miracle. Like finding Tiago on the beach. Like bringing him home a week after he'd fallen into a coma and almost died. She'd probably met her miracle quota for the week. For her lifetime.

But hopefully Peter, being the upstanding guy he was, would at least keep his relationship with Tiago. And somehow she would find a way to work with him in a professional manner despite her self-inflicted broken heart. She couldn't blame the guy for walking away after she'd shoved him out of her life and told him he didn't belong with her. And then she'd proceeded to ignore him. Her one text up until last night had stated *We're fine. Leave us alone.* It didn't exactly inspire a lot of warm, fuzzy feelings.

So of course he'd ignored her messages last night. And today.

Ronnie loaded her arms with balloons, bouquets, and stuffed animals, and finally managed to open the door to the apartment. She plopped everything on the dining room table.

Tiago followed behind with a few more items, the softer things that wouldn't hurt his arm. He sniffed. "What's that smell?"

Not that she could smell much over the flowers she'd just carried in, but a hint of fresh paint scent lingered in the air. "Megan asked if they could do some touch-ups on one of the walls while we were in the hospital." It had seemed like a strange request when her friend had asked a couple days ago, especially since they had painted everything before Ronnie and Tiago had moved in. But it wasn't like she would say no to anything Megan asked.

"Can I go see Josh?"

"And leave all this for me to put away? Nice try. Go unpack. And you're gonna have to take it easy if you're going to be ready for the play tomorrow. Maybe you should take a nap before tonight's rehearsal."

"Aw, Ronnie, come on. I'm not a baby, and I can unpack later. Now that I don't have that other medicine, I don't get so sleepy."

"Unpack now." She shushed him with a kiss on his head and gently shoved him toward his bedroom.

As soon as he was in his room, Ronnie checked her phone again.

Still nothing. She sank into a chair and tried to push back the tears. What did she expect? That after the way she'd treated him, Peter would be waiting for her?

She wiped her cheeks and took a deep cleansing breath. At least she wasn't alone. Not according to Pastor Dan.

He wants us to experience life with Him inside us. He wants to carry us through the hardships. Join in our celebrations. Hold us when we're hurting.

This definitely qualified as hurting.

Lord, help me get through this heartbreak one day at a time.

It wasn't a fancy prayer, but Ingrid had said it didn't matter. That God knew her heart and could translate just fine.

She waited but heard nothing. Felt nothing. Guess she just needed to trust that God knew what was best and move on. With a heavy sigh, Ronnie stood and went through the stack of mail on the counter. After trying to find a place for all the balloons and flowers and cards, she was left with her duffel to unpack.

She hitched it up to her shoulder and with heavy feet, she opened the door of her bedroom. She took two steps in and gasped.

Oh. My. Word.

She dropped her bag and moved to the foot of her bed. Her hand covered her mouth. There was no holding back the tears that streamed down her face now.

Above her bed was a huge magenta heart painted on the wall. A heart that matched the hundreds of deep pink roses set around the room in different shaped vases and jars. What in the world?

But before she could take it all in, a knock sounded at the door.

Tiago burst out of his room. "I'll get it!"

In a daze, Ronnie followed him. Tiago threw open the door to reveal Peter standing there with Blue and one more pink rose.

The kid actually hugged Peter around the waist. "I knew you'd come!"

Peter chuckled, set Blue down, and hugged Tiago back. "I missed you too, little man."

Blue barked and jumped in on the action. Tiago laughed and

let her lick his face. "See, Ronnie, I told you everything would work out if you would just call him. Does this mean we can stay in Deep Haven now?"

Since she couldn't speak past the emotion clogging her throat, Ronnie nodded.

Tiago—looking for once like a happy, normal ten-year-old boy—whooped in delight and grabbed Blue's leash hanging by the door. "Now can I please go see Josh? Blue probably needs to go outside. And I unpacked."

"Go ahead." Ronnie choked out the words with a grin of her own.

"Don't be gone too long. I was hoping we could go get some dinner together. Maybe ice cream too." Peter gave him a high five as her brother rushed out the door.

And then his attention zeroed in on Ronnie.

He walked toward her with his one pink rose. "I should've known you'd be early. I was hoping to be here when you arrived."

"I can't believe you're here at all," she whispered.

Her feet were cemented in place. But Peter took another tentative step toward her. "Veronica? Are you okay?"

She nodded again, trying to hold back the sob in her throat.

"I know you said to leave you alone, forget about you, but…I can't."

She swallowed hard. "Tiago was hoping you'd come."

"He was, huh? And what about you? Because, Ronnie, I've been going insane without you."

She finally looked him in the eye and caught a shimmer in those hazel wonders. He held out the rose. "This is for you."

Her hands shook as she reached out for it.

"It's the brightest pink one Claire Atwood could find. Even though she's still on maternity leave, she came into the florist shop and helped me in person."

His nervous babble and shy smile drew her toward him. "I

suppose I have you to thank for that heart on the wall of my bedroom too?"

He moved closer. "It's not Berry Kiss paint. The closest I could find was Razzle Dazzle Rose. And let me tell you, the guys at the paint counter had a field day with that. But if you don't like it, you can paint over it if you want. Cole said to paint the apartment whatever color you like."

The vision of Peter asking for Razzle Dazzle Rose paint made her giggle. Then she noticed the blue and green bruising around his left eye. "Oh, Peter, your eye. That looks like it hurts." She instinctively reached out to examine the bruise, but he stopped her hand. Clasped it to his chest.

"Not as much as hurting the woman I love."

She dropped the rose. "Love?"

He took her other hand as well. "I'm not sorry I held you back from the building, but I am sorry I hurt you. You have to understand, though—I couldn't let you go into that building, Veronica. I couldn't."

"And what if Tiago had—" Ronnie couldn't choke out the word. She turned away from him.

"Then I would've kept holding you and we would've gone through that together. I know you told me to leave you alone, but I can't. I love you and I'm here for you. I'm here for Tiago. And you should…you should just get used to it, because I'm not going anywhere."

She turned to face Peter. "What about your family? They hate me. They blame Tiago—"

"My job is not to please them. It's to stand up for the truth. And the truth is that you are worth fighting for."

She heard the words, but still didn't believe them. "Vivien told me you fought Elton." She bit her lip. "But that's craziness. Family is everything to you. What possessed you to do that?" She stepped closer, hope soaring as she waited for his answer.

"I thought it was obvious. I'm crazy for you. You make me do things I would never do." He reached out for her again. "But I'm a better man for doing them. You give me courage to stand up for what I believe in. And yes, family is everything to me. If you'd let me, I want to build a family with you and Tiago."

The last bit of hesitation melted as she moved in and rested her hand over his heart. "Sure you have enough room in that big ol' family of yours?"

"Always." He leaned down, and she gladly surrendered to his kiss.

EPILOGUE

"*H*urry up! All the good seats will be taken." Peter tugged once more on Ronnie's arm as they stood outside the auditorium entrance. It seemed like everyone in town wanted to see her and hear about Tiago's recovery. And, yeah, it was good to see how many people cared, but couldn't they wait until *after* the performance?

"Look who's bossy now!" Ronnie smirked and kissed his cheek.

Well, that was one way to distract him.

He pulled her close for a real kiss just as Seb came up to them. "Am I interrupting anything?"

Did he really have to ask?

Ronnie laughed. "Yes, but that's okay because we were just going in to find our seats."

Seb handed her a folder. "I'll make this quick then. I'd like you to look over the contract there. We've changed your ninety-day clause. As far as Deep Haven is concerned, we think you are the best fit for the CRT medic. But feel free to take your time and think it over." Then he leaned toward Peter. "Make sure she signs it, Dahlquist," he said in a stage whisper.

Ronnie appeared speechless.

But Peter had questions. "What brought on this change?"

Seb offered a nonchalant shrug. "Nothing."

"Really? Just out of the blue, you decided to change the contract?"

Lucy Brewster came and poked Seb's side. "That's not what he told me." She held out a hand to Ronnie. "I'm Lucy by the way. Seb's wife."

Ronnie shook the offered hand. "And you own World's Best Donuts, right? I need your recipe for roly-polys. The lemon ones are my favorite."

But Peter had tasted Ronnie's baking. And more importantly, he wanted to hear what Seb had to say. "Why don't you leave the baking to Lucy and let's hear why Seb wants to change your contract all of a sudden."

"Fine. I heard a little rumor that Ronnie was thinking about finding a new job, and I didn't want to lose the best paramedic I've had the privilege of working with."

Lucy nodded. "Now *that's* what I remember you saying."

Ronnie grinned. "I don't need to read over the contract. I'll sign it right now."

"I won't argue with that." Seb handed her a pen and she signed on the last page. It was official. She was here to stay.

The lights in the commons flickered. Showtime.

Megan and Cole waved them down to the front row of the auditorium where they had seats saved for them. Seats right next to Peter's mom and dad.

His mom snapped pictures every time Tiago was onstage. Dad must be coming around to the idea of Ronnie and her brother being part of the family too, especially since he'd talked with Tiago about football over dinner last night.

And while the original musical he watched with Ronnie on their first date was about the most depressing thing Peter had ever seen, this version, a children's comedic version—*West Side*

Toy Story, about two rival toy companies in Manhattan—had the audience in stitches.

Tiago sang with the rest of the cast for the ending number and waved at Peter and Ronnie before taking his bow.

Yes, there was no doubt—Peter had found what he wanted most in life. He'd found something worth fighting for.

CONNECT WITH SUNRISE

Thank you so much for reading *Crazy for You*. We hope you enjoyed the story. If you did, would you be willing to do us a favor and leave a review? It doesn't have to be long—just a few words to help other readers know what they're getting. (But no spoilers! We don't want to wreck the fun!) Thank you again for reading!

We'd love to hear from you—not only about this story, but about any characters or stories you'd like to read in the future. Contact us at www.sunrisepublishing.com/contact.

We also have a monthly update that contains sneak peeks, reviews, upcoming releases, and fun stuff for our reader friends.

As a treat for signing up, we'll send you a free novella written by Susan May Warren that kicks off the new Deep Haven Collection! Sign up at www.sunrisepublishing.com/free-prequel.

OTHER DEEP HAVEN NOVELS

Deep Haven Collection

Only You

Still the One

Can't Buy Me Love

Crazy for You

Then Came You

Hangin' by a Moment

Right Here Waiting

Deep Haven Series

Happily Ever After

Tying the Knot

The Perfect Match

My Foolish Heart

Hook, Line, & Sinker

You Don't Know Me

The Shadow of Your Smile

Christiansen Family Series

Evergreen

Take a Chance on Me

It Had to Be You

When I Fall in Love

Always on My Mind

The Wonder of You

You're the One That I Want

For other books by Susan May Warren, visit her website at
http://www.susanmaywarren.com.

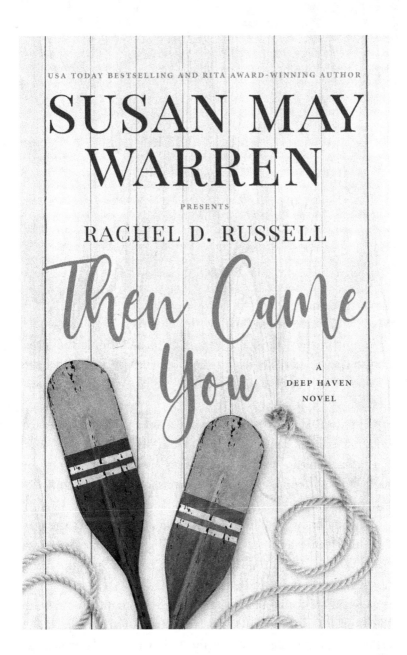

USA TODAY BESTSELLING AND RITA AWARD-WINNING AUTHOR

SUSAN MAY WARREN

PRESENTS

RACHEL D. RUSSELL

Then Came You

A
DEEP HAVEN
NOVEL

Turn the page for a sneak peek of the next Deep Haven novel,
Then Came You …

Vivien Calhoun needed a man within the next five minutes.

Unfortunately, the Sunday Fish Pic crowd filling the Deep Haven Coast Guard station parking lot brimmed with either the townees who knew her or tourists who'd come with their families in tow.

But she'd do anything to avoid a mortifying face-to-face with her evil half sister. Sabrina Calhoun stood on the sidewalk, her blonde hair loose, in a teal mini and white tank. She might look innocent enough to the casual observer, but Vivien knew the truth.

Sabrina knew how to draw blood and the fact that she was here in Deep Haven, on the North Shore of Lake Superior, couldn't bode well for Vivie. What on earth was she—the ruthless mean girl—doing in Vivien's hometown?

Vivie didn't care—she just knew that she couldn't be seen as the loser in the unspoken war between them. She glanced at her reflection in the side mirror of the 1954 Chevy Bel-Air next to her. Excellent. The August heat hadn't unseated her false lashes. She tossed her long sable locks over her shoulder and promptly whittled down her extensive eligible-bachelor criteria to three stellar qualities in a man.

Single, attractive, and present.

She scanned the crowd of the Fish Pic car show, hoping Sabrina hadn't yet spotted her. Maybe she could buy a few more minutes to execute her plan.

There, standing near a red Mustang. Tall, blond, and, *wow*. Definitely not a local. Pale blue eyes took in the festival-like atmosphere and a brush of whiskers darkened his jawline. Short-cropped hair. His tan said he spent a lot of time outdoors and he had muscles to boot. Oh, she'd cast him as a hero any day.

The newcomer couldn't possibly be single—she jockeyed into position to view his left hand. No ring. No indentation. Not even the faintest hint of a telltale pale line.

No. Way. Today might be her lucky day.

Mr. Hottie was her man.

She pressed her lips together, ensuring full coverage of her hour-old lipstick, smoothed her vintage sundress over her hips, and wove through the crowd, keeping her eyes on the stranger. He wore a faded green T-shirt over his tan cargo shorts. Definitely ready for an adventure. His blue eyes landed on her with the kind of arresting gaze that caused a woman to surrender.

"Vivie!" Her roommate snagged her arm, drawing her attention away from the target. "Did you already announce the Labor Day weekend play?"

"No, Ree, and you have terrible timing." She pulled Ree Zimmerman behind a green 1970 Chevelle parked on the scruffy grass at the edge of the lot. "Get down," she hissed.

"Have you lost your mind?" Ree squatted down beside her and tucked a wave of her long blonde bob behind her ear. "Why are we hiding?" She adjusted the cuff of her denim shorts and straightened her Mad Moose Motel T-shirt.

"Because for some reason, Sabrina is here." Ree was one of

the few people who knew the truth about Sabrina. Vivien flicked grass blades from her sundress before pulling Ree's back away from the sleek car. "Hey—be careful. Don't scratch the paint."

"Sorry." Ree scooched away from the car. "Why would she be here?"

"I don't know." Because, really, seeing Sabrina was more than enough reminder of everything that had gone wrong in Vivien's life.

Ree popped her head over the Chevelle. "I think I see her. If she's the blonde in the teal skirt that seems to be missing a few inches of fabric at the hem, she just went around the corner toward the music stage." She slid back down next to Vivien. "I wonder what she's doing here."

Vivien blew out a breath. "No doubt trying to make my life even more miserable than it already is."

"Well, I'm still trying to finish up the news story on the community theater event. I need a few quotes from you to polish it up."

"Right now? I'm a little busy." She gestured toward the car they hid behind.

"Now's a perfect time. I tried to do it last night, but you came in too late and I have to get the article to press this afternoon." Ree shuffled through her purse and withdrew a piece of note paper and pen. "Okay, sorry, reading through my notes here— so, you're opening up the community theater. How will that support your return to Broadway?"

Vivien's stomach turned. "I don't—um, I think I'm done with that." She smiled and declared, "For a while."

"What? That's always been your dream. Why aren't you going back?"

"I didn't say I wasn't *ever* going back." Vivien shook off the waves of nausea and straightened her back. "You know what? I just want to focus on being behind the scenes this summer. Give myself time to decide what I want to do."

"Are you kidding me? You were born for the stage."

Maybe born for it, but a stalker, a two-timer, and an on-stage disaster had pretty much destroyed those plans. "I'm ready to be a director." She gave Ree another assuring smile. "For now. I mean, I'll go back, of course." Someday. Maybe.

Ree's jaw dropped open. "Of course? Please. I have been your best friend since second grade. I know your tells. What's the deal?"

The problem with dear friends is they didn't always know when to let something go. "The best directors have been on the stage, Ree. I think it's great to do both. Diversify. I mean, look at Robert Redford. Angelina Jolie. Jodie Foster. So many." She waved her hand in the air, dismissing the discussion.

"Viv—"

She patted Ree's shoulder. "I'll show you I've still got it. See Mr. Hottie by the red Mustang?"

Ree took a look. "I take it you don't mean Nathan Decker."

"Obviously not. No, Mr. Hottie, the guy talking to Nathan." Vivien leaned forward and took a quick peek to make sure Sabrina hadn't come back through. "He's going to be my plus-one for a little while so I can rob Sabrina of her smug, self-serving victory." She winked. "He just doesn't know it yet."

Ree's mouth fell open, her eyes wide. "I thought you said you were done with relationships. I'm pretty sure you used the word *indefinitely*."

"I am. I simply need a plus-one for today. A stand-in."

Ree tugged on her arm. "Viv, you can't do that. You don't even know that guy."

"Oh, watch me." She fluffed her dark waves. "It's not like I'm preying on a defenseless man, stealing his fortune. I just need him for the next few minutes and it really doesn't look like he has anything else going on." Besides, it was just another role for her to play in life.

"I can't talk you out of this, can I?"

"Nope."

"Well, then I should warn you Sabrina's still on the prowl." Ree pointed with her pen toward the judges' booth where the prima donna was engaging locals in conversation, her laughter less than genuine.

"Then, take notes, my dear. This is how it's done."

Vivien stood and made her way around the Chevelle to the red Mustang as Nathan departed. The man turned, his eyes meeting hers across the hood of the car. He stilled. Stared.

"Nice ride." Vivien smiled, looked down, and ran her hand across the pale interior of the convertible. "Is this the 225 or the 271 V-8?" She raised her eyes back to his.

He tilted his head, smiled. "You know your cars. The V-8."

Oh, yeah, she knew the beautiful car had the V-8 under the hood. "This must be your first time in the car show. I'd definitely remember this car." And its driver, who managed to look even better close up. She stepped closer and a faint hint of cologne, a blend of citrus and sandalwood, reached her. A woodsy, masculine scent that made her want to lean into it.

"Thanks. It's actually not in the car show. She's just my baby."

Definitely not married.

"Oh?" She held out a hand to him. "Vivien Calhoun. And you're...?"

"Late." He said it with a twinkle in his eyes and pulled his car keys from his pocket.

She laughed. "Okay, Late. Hey—I need your help with a little something—you look like the kind of guy who'd help out a girl in trouble."

He frowned. "What kind of trouble?"

Sabrina had started wandering through the cars.

Vivien placed a hand on his arm, gave it a little squeeze. He stopped in his tracks and looked down at her, a little blaze in his eyes. "Here's the deal. All I need is for you to take a walk with me—you know, like we're...together...so Ms. Venom-for-Blood leaves me alone." She tilted her head toward the blonde interloper who'd started toward them.

He gave Sabrina a casual glance and turned back to Vivien. "Ouch." He smiled, something slow and teasing. "What if I told you she's my date?"

"Oh, hon, if she's your date, then you really do need me to save you."

A rich, warm laugh broke free. The kind that thrummed through her like a favorite show tune. "I thought I was saving you."

"We can save each other."

He laughed again. "I'm sure she can't be that bad."

"Trust me. If you consider the totality of her transgressions, she is exactly that kind of terrible, no-good, very-bad person."

Several drivers started up their engines, the rumble so deep she could feel it in her chest.

"I'm really sorry, but I need to get going." He stepped away.

"Ten minutes into town and of course, I run into you." Sabrina sauntered over, ensuring she was loud enough to draw stares. Sabrina was beautiful, with her long legs, perfect white teeth, and deep blue eyes.

But Vivien did have acting chops. She wouldn't have landed the role of Belle in *Beauty and the Beast* in New York if she didn't. Vivien turned. Flashed her megawatt smile. "Oh, Sabrina. What a...surprise." She seriously doubted it was the fishing contest or smoked walleye that brought Sabrina to the remote location.

"What are you doing here?" Sabrina waved her hand in the air. "Oh, that's right. All those things that happened in New York City caused you to turn tail and practically run out of—"

She covered her mouth, her snotty smirk still visible. "Oh, there I go. Sorry. Well, I know that was probably so humiliating, I can't even imagine how mortified you must have been when—"

And a little piece of Vivien broke away. Because Sabrina was right. Flames of embarrassment heated Vivie's face, burning hotter than the summer sun. And, just like in New York City, she stood alone. All eyes on her.

"Hey, Viv—you ready to go?" The voice, rich and deep and solid reached right through the chaos of emotions, grabbed her, and held on.

She blinked, felt a solid hand slip around hers, and turned to see her hero nod toward his car. "The parade is about to start."

Sabrina's eyes painted Mr. Hottie in slow motion, up and down, landing on his hand joined to Vivien's.

Yeah. Hottie for the win.

Vivien swallowed, nodded, tossed her goodbye to Sabrina. "See you around." Or not. Handsome held open the passenger side door and she slid in. The daggers in her back from Sabrina didn't even hurt as they pulled away.

"That. Was. Awesome." Vivien turned, blinked away the moisture in her eyes. "Did you see her face?"

Her rescuer nodded, his face tight.

Oh. "Hey—I'm sorry. I didn't mean to make you even later."

"It's okay." He tilted his head toward Sabrina's indignant figure behind them. "I have little use for people like that."

"Well, thank you."

He nodded. "Clearly a friend of yours." He looked over at her and winked.

And that made her smile. "Right. You can drop me off at the end of the parking lot and I'll catch a ride with my roommate." She could find some other way to avoid Sabrina the rest of the afternoon.

He stopped the car. "Oh no."

"What?" Vivien followed his gaze. "Oh no," she echoed. Cars

had pulled out in front of the Mustang and behind. The car show entrants. "Um, looks like you're going to be in the parade after all."

"I was kidding."

She started singing. "You've got to... Live a little... Laugh a little..."

"I don't think you understand—I—" He made a face. "This is bad."

"So, what's your name? I mean, if you're going to be my plus-one for the parade, I should at least know your name."

"Plus-one?" He shook his head. "Boone Buckam. And I can't believe you got me into this."

"Well, Boone Buckam, you're about to find out exactly how much fun Fish Pic can actually be. Think of it like it's a happy accident."

He gave her a look and she shrugged her shoulders, kicked off her heels and began waving to the crowd that lined the streets—their hands filled with everything from cotton candy to fish burgers, the spoils of a day spent at the community celebration.

"What are you doing?"

"Have you never been in a parade before? You've got to wave to your adoring fans. Like this." Vivien took off her seatbelt and stood, letting the breeze lift her hair. "See—those are the Christiansens." She pointed to John and Ingrid, who stood with their son Darek, his wife Ivy, and their own children, Joy and Tiger. Ingrid stood with her husband's arm around her, her short bob haircut still stylish as ever. "Well, that's some of them. They own a resort on Evergreen Lake. John's the family patriarch." She looked to see if he was paying attention. "Big family."

"I see." He put on his sunglasses. They made him look very James Dean, thank you, Classic Movies channel. "For someone trying to make a great escape, you seem pretty comfortable in front of a crowd."

She turned back to Boone. "I'm an actress. Well, I was. I'm focusing on directing next. A community theater summer program."

"I see."

"Oh—and that's Cole Barrett and his wife, Megan. He's part of some new Crisis Response thing they've started up here. Also a deputy sheriff."

She cast a look at Ree on the sidewalk, whose wide-eyed laughter was drowned out by the raucous cheers of the crowd on either side of her.

Well, Ree knew better than anyone how easily Vivien could put on a show. How much easier it was for her to be someone else.

And her newfound chauffeur-slash-fake boyfriend certainly wasn't slowing her down. He drove through the parade, his mouth in a tight half smile, as if he might be enjoying himself.

The parade wound its way back to the Coast Guard station's lot, the crowd gathering for the judges' awards. They parked in the lot, watching the rest of the cars pull in and letting the breeze lift the heat of the day off them. The station stood at the end of the peninsula, the harbor on one side and the open waters of Lake Superior on the other. The two-story white building stood like a sentinel over the ever-changing waters.

She scanned the crowd. No sign of Sabrina.

"Are you sore?" Boone leaned in.

There it was again. Faint cologne mixed with heat, a little earthy and intoxicating.

"From what?"

"All that waving." He lifted his hand, gave her a perfect royal wave, his hand rotating side to side on his wrist.

"You know, you're actually pretty funny for such a serious guy."

The microphone let out a squeal before the emcee, Ed Draper, began the drone of naming award winners from the stage at the end of the lot. Funny, the dog sled guy was manning the car show. Ed had always reminded Vivien of a younger Paul Newman. His graying hair had never diminished the classic handsome features and his clear, bright blue eyes. Edith must have exercised epic powers of persuasion to convince her son to participate in Fish Pic this year. One by one, various participants made their way to the stage to collect their trophies.

Vivien turned back to her driver. "Thank you. I owe you one."

Boone slid his sunglasses back on his head and held her in his dangerous blue eyes. "You're welcome."

"I'm sorry I made you super late for whatever your thing was."

"It's okay." He lifted a book from the center console, shoved it under his seat before she could read the title. "I'd planned to lay low. Relax."

"Hey—that's you." Ree had appeared next to the Mustang.

"What's who?" Vivien asked.

"You guys won." Ree was pointing toward the stage.

The crowd had turned, applauding, eyes on the 1965 Mustang.

Ed held a trophy, staring at the paper in front of him, his voice booming over the mic. "I don't see an entry number or name, here." He looked up, pointed to the Mustang again. "Vivien, would you and your...uh...friend come claim your award?" The crowd began to clap again.

"You've got to be kidding me." Boone shook his head.

"You shouldn't be so surprised that your baby won."

"We're not even entered."

"Go, you guys, go." Ree waved her hands to usher them out of the car. Boone stood, rooted into the ground.

"Oh, come on," Vivien slipped on her shoes and grabbed Boone by the hand. They made their way to the stage to stand next to Ed.

Ed tried to hand the trophy to Boone, who didn't take it.

Oh, please. They'd won an award for Pete's sake. Who turns down an award?

Vivien took a bow to the applause and accepted the heavy glass award, hoisting it over her head, bringing it down to cradle in her arms.

"Hey—can I have the mic?" Vivien held out her hand to Ed.

"Um, sure." He gave it to her and stepped back.

"Hi, everyone. I'd like to thank you for coming out to the Fish Pic car show today. Let's give a shout-out to Ed Draper, who helped organize the event with the local booster club. I'm super glad I could share this afternoon with my dear friend Boone."

Friend might be a stretch, but, oh, well. If Sabrina was still stalking the grounds, Vivien wasn't going to give up on the charade. "And, wow—the People's Choice award? Thank you. I'd like to announce we'll be holding auditions for a summer community theater event on Wednesday evening at the Arrowood Auditorium in the high school. While the last show had a youth cast, this time all you adults get to give it a go. I'll have a short synopsis and character list at the library community events' table. We'll be performing *Then Came You*, and I can't wait to see you all Wednesday at the playhouse." Murmurs rippled across the crowd.

"Thank you again." Vivie held up the trophy. She imagined for a moment that she held an Oscar and smiled for her adoring audience. Well, a girl could dream, right? The crowd cheered one more time.

She stepped away from the mic and followed Boone off stage while Ed announced the end to the car show portion of the activities. The crowd dispersed and Vivien found herself facing Boone across the open convertible.

"People's Choice. Not a bad way to end the ride." And, shoot, she wasn't sure why, but she didn't really want it to be over. She swished the skirt of her sundress side to side. "What about my ice cream?"

"What ice cream?"

"Oh, come on. Every convertible ride ends with ice cream."

He rubbed his hand across his face, a curve at the corner of his lips.

"Is that a smile?" She squinted at him.

He shook his head. "Get in. I'll take you home."

"Ice cream first?"

"Fine."

She pointed the way while he drove three blocks to the Licks and Stuff ice cream shop. They stood in line among the rest of the Sunday afternoon crowd, and Boone leaned in, his voice low. "What do you recommend?"

The close tenor of his voice did annoying things to her pulse. Like, sent it into the staccato of a marching drum. Clearly, she hadn't been around any eligible men recently. And he was hardly anything less than cover-model material, so she could let her heart beat a little. It did a girl good.

"You have to try the Moose Mocha Madness in the home-made waffle cone." In answer to the question on his face, she added, "Espresso ice cream, chocolate chunks. A little hunk of paradise in a confectionary masterpiece."

"When you put it that way..." He turned to the server, a cheery high school girl with a nose piercing and several purple streaks in her dark hair. "We'll have two of the Moose Mocha Mad—"

"Just one—" Vivien interrupted.

"What?" He raised his brows.

Vivien looked over the ice cream display. "One double-scoop Moose Mocha Madness in a waffle cone and one..." She perused the colorful vats. "One Ravishing Rainbow sherbet in a sugar cone."

"I hope the Moose Mocha Madness is for me, because I think

I'd lose my man card if I ate the Ravishing Rainbow sherbet," Boone said as he paid for the cones.

She laughed. Um, no worry there.

He handed the sherbet cone to her and held the door for her on their way out. He slid under the window awning into the shade.

"We're not eating these in the car."

She pressed her hand against her chest. "I would never."

He started toward a bench along the sidewalk, weaving through the Fish Pic stragglers who smelled like sunscreen and smoked walleye, the din of children's chatter competing with music from the stage. "I thought you said the Mad Moose Mocha was the best." He looked from his oversized frozen treat to her bright sherbet.

"Moose Mocha Madness." She licked the melting top off her scoop, the sweet-tart raspberry melding with the orange sherbet on the roof of her mouth. "And, it is, but I don't know. Today felt like a rainbow sherbet kind of day for me."

"I didn't realize that was a thing."

"Oh, yes. There are days for chocolate chunk, days for mocha madness, days for sherbet." She considered her cone for a moment. "I suppose there are even days for vanilla."

"You don't strike me as the vanilla type."

"Well, I haven't had a vanilla day, but I'm leaving open the option that there could be a vanilla day."

"Hmm. I see." He took another bite of ice cream. "This is really good, by the way."

"I told you so. I know my ice cream flavors." The band had started playing in the park and the smells of cheese curds and smoked fish floated on the breeze. Families still crowded the downtown streets, squeezing the last hours out of Fish Pic.

They watched a metallic blue Impala drive by. "Oh, that's a nice sixty-four," she said.

"You seem to know a lot about classic cars."

She turned from the car, her eyes settling on him. "I've always had an eye for fine things." Oh, sometimes she wished she could filter what came out of her mouth better. But he was standing there. Tall and strong and utterly adorable with his double-scoop waffle cone. "I'm actually car-less right now. I moved back here a few months ago from New York City." She lifted a shoulder. "Didn't need one there."

"I see. But, you're in the market for one?" He took another bite of ice cream.

Well, hmm. "Not yet. I'm not sure when I'll be heading back to the City." She took a bite, savoring the tang. "You're not half-bad at this acting stuff. You're not, like, some soap star from Hollywood, are you?"

He cut her a look over his cone and sat on one of the benches along the sidewalk. So, that was a hard no.

"What do you do then? What brings you to the village of Deep Haven?" She sat down next to him.

"Village?"

"Well, we are quaint. I think it sounds so much more picturesque than 'town.'"

He looked like he was running an inventory of exactly what to say, finally settling on, "I'm a detective. Taking a vacation."

Oh boy. "A detective? As in a police officer?" Vivien's heart rate ratcheted up a few notches. "And I asked you to impersonate someone else? Good grief, why didn't you say something?"

And there was that warm rumble of laughter again. "Well, technically, I didn't impersonate anyone else. I just pretended to be something I'm not."

Oh, like every day of her life. She shot him a smile. "Aha. So, we'll consider it an undercover operation."

He seemed to be considering her, as if she intrigued him. Maybe the detective in him. "If you'll tell me about this theater thing. So, you said you're an actress?"

"I'm not currently acting. I'll be directing the show I announced."

"Well, Garbo." He tossed his napkin into the trash and stood. "I'll give you that ride home now, if you'd like."

Garbo? This guy was trouble of the most scrumptious kind. "Just so we're clear, I wouldn't normally accept a ride home with a strange man. Which probably sounds funny since I rode in the parade with you, but that's different. I may be—I may come across as—dramatic, but I'm really just a small-town girl." She refrained from breaking out into "Don't Stop Believin'."

"A villager."

And this time, she laughed. "Yeah. I'm just a villager with big dreams. Hoping to shine."

She followed him back to the car. "But, if you're really a cop —and maybe you need to show me some credentials—then, yes, I'll let you drop me off."

He pulled his wallet from his cargo pocket and flipped it open.

Oh, Handsome really was a cop. "Thank goodness." She tugged off her heels and slid into the seat. "I did not want to have to walk home in these. They look super cute, but let me just say, they are painful."

"I'll take your word for it." He closed the door and slid into the driver's seat. "You know, the solution would be to wear something more practical."

"Practical?" Hardly. She wasn't the kind of person who could get away with practical. "Oh, you can't imagine. A girl's got to keep up appearances. The world is a stage, after all."

"Indeed," he said.

"Head up the hill, past the gas station," she said, pointing the way. "That cute yellow house—we call it the Butter House—go down the street past those big dogwood trees."

He followed her directions. "Here?"

She urged him to keep driving. "Go past Edith's house—it's

the one with the pink gnome in the front yard. Stop at the blue bungalow on the corner."

"Oh, you mean the one with the giant walleye and salmon eyeballing the neighborhood?"

"It's a walleye and a trout." She grinned. The gentle breeze swung the two 4-foot-long papier-mâché fish from the porch rafters. "That's the one. Well, mine and Ree's. Until she gets married and moves into her fiancé's gigantic log house. She's my best friend and the town journalist." Why was she babbling?

He pulled up to the curb.

She glanced at him. "Thank you again. You nailed the role."

"You're welcome."

"Will I—will I see you around?" Oh, shoot, and now she sounded needy. She shot him a smile, picked up her high heels, and stepped into the grass. "I mean, how long are you here for?" Lovely. That made it sound like a prison sentence. She shot him a smile, a little big, like she might be on the local tourist council.

"Five weeks." He picked up his book and waved it. "I plan a ridiculous amount of reading by the lake." His tone held something of sadness. Or regret?

And she dearly wanted to ask, but before she could, her eyes fell on the foreign objects lying across her porch floorboards.

She stilled, her breath caught.

No. That wasn't...no, this could not be happening again.

"What's wrong?" Boone asked.

She turned back to the car, stepping over to block his view of the porch. "Oh, nothing." She waved him off. "Just a neighborhood prank from the boys next door. I'll see ya."

He paused, as if he had something else to say and she gave him another flash of smile until he pulled away.

She had the sinking sense that Sabrina wasn't the only person who'd found her in Deep Haven. Those roses looked exactly like the last ones she'd received from her stalker.

ACKNOWLEDGMENTS

A whole village was needed to raise this book baby. Seriously. A whole lot of people!

First, I want to thank Susan May Warren and Lindsay Harrel. Thank you for taking a chance on me. You've been very patient and encouraging with this rookie. I've learned so much from you both. You're quick to point out the good as well as the "needs some work." (And let's be honest, it needed a lot of work!) Not only are you both incredible authors in your own right, but you're also generous hosts, gracious teachers, and true friends. I'm so grateful for you both.

Editors Barbara Curtis and Rel Mollet helped make this story the best it could be. As someone who has a hard time with the details, God knew I'd need people like you on this team. Thank you!

Throughout this whole process, I was never alone thanks to my fellow Deep Haven authors Andrea Christenson and Rachel D. Russell. Can you believe it? We did it! From brainstorming to late-night texts, random questions, and big-story problems, you two were there for me. I have loved collaborating with you and walking this road together. Let's do it again!

Linda Day, there are endless reasons I'm forever thankful for you. One of those reasons is that Ronnie would be pretty pitiful if not for your paramedic expertise. Thank you for helping me with the medical scenes and walking me through the procedures. Anything inaccurate is my error alone, because we both know I will never be as cool as you. Fun girls rock!

Arlene Warga, thank you for taking me through the fire hall and answering my gazillion questions about firefighting. There are probably *still* things I didn't get right, but that's my fault. You and your crew are the real heroes.

My writing amigas, Gail, Mollie, and Julie have walked this road with me each step of the way, cheering me on, lifting me up, and sometimes holding me together. Gracias, ladies. I love you all!

My Novel.Academy prayer huddles have prayed me through this whole process! I hate to think where I would be without you. Alena, Sharon, Shirley, Dee, Becky, Diane, Karen, Janda, Dia, Joni, Kelly, and Teresa, I can't thank you enough.

To my MBT gals, you are the best! Tari, Lisa, Mandy, Kariss, Jeanne, Andrea, Alena, and Tracy. Y'all have been with me from the beginning of my writing journey. Hugs to each of you.

Sonja, Karen, Angela, Bethany, and Elizabeth, you have been my lifeline before I ever started writing and you have continued to cheer me on every step of this journey. I thank God for each of you. I know you have my back.

So many extended family and close friends made this book possible in a million big and little ways. Thank you for pouring into me and my family.

And just like so many days when you were pushed to back of the line as I struggled to finish, I end these acknowledgements with the most important people in my life. Jesse, Anders, Evie, Lucy, and Trygg, you have put up with a lot in the process of writing this book. You kept me fed, sane, and encouraged. You were the first to celebrate with me. The first to pick me up when I was frustrated or falling apart. Any accomplishment of mine would be nothing without you. You all are the sunshine in my life, my reason for getting up each day. You are my heart.

And to the Author of my life, all glory to You!

ABOUT THE AUTHORS

USA Today bestselling, RITA, Christy and Carol award-winning novelist **Susan May Warren** is the author of over 75 novels, most of them contemporary romance with a touch of suspense. One of her strongest selling series has been the Deep Haven series, a collection of books set in Northern Minnesota, off the shore of Lake Superior. Visit her at www.susanmaywarren.com.

After growing up on both the east and west coasts, **Michelle Sass Aleckson** now lives the country life in central Minnesota with her own hero and their four kids. She loves rocking out to 80's music on a Saturday night, playing Balderdash with the fam, and getting lost in good stories. Especially stories that shine grace. And if you're wondering, yes, Sass is her maiden name. Visit her at www.michellesassaleckson.com.

CPSIA information can be obtained
at www.ICGtesting.com
Printed in the USA
LVHW111555190521
687895LV00004B/814

9 781953 783059